JUST LIKE DADDY

JUST LIKE DADDY

ANDRE BROWN SR.

ARPress

ILLUMINATING IDEAS,
EMPOWERING VOICES

ARPress
45 Dan Road Suite 15
Canton MA 02021

Hotline: 1(888) 821-0229
Fax: 1(508) 545-7580

Ordering Information:
Quantity sales. Special discounts are available on quantity purchases by corporations, associations, and others. For details, contact the publisher at the address above.

Printed in the United States of America.

ISBN-13:   Softcover   979-8-89676-693-3
            eBook   979-8-89676-694-0

Library of Congress Control Number: 2025924877

Contents

CHAPTER ONE

Waking up with a hard-on for a young boy Romeo's age was typical, especially one growing up around a father like Big C, who himself was a ladies man. This hard-on was different for Romeo, he thought. It was more like something was pulling him out of bed, and being awakened in the middle of the night by a sudden urge to pee, gave the little guy the strangest feeling. Getting out of bed was one of the hardest tasks Romeo ever had to tackle. Usually he'd just lay there and imagine he was in the bathroom standing over the toilet, which in turn might cause him to piss in the bed. This time was different. This time the little fella' used all he had in him. He rose in his bed, threw back the covers, and tossed his little feet over the side of the bed down into his house shoes. As he stood to his feet, he stretched out his arms and yawned. He then began to clear his vision by knuckling the crusty sleep out of the corner of his eyes. Romeo headed to the bathroom still rubbing his eyes stumbling down the dark hallway like a nine year old drunk. He pauses to the sound of voices coming from the living-room area. When he reaches the doorway entrance to the living-room, he looks across and sees his dad, Charles Jackson, a.k.a. Big C in the kitchen. Romeo lit up like a Christmas tree. His dad is everything good under the sun to him and nothing could ever change the way he felt about his hero. It was engraved in his little heart. Romeo craves the day he's old enough to be just like his daddy. He notices his dad is not alone in the kitchen. He squinted to focus his sight, then recognized his uncle Kadafi, a.k.a. KD, was also in the kitchen, along with another man the little one never seen before. Romeo took two small steps back and tucked himself in the darkness of the hallway in hopes not to be seen by anyone.

Big C was in the kitchen conducting a drug deal with his ex-brother-in-law KD and one of KDs' homey's Wacko. When Romeo noticed all of them in the kitchen together he got real curious as any typical young boy at his age would, and began to wonder what it was they were doing in the kitchen this late at night. He did know that if he gets busted being nosey that would be his ass in a sling, so he kept real quiet. Big C was standing at the table counting stacks of money that KD was handing him out of a brown paper bag, while Wacko was loading bricks of cocaine into a dark blue duffle bag.

"Hold up Wack . . . Let me weigh that shit fo' ya'll cuzz" stated Big C

Wacko slid the duffle bag across the table as Big C turned to retrieve his triple beam scale from under the sink. Romeo was still tucked away in the darkness, quiet as a church house mouse, and paying close attention to every move being made in the kitchen. It appeared strange to him the way his uncle and the other man staring at his dad while his back was turned. As he continued to look on that strange demanding urge to pee returned. Before Romeo could make a move towards the bathroom he noticed his uncle pulling a gun from under his shirt. He didn't quite understand exactly what was happening until his uncle pointed the gun at his fathers' back. Romeo's entire body tensed as he watched fire blaze from the barrel of his uncles' gun and his dads' white T-shirt turned red right before his eyes. Romeo closed his eyes hoping this was a dream and his hero was going to be okay. This had to be a dream, he thought. It was somewhat confusing to the little fella' because he saw the fire but never heard the actual shots. When he opened his eyes he saw KD and that man grabbing everything off the table and stuffing it down into the duffle bag then heading for the front door. KD looked towards the hallway and fear stabbed Romeo in the chest as he was frozen in the darkness hoping not to be seen. That demanding urge to pee was no longer just an urge.

CHAPTER TWO

It was a bright and warm summer morning. Romero was out in the spacious front yard of his mother's home playing soccer with his son Romero Jr. this bonding was a practice that Ma' Ma' instilled in her son, Romero, as a young boy. Romero grew up without his father. Therefore, Ma'Ma, was challenged with the task of raising a boy into a man on her own. She tried hard to keep him away from the streets, a place she feared. A place she feared losing her son the same way, if not worst, the way she lost the love of her life.

Romero Jr. loves his father, even though most of their time is spent apart. Out in the yard on this morning, Romero Jr. enjoys the time. He rears back and kicks the soccer ball as hard as he can towards the makeshift goal and his dad.

"Bet you can't stop this one papa!" He yells.

"Oh yea . . . Watch me ay" Romero said as he dove for the ball, missing it purposely. His son believes he's just out done his father on the soccer field and jumps for joy. Romero gets to his feet just as Junior runs and takes a flying leap into his dad's heroic embrace.

"I did it . . . I did it papa . . . I scored on you!"

They both laughed and yelled out together, "G-O-O-O-O-O-O-AA-A-LLL!!!"

Romero enjoys the warmth of his son's heart beating against his chest, as well as his happiness of scoring a goal on his papa.

"Awe you got me little one . . . I can't believe it . . . You da' champ ay"

Ma'Ma' was watching the two them play in the yard from the doorway of the front door. The love shared between them, she believed, was blessed. It brightened her day every time she was blessed with the privilege of seeing it. She gasped for breath, as she used all her strength to hold back the tears that were trying to escape her eyes. There is an ever present desire for Ma'Ma of seeing her son out in the yard playing with the father he never had. With this thought, her tears almost always made their escape.

"Ma'Ma' . . . I scored on my papa . . . Did you see it?" yelled, Romero Jr.

"Yes mijo . . . I saw you . . . you did good too".

Ma'Ma' quickly brushed at her cheeks removing the tears from her face before they got close enough. As Romero and his son made their way to the door Ma'Ma' stepped in front of them and kissed her grandson on the cheek. It was full of, congratulations, and lots of plain old grandmotherly affection. After the kiss from Ma'Ma', Romero and his Jr. went into the kitchen where he drowned the little one with a bunch of wet ones of his own.

"How bout some juice for yo champ" Stated Romero Jr., throwing his hands in the air still celebrating his goal. Romero released his grip on his son and sat him down at the kitchen table. He turned to the refrigerator and opens it.

"Ay little one, you wanna' go to the park and play with Romeo ay?" Asked Romero.

"Ooooh . . . yeah papa . . . is he bringing Bootsy

Ma'Ma' was now standing in the doorway of the kitchen still admiring the love. As she overheard the conversation her boy's were having. She had a gentle smile on her face as she stood there listening.

"Bootsy! Who the hell is Bootsy, little one?" Asked Romero.

"Papa you know who Bootsy is . . . That's little Romeo's puppy"

"Pupppy! Boy that aint no puppy . . . That dog is bigger than both of us ay!"

"When are we gonna' get a puppy papa . . . Why wont Ma'Ma' let us?"

Romero comes over to the table and sits a glass of juice in front of his son. Pulling a chair from under the table for himself, he noticed Ma'Ma' looking on from the doorway. He knew then to be careful how he answered his sons' question.

"Well, you know small fry, I think it's partly my fault ay . . . When I was little like you I wasn't as sharp as you are. So I really didn't understand how to take care of a pet ay . . . but I'm sure you could do a better job than me ay. Maybe you should ask Ma'Ma'"

Ma'Ma' chimed in aggressively.

"No! No! No! . . . Your papa don't know how to raise a puppy right mijo . . . He always make them mean"

"Ma'Ma', Pit Bulls are supposed to be mean, so they can protect you ay" Stated Romero as he laughs and responds to Ma'Ma's reason for saying no. Ma'Ma' cut his words with another sharp "No! No! No!", and pointing directly into her son's face. It looked as if she was playing a starring role in a movie as somebody's Big Mama.

"But Ma'Ma', what if I raised it?" Asked Junior, looking up at Ma'ma' with his sweet little innocent eyes.

Ma'Ma' strutted over to the refrigerator throwing her hands in the air, mumbling a flurry of Spanish obscenities, while staring straight at Romero. She quickly opens the refrigerator, grabs the jug of juice, walks aggressively back towards Romero staring him down with an evil eye, still mumbling, as she gently poured her precious grandson a little more juice. The look on her face portrayed a sweet and very loving Hispanic grandmother, however, her words said different as she began to speak.

"What if you raise it? Ay eres igual a tu padre!!!!" Stated Ma'Ma' . . . Which means . . .

". . . Ah you're just like your papa!"

Romero smiled and chuckled at Ma'Ma'. He loved the way she expressed her love for her family. He felt she held everything together. He felt he needed her to hold it all together, because sometime that responsibility can get a bit overwhelming for him.

"See what you started little one" Stated Romero

He grabbed a hold of his son soon as he finished his juice, by scooping him out of his chair, tickling him, and again drowning him with kisses.

"Com'on champ . . . Lets go"

Ma'Ma' put the jug of juice back in the fridge as her two boys made their way through the front door to leave. "Ma'Ma'" Romero called out. "Me and the little one are heading to the park . . . You need anything?" He asked.

For a brief second Ma'Ma' didn't respond. She just stood in the doorway of the kitchen and stared out at them.

"I love you Ma'Ma'" yelled Romero Jr.

She turned away and headed back into the kitchen throwing her hands into the air again.

"Ay vamonos!" She shouted as she disappeared from sight.

Romero and his junior looked at one another, laughed, and headed on out the door. Ma'Ma' sat at the kitchen table. A few tears flowed down her cheek as she sat and reminisced on losing her husband to the mean streets of L.A.

"He was a good man" She repeated to herself over and over again.

She closed her eyes in hopes in regain her composure. Then she began to pray out loud.

"Lord . . . I come to you in this time of need, in the name of Jesus . . . I asked you to watch over my boys Lord . . . I've already lost one to these devilish streets . . . please don't let the devil take these that I have left . . . Watch over them Lord . . . por favor . . . In the name of your son Jesus Christ hear my prayers . . . . Amen"

Ma'Ma' took a deep breath, wiped at her tears, and went about her way as she felt her burdens being lifted.

CHAPTER THREE

Romeo rises out of a dead sleep in cold sweat. After fifteen years he's yet haunted by that demanding urge to pee, which leads him down that dark hallway to witness his father's demise. Then, nine years of age, now twenty-four, Romeo has his own family and his own reputation. He quickly awakens, shaking off the sleep, startling his girlfriend Janisha, and breathing hard.

"What's wrong babe?" asked Janisha.

"Nothing . . . I'm cool" Romeo quickly responds, staring at the ceiling.

Romeo jumps out of bed with only his boxers on. He has a muscular build from all the exercising he was doing while he was locked up in jail. He has a few jailhouse tattoos. One in particular was a big block letter "M" on his right bicep. This symbolized unity between his extended, "The East Side Mafia Crips". Romeo moved swiftly through the doorway of his bedroom, frightened from that nightmare he darts down an unlit hallway leading to the other rooms in the house. The first door he came upon belonged to Da'Nisha, (DJ) his girlfriend's daughter. Romeo opened her door cautiously, looks in, sees that DJ is safe, and lets out a sigh of relief. He took a few more steps down the hallway to a door with a big nameplate the reads "Junior" again, Romeo cautiously opens the door. When he sees that the covers is thrown back and no ones in the room, Romeo's heartbeat sped up to double time. Scrambling through the house fiercely now, Romeo's heart is racing and in turn has him racing. He's checking under beds, in closets, and behind every door. Finally, he reaches the front area of the house where he hears Janisha talking to his little one in the kitchen.

Janisha bent over and gave little Romeo a sweet motherly peck on the head.

"Good morning Nisha" Little Romeo said with a smile.

"Good morning handsome . . . What'chu' doing? I think your daddy is looking for you"

"I'm fixin' me and my daddy some breakfast . . . Nisha, do you know what kind of cereal my daddy like?"

When Romeo recognizes his son's voice, he leans up against the wall in the living-room, shutting his eyes to regain his composure. Just the thought of something happening to his mini-me would literally kill him. Sometimes Romeo imagined how his father felt about him, and wondered what he was feeling now. After regaining himself, he peeled away from the wall and joined his little one and Nisha in the kitchen.

"What kind of cereal your daddy like?" Asked Nisha.

"Umm . . . Honeycomb and Dig'em Smacks!" He shouted.

Nisha looked somewhat confused at Little Romeo's response. "You mean mixed together?"

"Yea . . . I thought chu' knew"

"Well handsome, what about me and Danisha?"

"N-i-s-h-aaa" Little Romeo dragged out in his sweet little tone. "You and DJ don't eat cereal . . . Ya'll eat bacon and eggs and toast and jelly and stuff." He shrugged his shoulders and gave his baby face look. "I don't know how to cook that stuff"

Romeo was still gathering himself together as he stood in the shadows, listening to their conversation. The sweet sound of his mini-me's voice calmed him. Romeo remained standing there a few more seconds just smiling at his little fella.

"Hey lil' man" Romeo said softly as he finally joined them in the kitchen. He held his arms open to welcome what he knew was coming next.

Lil' Romeo quickly turned to the sound of his daddy's voice. All in one motion, he turns, runs, and leaps into the air.

"DADDY!" He screams, launching himself into the air, knowing his hero would catch him.

"Hey champ!" Exclaimed Romeo.

He caught his little fella in mid flight and embraced him with a fatherly warm squeeze. Romeo closed his eyes as he held his joy and counted his many blessings, especially the one he was holding.

"Daddy I fixed you some cereal . . . its Dig'em Smacks and Honeycombs too"

"Whaaaaat . . . You know what daddy like huh?"

Romeo put his son down and leaned in and gave Janisha a kiss. She was sitting at one of the barstools by the kitchen bar.

"That's so cute," she said. "He gon' be just like you"

"And what's that like?" Romeo shot back as he wrapped her up into his arms.

"You know what I'm talking about . . . He be battin' them pretty browns just like you do . . . A little heartbreaker, just like his daddy"

"Girl you trippin' . . . My little man ain't trying to be no playa'"

"Oh . . . So you saying you a playa'?"

Romeo's whole faced changed. His mind was racing trying to find an exit out of this line of conversing, Nisha was heading into.

"Hey look!!! Here comes Miss Crabtree!" He shouted, throwing the attention on DJ.

"Oh please . . . . Don't start . . . its way too early for your jokes"

With a sassy attitude as usual, DJ shot some of her prized sarcasm at Romeo. He always said, "she was sixteen-going on thirty". Romeo, however, does an outstanding job with putting up with her sometimes foul mouth. It's mainly because of his relationship with her mom. Who wouldn't, Danisha is one of the finest bitches in the hood. She has the body of a goddess, ass out of this world, prettier than a newborn baby, and a sassy ass attitude . . . which can be a bit overwhelming at times.

"Ummm, can I get some money so I can go to the mall with my friends after school?" DJ asked.

Silence surrounded the room.

"Dang girl . . . slow down and catch yo' breath before you pass out . . . wow!!! No goodmorning or nothing" Romeo fired back. DJ gave off a short sigh, like she was finally fed up with Romeo's old ass smart mouth. Although Romeo was only twenty-four. However, to some teengers, that's ancient.

"Please, can I have fifty bucks?" asked DJ.

Romeo, being the thug that he is, an eye for an eye type of nigga, couldn't resist the conflictual welcome DJ was putting in front of him.

"Hold it! . . . . I thought you said it was too early fo' jokes . . . . Did she just say please?"

"Mammaaaa! DJ screamed.

If she were a white girl, she probably would've turned peachy red in the face. But her dark chocolate complexion hid her almost blatant irritation of Romeo's sarcasm. Nisha noticed her daughter taking some inevitable blows from Romeo. She stepped in between them to put a stop to the verbal brawl.

"Baby give that girl some money" Nisha said in her, I'm gon' break you off some of this fantastic pussy later," voice. She got a little closer to Romeo, resting one of her hands on his bare chest. He still showed no remorse, only restraint.

"Umm . . . Yes I did say please" DJ shot yet another un-called-for response. This one was accompanied by a smart-ass like twitch in her neck.

"Awe shit!" Romeo said. "There it is again"

He pushed Nisha out of the way gently and continued his verbal bashing.

"Baby check her pulse . . . Check her temperature . . . She may be coming down with a fever or something, and we can't let her go to no mall with a fever . . . . She keep saying please . . . . Shiiiit, she scaring me"

"Mamaaa!" Again DJ cried out for help from her mama.

"Baby stop . . . Now that's just evil" Stated Nisha as she caressed Romeo's chest.

"Okay . . . Okay" Romeo finally conceded. "Hey lil' man . . . could you run and grab pops pants real quick out of my room?"

Little Romeo took off like a jet from the run way. He shot through the house an was back in a flash.

"Thanks champ"

Romeo dug into one of the deep pockets of his Sean John Jeans and retrieved a wad of money. Of course this was intended to shoot yet another blow at DJ, but Romeo held back and peeled one of the hundred dollar bills off the top the wad and handed it to DJ. When she saw this, she lit up. She almost said thank you. Instead she welcomed the money into her hands with a, "can I keep the Change", remark.

"Umm, I don't know . . . Ask Lil' Romeo" Said Romeo

"Can I keep the change Lil' Romeo?"

This was the sweetest sisterly voice little Romeo has ever heard her speak. He smiled. Now when it comes to the little one, yes he's very sweet, and a joy to be around, but let's not forget . . . he's just like daddy.

"Oh! Now you wanna be super nice and sweet all of a sudden" Stated Lil' Romeo.

He sounded just like a little man. He was rubbing his little hands together like, I got you right where I wanted you now.

"Well, well, well . . . let me see" He said. Then he dragged out his demands to her.

"I . . . need . . . you . . . to buy . . . . me . . . . a . . . braaaaannnnndddd new . . . . basketball game . . . . for my Playstation"

"Dang little Romeo . . . them games cost more than I got"

"Umm daddy . . . she gon' need some more money . . . Maybe another one hundred dollars . . . one for her and one more me, please"

He sounded like a two and a half foot dictator, until he said please. Romeo yeileded to the little dictator's request and handed DJ another hundred.

"You make sure you get his game too . . . and you be careful at that mall too" Stated Romeo.

"Bye", was all DJ said before she shot out the door with the two hundred dollars. Romeo just looked in disgust as she flew out the door. He thought to himself, maybe she don't know how to say thank you. A smile to his face when he thought about how her mom says thank you.

He shook his thoughts and came back to reality.

"C'mon lil' one . . . let's get geared fo' the day"

He scooped lil' Romeo up in his arms again like he was his favorite pillow.

"Wait a minute daddy . . . What about our cereal?" asked lil' Romeo.

He put his son back down, slipped on his pants, and he and lil' Romeo sat the table and enjoyed their soggy cereal together. Peeking up from the bowl he noticed Nisha strutting down the hallway to the bedroom. It seemed that every time she turned her back to him, he'd get suspicious of why she's really here. Knowing his feelings deep down tell him, it's the lavish lifestyle and the respect as well as the recognition of being Romeo's girl. Despite the truth in his thoughts, Romeo, yet again ignores his feelings.

CHAPTER FOUR

Romero and his junior already made their way to Cherry Park, in Long Beach. They pulled into a parking space and sat there for a few while Romero made a phone call on his cell. Junior was quietly in the back seat strapped in playing his video game. This was every kid's dream, to be able to ride with pops and have all the luxuries but maybe a few extra minutes with papa.

The music was playing was playing low in the truck. Romero was rolling the new 2009 Cadillac Escalade, twenty six inch Giovani Blades, Vouge rubber bands, a deep wine Burgundy paint, Gucci interior, T.V.'s everywhere, and more wood than Home Depot. Talk about lavish. Romero took pride how his homies and the streets viewed him. He had to have the best and only money could get him that, in his eyes.

Romero built his drug empire from the bottom up on his own. He learned about the streets simply by being in the streets and becoming a part of them. It sort of came natural in a way. Everyone that knew him knew of his father, and they always told him that he was just like his papa . . . even his own mother. Although he never knew his father personally, he still understood it as a lot people respected his father to the utmost. So whenever he heard this from people, mostly his uncles Juan and Tony, his father's brothers, Romero just smiled.

Fear, respect, honor, and loyalty are what Romero's empire thrives on. Most of his loyal compadres are hispanic as he is. Some are Caucasians, which are half assed confused or just plain scared shitless of being left out of something that they may feel is of importance. Romero has three main homies he really has love for, Sneaks, Monster, and Pelon. He refers to them as his "Three Amigos" on occasions. Monster is like his right hand. He kept the other two around just in case he needed a pawn or two to push or sacrifice. While Romero sat in his truck waiting on Romeo, he called his paint shop. Romero jr. continued to play video games in the back seat.

◇

A couple of blocks away, Romeo and his son were stopped at a red light. The music was blaring through the metal of his eggshell white with a blue pearl, 1982 Malibu Wagon-SS. It was white leather interior with blue piping, blue carpet, and a blue head liner. This ghetto fashion had Crip written all over it. Even the faces of all twenty-six Kenwood speakers were blue and sitting on twenty-two inches of blue hundred-forty-fo' spokes of Daytona's. One thing a thug knew in L.A., was how to roll in the spot light. At the light lil' Romeo and his dad bobbing their heads to the beat and siging along to Heat Waves' "Always and Forever". They looked like twins, expecially the way they sung and swayed. It sounded like two pigeons that just flew through a Hennessy Factory and now trying their luck for American Idol. This was truly some genuine bonding between a father and his son. In these neck-of-da'-hoods, this is a definite need.

Finally Romeo pulls into a liquor store parking and parks.

"C'mon Romeo, lets grab some snacks before we hit the park . . . tell Bootsy to watch the car" Stated Romeo.

Lil' Romeo unhooked his seatbelt and called out to his puppy Rottweiler. Imitating his dad, the little dictator verbalized a command to Bootsy.

"Bootsy . . . . watch the whip puppy" He said in a raspy deep tone.

Bootsy rose up on all fours in the backseat. What lil' Romeo was referring to as a puppy . . . was in no way that by looks. Bootsy is a hog of a dog. Damn near as wide as the backseat with a head almost as big as a beach ball. This was no puppy, weighing in at 137 pounds, a puppy bear maybe. The only thing that made him a puppy was the fact that Bootsy was only eleven months old and playful as a four year old child, however, he looked and growled full grown. Lil' Romeo caught up with his dad in the store. Everything he grabbed he grabbed double. One for him, and one for his dad.

"Daddy I want some of these powder donuts and some milk . . . Chocolate Milk"

"Mmmmm . . . . I think I want the same thing" Romeo responded.

"You always get what I get daddy that's why I always grab two"

"That's because you're just like me little one"

"I thought chu' knew"

They both laughed it off with a pair of smiling faces. The lady at the register was smiling too. She told Romeo how cute his son is. Romeo just smiled and requested some chocolate blunts. When they returned to the car, Bootsy was still standing at attention and on guard. Lil' Romeo pulled tow long beef sticks out of his goodie bag and Bootsy leaped over onto the passenger side front seat. Lil' Romeo climbed in and hopped on his throne which is the middle armrest right next to his daddy. He unwrapped one of the beef sticks and awarded it to his puppy for his bravery and obedience.

"Good puppy Bootsy" He said as he fed his baby bear a treat.

As they pulled off, Romeo smiled at the similarities shared between him and his junior. The little tyke was genuinely his mini-me. As they continued to hit a few more corners, they also continued their karaoke their way to the park.

Back in the park, Romero and his little one were on the basketball court shooting some hoops. Jr. was bouncing the ball furiously, going in for the score while papa was playing his kindergarten defense. They both turned when they heard some loud music approaching. Romeo was pulling into a parking space in the parks lot. Romero Jr. and little Romeo spotted one another in the distance. Their smiles lit up the park. Romero Jr. dropped the ball and took off in little Romeo's direction.

The driver's side door flung open on the wagon. Romeo stood up out the car and little Romeo followed. He jumped out from behind the door and darted towards Romero Jr. with what seemed to be a bear's cub running behind him. Bootsy was running and just as excited as the kids were. When little Romeo and Romero Jr. finally made contact, it was a tight hug, instead of hi-fi's and handshakes. They were so happy to see one another they both fell to the ground still bound by the hug. Bootsy joined in by bouncing his big ass around the boys and barking in stereo. When they got up they booth took off running with Bootsy chasing them.

"C'mon puppy!" Yelled lil' Romeo.

He threw a tennis ball that he'd brought from home to play with Bootsy. Bootsy darted out in front to retrieve the ball and they continued to run after him. Romeo looked on and watched the two of them have fun like they've known each other for twenty years.

"What it do, my knott?" Stated Romeo as he and Romero made contact and greeted.

Romero returned the greeting with smooth player like, "What up gee"

They first connected by a handshake which went into a brief embrace, then back out to a dab of the fist.

"I know you got some of that fire love one," Stated Romeo.

"All the time homeboy . . . you got the blunts?"

"Fo'sho' my nig"

They sat one of tables that was nearby, Romero pulled out an ounce of some of the finest Bud, Los Angeles had. Being da'man, he was the connect to any and everything illegal. Romeo immediately began breaking down one of the blunts when Romero pulled out the bag of weed by splitting it down the middle from one to the other with one of his fingernails. Then he dumped the tabacco out onto the ground under the table.

"What'chu waiting fo' fool . . . twisit one!" exclaimed Romero.

"Boy you ain't said nothing . . . I got the thang right here ready"

Romeo grabbed some of the weed off the table. He took three of the fattest buds out of the bag and broke them down to flakes. The shit was sticking to his fingertips like it had glue in it. It looked like emeralds with sprinkles of crushed diamonds and scent that sucked you in like a singing mermaid. This was definitely what most may call, "The K.G.B. (Killa' Green Bud). Romeo started filling the blunt with as much of the bud as he possibly could fit in it. Romero was laughing at the way Romeo was looking like he was performing a surgery or some kind of ritual.

"Damn homey . . . you rolling that shit like its part of your religion ay"

Romeo didn't respond, he was too busy stuffing and making sure every speck got in. When he finished thumbing and tucking it, he licked it from one end to the other and wrapped it on up. He pulled his lighter from his pocket, flicked it on, and dried the wetness from his licking up. The he looked up at Romero.

"It is a religion love one . . . cause when you smoking on shit like this you can't rush perfection my nig . . . and you got to stay faithful" Stated Romeo.

"yo' ass is sick boy . . . just light the damn blunt fool" said Romero is jokingly fashion.

The both of them laughed in unison. It was as if they were brothers out at the park on a sunny day enjoying each others company. Romeo lit the blunt and took a long and hard toke. When he inhaled it, he felt like coughing up his insides. He passed it right away to Romero as he exhaled the smoke along with some slight coughing.

"Whew shit . . . thass' some gas loco!" exclaimed Romeo.

Romero took the blunt while laughing at Romeo. He takes a full pull himself, then holding the smoke in. He shut his eyes to concentrate on his own ritual . . . getting high. Romero exhaled the smoke and passed the blunt back to Romeo, then he started talking the business.

"Check this out ay" Romero said. "I'm kind of going against the grain on this shit homey . . . But you my boy, and you know I got love for you ay . . . So this whass' up ay"

Romero hit the blunt again, let the smoke out slow and easy, let it marinate on the brain a little, and then broke down the deal to Romeo who was listening attentively.

"Each kilo ay . . . Ten a piece to you . . . Take yo' time carnal . . . feel me"

"Yeah I feel you" Romeo said. "But my nig . . ."

Romeo pauses and takes another toke from the blunt, looks seriously into the eyes of Romero, and the n glanced at the boys playing with Bootsy.

". . . Look homey . . . as I was saying . . . I feel ya' . . . but we ain't gon' put them two between no political bullshit . . . I."

Romero cut Romeo off real quick as if he was offended by what Romeo was about to lead up to.

"What da' fuck holmes . . . I ain't talking bout no politics fool . . . I'm talking bout the po'po'

Seeing you coming through all the time . . . They know the war is on with Mexicans and Blacks ay and them motherfuckers is far from stupid ay . . . so what I'm saying homey, is we don't wanna give them nothing else to think about . . . feel me."

"Right right . . . I feel you . . . but believe me, when I slide through, I'mah' be under the radar fo'sho'"

Romeo passed the weed back to Romero and at the same time blew out a cloud of smoke. "Here love one"

Romero had to concentrate a little harder when he grabbed hold of the blunt. The weed was taking effect so he really had to focus.

"Look Romeo . . . I'll call you later homes . . . in a few hours ay, so be ready ay . . . oh yeah . . . I got some mo' of that fire fo' ya' too . . . free of charge ay so stay by the phone"

"Okay . . . now puff puff pass motherfucka'!" exclaimed Romeo

"Yo' ass is high as a motha' fool . . . damn boy look at cho' eyes esse'"

"Yeah thass' some gas love one"

They started laughing and coughing uncontrollably, and tears ran from Romeo's eyes from the smoke. Out of nowhere, Bootsy jumps on top of the table startling Romero and Romeo. He snatched up the bag of weed in his mouth and took off with it towards the car. The two little ones began laughing like crazy as if they had shared a blunt or two of their own. They enjoyed the show as their dad's was chasing after Bootsy looking like two of the original Three Stooges. Bootsy ran around for a bit then finally jumped in through the window of Romeo's wagon Romero and Romeo both stopped running and looked at one another in exhaustion.

"Ay fool!" Romero exclaimed, breathing extremely hard. "What the hell is up with your pet bear ay?"

Romeo leaned over on his driver's side fender to assist in holding himself up. He shook his head and just laughed in response to Romero's comment. When he was able to look up he noticed the two little mini-me's coming towards the car laughing their asses off.

"Look homey", Romeo said catching his breath. "I'm willing to bet that them two little rascals is behind this shit"

Romero looked up in the boy's direction. All he could do was laugh with the little breath he had left in him.

"Gotta' love'em," he squeezed out.

They caught their breath as the boy's were walking up. Romeo stuck his hand out and shook hands with Romero. Little Romero and little Romeo did the same. Before Romeo could crank up his motor, Romero hollered out, "holla' at'cha' tonight carnal" Romeo gave a thumbs up. When he got all the way inside the car Bootsy jumped in the backseat and little Romeo climbed onto his throne. This was routine when these three got together. Once the car started, so did the oldies, and off they were once again rolling and bobbing their to some music that's way older than the both of them.

Romeo tried his best to spend as much time as possible with his son. Fearing the pain he went through as a young boy witnessing his father's demise, will someday come to haunt his own son. Little Romeo's mom, Renee', couldn't put up with the dangers of Romeo's lifestyle. She always tried to talk to him and remind him of his loss and the pain he endured. To Romeo, Renee's is a beautiful sweet flower, and the way he had chosen to live his life, he didn't believe she should be a part of it. He didn't believe she or his son should endure such pain. Romeo believed he made the worst decision of his life when he chose to let his sweet Renee' go. Of course he loved Renee', she was his Juliet, a dark deliciously sexy Juliet for that matter. Their harmony came to an abrupt end one night while they were enjoying a meal at T.G.I. Fridays. Romeo ended the night with a shootout between him and rival gang members. It wasn't all his fault, yet Renee' couldn't understand, being pregnant at the time. The thought of what could've happened that night, stuck with her and eventually pushed her away.

Romeo and little Romeo hit a few more corners bobbing their heads. Finally they pulled into the driveway of a nice quadraplex. There was one large unit in the front with three smaller units in the rear. All of the units were decent living spaces, although they were located dead smack in the heart of the ghetto. A few cars were parked out front. There was dark blue El Camino, a Chevy Short Block Malibu on dubs, and a very sexy Charcoal-Gray Six-Foe Chevy. With Romeo's wagon included, these four cars stood out like fo' of the badest bitches on the block. Romeo parked and cut the motor on the wagon. He, his son, and Bootsy hopped out in unison. The windows rolled up, the music stopped, and the alarm set itself automatically when Romeo closed the door. As they were about to head to one of the back units, the front of front house opened.

"Heyyy Romeo" K'K said as she stepped out onto her front porch, obviously flirting. "I see you got your two bodyguards with you today"

Romeo was almost successful in ignoring the nosey bitch, but he courteously responded.

"All the time," he said.

To Romeo she was sexy in an irritating way, and that just wasn't cool. Knowing that, he kept his immediate attention directed on little Romeo and Bootsy. As the three of them made their way to the back, K'K shot yet another flirtatious comment as they disappeared from her view. "I sho'll be glad when I get the chance to guard that body Boo Boo"

Romeo just kept the line moving.

CHAPTER FIVE

Romero took Romero Jr. straight home. He Knew that Ma'Ma' would piss a bitch, if she had known that he had her grandson at the park running around while he was smoking and conducting drug deals. Romero turned the music off before pulling into the driveway of Ma' Ma's house. This was Ma'Ma's home, but it was purchased with drug money from Romero's drug dealings. He parked but didn't cut the motor; just let the little one hop out. Romero dug into one of his pants pockets and retrieved a wad of cash, handed his son a crispy fifty, and tooted his horn. As soon as Ma'Ma' opened the front door Romero pulled off. He didn't dare go inside or let her close enough to risk her seeing how red his eyes were, especially after the earlier episode. Junior ran in the house and Ma'Ma' immediately shut the door without a word.

Romero continued to float through traffic in his Escalade, leaned back in a gangsta's lean and soaking up all the stares from the other drivers and on-lookers. Shining like brand new money, is how he felt. He continued to spin some lefts and rights until he pulled into a Wenchell's Donut and parked. As he sat inside his truck he decided to make a phone call on his cell. The conversation was brief. In fact he just gave an order and hung up.

"Ay esse . . . Meet me at the paint shop ay . . . and call the homies too"

After hanging up the call, he got out the truck and went inside. His stay in the donut shop was just as short as the phone call. He came out eating

24

one big, nice, glossy, glazed donut like it was the last one on earth. This was the aftermath of the effects of the K.G.B. Jumping back into the truck again; he pulled off striking his red carpet pose. Leaned back with one hand on the steering wheel, and an I'm the shit look on his face. As he pulled up to a red light he checked every mirror and direction. This is a habit of almost every street thug, especially one within the city limits of L.A. No one ever knows who's lurking in the shadows of these mean streets to take what they aint got, or even take a life. As Romero checks his surroundings, his free hand grips onto his beefy forty-five pistol he had lying on his lap. The light turned green and off he went making the motor roar through the dual exhaust system. He hit a couple of more corners and up one or two more blocks before he finally pulled into the paint shop's parking lot. This is where Romero conducts most of his business, legal and illegal. He noticed Monster's car was already there so he parked right next to it. Romero got out and tucked his pistol down in the waist of his pants and allowed his cocaine white T-shirt to hang over and conceal it. When he entered the shop he saw that everyone was there that needed to be, Pelon, Sneaks, and of course Monster.

"Whass' up fool!" Exclaimed Pelon.

Romero gave him a head nod in response and kept the line moving into one of the offices of the shop. It was like routine as they all followed him knowing that when Romero acts this way it was business time. Pelon was the last one to enter the office. He closed the door as soon as he was all the way inside.

"Ay homes" Romero began. "Remember that vato I told you I was thinking bout bringing on board ay?"

Pelon looked at Romero with a smirk on his face.

"You mean that black fool ay?" He said.

It was brief silence in the room before Romero broke it with his response.

"Yeah . . . that one ay . . . well I'm not thinking about it no more . . . I'm bringing him in ay"

"Hold it esse!" Pelon exclaimed. "we don't fuck with the black's ay" He continued.

Romero instantly flared up in anger.

"Who da' fuck is we motherfucker!!! I run this shit esse!" Stated Romero.

Pelon felt Romero's words hitting him like bullets so he backed off. "I'm just saying ay . . . what the homies gon' think fool if we start dealing with them fools ay?"

Romero pulled his pistol from under his shirt and laid it across the desk that was in the office. "There you go with that we shit again fool . . . who da' fuck is we esse?" Romero asked in a more aggressive tone. He paused for second and gathered his thoughts he continued.

"Look holmes . . . don't come at me like that ay . . . I started this shit esse and I do it my way ay" Romero stated calmly.

With that statement, it became perfectly clear to everyone that Romero's mind was already made up.

"Ay holmes . . . what you need us to do ay?" Monster asked, bringing Romero's attention back to the business at hand.

"I need twenty bricks ready when my boy get here ay . . . and have Sneaks go upstairs and get me two pounds of that Cush ay . . . I told my boy I'll look out fo' him on somptin' extra ay" Romero answered.

He picked up his office phone after passing out his orders. Again this call was short, just as the last ones were. Romero knew never to talk business over the phone unless it was about getting your car painted. Monster and Pelon left the office together. Pelon was furious about doing business with some blacks. It was obviously written on his face. Sneaks took off up the stairs to the stash-room as requested. He was monster's younger brother who just took orders and asked no questions. While Sneaks was upstairs, Romero stepped out the office and noticed

Pelon and Monster standing over by the shop's vending machines chit-chatting. He remained in the cuts so that they was unable to see him watching. Although he couldn't really make out exactly what was being said between the two, he did make his own assumptions by their body language. Romero understood Pelon's personal qualms with blacks. His older brother was killed in major penitentiary race riot, by two black crip's over the phones. With Pelon, forgiveness was not in the script.

"Whass'up esse . . . you vatos got the shit ready ay", he asked as he stepped out from the shadows.

"It's ready ay . . . and Sneaks already put the twenty piece with the pounds ay" Stated Monster.

Romero gave Pelon a look he didn't quite understand . . . a look he really didn't want to understand. Sneaks was then making his way down the stairs with everything inside of a duffle bag.

"Damn esse . . . this shit is heavy ay" Stated Sneaks.

"Don't worry junior . . . Romeo's a big boy, I'm sho' he can handle it" Romero stated sarcastically.

Pelon took the bag from Sneaks, took it into the office, and slid it under the desk. Romero approached Monster and stuck his hand out for a shake. He did this to feel him out on this joint venture.

"Whass' up esse?" Asked Romero

"Que vo esse?" Monster responded in spanish, which also means what's up.

"What you think about this ay?"

Monster threw his hands up in the air as in whatever. "Ay holmes . . . I don't want to get off into no bullshit ay . . . you made the call esse . . . so it is what it is ay"

"Ay holmes . . . I respect your opinion ay . . . thass' why I'm asking ay"

"Ay . . . you know I don't fool with them vatos ay . . . I don't trust'em and this shit just don't seem right ay"

Ay fool it ain't like I'm bout to marry the fools esse . . . It's just business fool and I know this vato got a lot of pull in his neck of the woods . . . that means mo'money ay"

"I feel you holmes . . . but we got more shit than just money to trip on ay"

Sneaks was now posted in the cut listening to the two of them talk, which to him seemed to be a somewhat of a heated conversation. He remained out of the way and didn't bother to interrupt.

"Ay fool . . . don't worry bout nothing ay . . . I got this shit under control fool" Stated Romero

"Whatever esse . . . I got yo' back ay" Monster responded.

They shook hands again and respectfully pounded one another fist. Romero then headed back into his office and made another phone call. This was the shortest one yet. When whoever answered the call, all Romero said was, "stay on deck", and he hung up the line. He then sat in the chair at the desk, took a few seconds to gather his thoughts, and took a deep breath. He pulled the duffle bag from under the desk and double checked the count. He confirmed it to be twenty bricks and two pounds of the cush. Although Romero trusted his homeboy's with his life, he understood that his loyalty was the one in question. Reason being, that teaming up with blacks was truly against the grain nowadays.

Politics played a vital role in Romero's organization. Some were necessary while others were simply ridiculous. Romero abided by the rules and regulations of the code, but getting money to Romero, ain't got nothing to do with no code, because to him, all money is green. His problem now was how his hands interlocked, took another deep breath, and came to the conclusion of a true gangster, whatever, whenever, whoever, and however. This was his shit and he'll run it the way he feels, he thought. He stood up from his chair, grabbed his truest friend-his forty five, tucked it once again, and then snatched up his cellphone from the desk. When he stepped outside the office he noticed that some of his shop workers had made it in to work.

Pelon and Sneaks had reconvened in the shops game room located in one of the far corners of the shop. The game room was filled with all sorts of entertainment for the customers. It had the original Ms. Pac Man, Defender, Centipede, and Donkey Kong. It was also equipped with the latest video games such as Playstaion, Ps Two, Xbox, Will, and Nintendo 64. All hooked up to plasma TV's posted around the room, and two pool tables. Sneaks, was sitting on one of the bing-bags smoking on some cush, and playing Double-O-Seven with Pelon. Like two kids, they were having the time of their life. Monster was out in the shop area hooking up some sounds in one of his homey's car. It was one them new Camero SS's, dark blue with the white racing stripes and set of sparkling twenty-four inch spinners. This was a rag SS and Monster had the top down showing off the white and blue Gucci interior. Romero walked over.

"What up ay . . . you finished with this one esse?" Asked Romero.

Monster was laid across the seat twisting on some wires under the dash.

"Almost holmes" He responded.

"Let me know when you done carnal . . . that fool Hector just called ay. He wanted to know if it was ready"

"Tell him yeah ay . . . by the time he gets here I'll be finished ay"

"Orale", which means Okay in Spanish, Stated Romero.

"Ay fool!" Shouted Monster. "Hold up ay . . . I want you to tell me how this shit sounds ay"

Monster rose up and got out of the car. He popped the hood and reconnected the battery cable, went back into the car and turned the key and the music came on. The volume was low but you could still tell that the sound was crystal clear. He put in 2Pac and Snoop CD and cranked up the sound. Romero immediately start smiling and bobbing his head to the beat while Monster sat in the car and played with the adjustments. When he felt it was just right for the ears he turned it down then off.

"Ay fool that shit was bangin' ay . . . the homey gon' love that ay" Stated

Romero.

"Yeah fool I put the homey some extra tweets in the back ay to balance the highs with a little mo' treble"

Romero shook his head in agreeance and stuck his fist out to compliment Monster with a pound-pound. Romero was really still testing the waters to see if Monster had the same hang-ups about the blacks as Pelon. Not that there was any fear in his heart, because Romero couldn't have cared less about what Pelon felt about the matter. He was just one of the knuckle headed homey's who didn't really know no better, and probably wouldn't understand no better, on respect for each other and reputation in the hood. The only difference would've been money.

Romero grew up watching his uncles deal drugs. One died and the other got out of the game early. However his uncle Tony did stay in the game long enough for Romero to suck up what he needed. He learned right off the back that money is power and power is definitely respect. Although Romero do have a lot of respect for Monster, even though his heart is still set on dealing with Romeo. He spun off from Monster and went back into his office. Monster gave no obvious indication of disapproval or approval to the matter at hand. Romero . . . well let's just say he didn't give a fuck either way . . . so he just kept the line movin'.

He flipped open his cell and made another call.

CHAPTER SIX

Meanwhile at the safe-house:

"Hey you two." stated Kia.

A sexy and very smooth skinned white girl stepped out onto the porch of unit A. You would assume that Nakkia is black if you only heard her talk, despite the color of her hair or skin. Her attitude, the way she walked, the shape of her apple-bottom ass, the way she styled her hair and just her ghetto swagger said she was black. A lot of black women didn't like Kia at all. Most of them felt that if the world were full of white bitches like Kia, their mere existence would be in jeopardy. To a thug, Kia was as real as they come, a thug's passion. She had her sights set on Romeo. Loved him, and would walked to the end of the earth for him, however, little Romeo had his sights set on her.

"Hi Kia" Spoke the little one. Blushing and flashing that handsome little smile of his.

"Hey sexy" Romeo said, chiming in with his greeting. He too was smiling and checking her out, flaunting her body in some sexy ass boy shorts.

"What it do?" Romeo added.

"What eva' you want it to, Boo." she responded.

She had the sweetest voice when being flirtatious. Those hot pink boy-shorts she had on was definitely flirting too, fitting her ass like brand new skin. She also had on a matching top that rode just above her belly button which showed off her diamond piercing, some pink and white Nike running shoes with no socks, a gold anklet with a diamond "R" hanging from it, and her hair was in five sexy corn rolls straight to the back.

"Hey little dude . . . run in and tell the homies I'm out here" Requested Romeo, tapping his son his shoulders.

Little Romeo responded with a swift "kay", then ran inside of unit C. Romeo walked over to Kia's front porch and took a seat on her banister. Kia approached him carrying a drink she was sipping on through a straw. She gently put the straw up to Romeo's mouth to share some of her drink with him, as Romeo's little homies filed out of unit C. Kia then leans in and whispers into Romeo's ear.

"Baby would you slide through later . . . I got a little somptin' somtptin' hot for you"

Even though Romeo knew what she meant by hot, he still obliged the conversation with a sweet question of his own.

"What'chu' got sexy?" He asked.

"You'll have to come through and see when you get the time"

She wiped a small drop of the drink from Romeo's lip with her finger the licked it off of her finger with a sexy swipe of her tongue.

"What up big Homey", yelled C-Loc as he approached the Porch.

Romeo stood up to greet his squad.

"What it do Mafia's?" He stated.

He hugged C-Loc, Dove Sac, D-Sac for short, was next in line. He was Romeo's young go-getta'.

"Chillin' chillin'," D-Sac said. "ay big homey . . . wha'd up with yo' boy?" He asked

"Ain't nobody called yet . . . thass' all we waitin' fo' righhht" Stated D-Kay, before Romeo could respond to D-Sac.

Romeo looked back at Kia and have her a light head nod.

"Ay girl do me a favor . . . take yo sexy ass to the store real quick and let me holla' at my little homies"

He dug into his pocket, pulled out a wad of money, and peeled her off a couple of hundred dollar bills.

"Here . . . get us some blunts and buy little Romeo some chips and shit"

Romeo turned around to Kia when she asked in her come fuck me tone, "can I keep the change Boo?"

"Yeah . . . Yeah . . . keep tha . . . Wait hold on . . ."

He turned towards BG, Baby Gunner. Who was just as the name said, gunner. Nigga's know that when BG was involved it was gonna' be gun play and some killing involved as well.

"Ay loco . . . where lil BG at?" Asked Romeo.

"He in the spot playing the game with lil Romeo cuz" Stated BG.

"Ay baby girl . . . get lil BG some shit too" Romeo added to his instructions for Kia.

"I got'chu' Boo . . . I'll be right back"

She stepped inside her unit to put her glass down and came right back out the door walking pass everybody without a word. KK was standing at her backdoor spying out at Kia through her security bar door, in which she can see out but no one can see in. She watched Kia's every move with pure hate and jealousy.

"Punk ass white tramp!" She whispered to herself as Kia passed her door. She was smoking on a joint and plotting on how she can get some of Romeo's lovin'. But first she had to get his little hoochie white bitch out the way.

Before Kia got all the way out of sight, Romeo called her back.

"Ay . . . Ay . . . where Chocolate at?" He asked, pointing at unit B's front door.

"Oh . . . she gone somewhere with her bad ass kids babe"

"Aright . . . good lookin'"

She turned and left again to continue her mission, and show off her ass-set trying to entice Romeo as much as possible to take a stab at some of her self-proclaimed good pussy. Kia had the highest degree of a burning desire for Romeo and everyone around them knew it. By the time Kia got to the end of the driveway and out of view, Romeo was back to the business at hand.

"Aright loc's" He stated

The Squad, D-Sac, BG, lil Flash, D-Kay, and C-Loc gathered in closer as Romeo continued.

"My boy gon' give us what we can move homey . . . we got's to get this shit cracking . . . . the faster we move the shit the mo'money we'll see . . . . and listen loc's . . . ."

Romeo's tone dropped into a more serious depth.

"We gon' be up against a lot oppositions cuz . . . we have to maintain our structure cuz . . . we family, ain't no big heads-little heads, or no big I's-little you's . . . feel me"

The Squad's attention was all directed at Romeo's preaching. They respected and loved Romeo realistically. Romeo, like his father, gave the love he needed in return and the respect he demanded. You would have to be inhuman not to cleave to his structure. Everyone in the ghetto is looking for a way out, and the widest doorway is the game to most, is the game. Although Romeo preached no big heads or little heads, the Squad still looked up to him as such just out of the love they had for him. Romeo began pounding one of his fist into his palm as if he were angry as he continued. The Squad recognized his seriousness and accepted it as just that . . . serious business.

"My knots," he said gritting his teeth. "This is where we bubble cuz . . . we gotta keep our eyes open and our ears to the streets . . . feel me . . . keep it together and stay getting this money cuz"

As Romeo and his fella's chit-chatted Kia walked back up just as sexy as she walked away.

"Hey boo", she said as she approached. This was her way of letting Romeo know that she was in ear range just in case he was saying something that he didn't need anyone else to hear, or just her way of maybe gaining some brownie points. Whatever the case, the timing was perfect.

Little Romeo came out of the front door of unit C with the cordless phone in his hand.

"Daddy . . . Uncle Romero's on the phone"

"Thass' the call cuz" Stated Romeo.

He trotted over to his little one and grabbed hold of the phone.

"What it do" he said answering the call.

"You know what time it is fool," stated Romero on the other side of the line. "I'm on my way to the shop ay . . . you ready to bubble boy"

"I'm like Sugar Free my nig . . . I stay ready" Romeo responded.

After hanging up the phone he called little Romeo and little BG back outside. Kia was standing right next to him, like this would soon be her permanent position in his life, with two separate bags containing the boy's goodies in one hand Romeo's blunts tucked safely in the other. The little ones ran out, grabbed their bags, and shot back inside to continue playing the video games.

"Hey slow down," yelled Romeo. "Before ya'll hurt yo'self" He continued.

The boy's ere too quick. They had already disappeared back inside before Romeo could finish his statement. Romeo shook his head and called little Romeo back outside.

"Little Romeo check it out lil homey, he screamed.

Both of the small tikes ran full speed back outside still gripping on their bags of goods, almost running over one another.

"Whoa!" Exclaimed Romeo . . . "Pump ya'll brakes on them Vet's you two . . . little one . . . daddy got to handle some biz . . . you wanna stay here with me or you ready to go home with mommy?" Romeo asked.

"Ummm . . ."

"He can stay here with me babe while you take care of whatever it is you got to do . . . I'll watch him for you" Chimed in Kia.

Romeo swallowed so hard, everybody heard it.

"What!" . . . Girl . . . hell naw . . . his mama a'kill both of us!"

"Oh yeah daddy . . . mommy called too . . . she said she was coming to get me . . . I told . . ."

"Why didn't you bring me the phone champ" Romeo stated, cutting his little ones words shot.

"Daddy I told her you was outside talking business wit the little homies"

The squad laughed at little Romeo's response. Romeo slapped his forehead and just smiled at his son while shaking his head.

"Awe shit . . . she gon' be pissed . . . I got chu' . . ."

"Umm huh" Renee' said, cutting through Romeo's words. "If you knew I was going to be pissed then why you got my baby over here in the first place," she continued.

Romeo immediately put on his baby please have mercy smile on his face when Renee' appeared from out of nowhere. He threw both of his hands into the air as if he were being robbed.

"Baby girl . . . I . . . I . . . I . . I . . ."

He couldn't get the words out to save his own life, so Renee' finished the sentence for him in her words.

"I . . . I . . . don't want to hear it Romeo . . . Com'on little Romeo lets's go baby'

Her tone changed to the voice of an angel when she was talking to the little Romeo. She turned back into a devil when talking to and pointing at Romeo.

"And you . . . you . . . you come here" Stated Renee' aggressively.

She and little Romeo headed up the driveway.

"Hi ya'll . . . Bye ya'll" She said as she passed the Squad. Romeo followed Renee' like he was her little puppy. He looked back and noticed the looks on his little homies faces and Kia's. Ignoring those laughing looks he turned back and focused his attention on his baby mama. He thought to himself, "How the hell did I let that one get away".

Renee' stole the show every time she stepped on a stage. Today was no different. Showing up at the safe house today, she shut Kia's show down. At least in the eyes of the two Romeo's, Renee' was and will always be their chocolate covered star. At Five-foot-one, long silky black hair, the prettiest brown eyes, a well proportioned one-hundred-twenty-four pounds, and an ass that looked like, on her is the only place it belonged. She continued out to her car holding on to little Romeo's hand, as Romeo continued to follow lkie a mesmerized little puppy. She pushed her car alarm on her key chain and opened up the passenger door for little Romeo to climb in.

"Mommy is daddy in trouble?" asked little Romeo.

"Baby . . . Yo' daddys' always in trouble"

"Com'on baby girl don't be tellin' him that."

"Hush!" snapped Renee' "And don't be baby girlin' me either . . . now . . . you know little Romeo takes his school pictures next week"

"Alright . . . I'll be there with the little dude . . . how much they cost?"

Asked Romeo.

Renee' walked around to the driver's side of her car, while Romeo squatted in the doorway of the passeger side. He belted his son safely in his seat and took another look at the chocolate perfection he let escape his world.

"Well the packet that I want cost $96.00 . . . we get a bunch of pictures too. But you know if you feel the need to give extra . . . ah., I'm cool with that too" Said Renee'.

She finally sat down inside the car behind the steering wheel. As Romeo began pulling money out of one of his pockets to give to her, she added some sarcasm to her game.

"You sure yo' hoochie won't mind?"

"Girl please! I don't give fuck about that girl like that"

"Stop cussin" She stated

She got back out of the car and walked around to where Romeo was now standing. He gave her half of the wad he pulled out of his pocket.

"Here . . . that should hold you fo' a few days"

She quickly recognized Romeo's slick way of having a sharp tongue.

"Yeah whatever" She said. "You need to bring yo' butt home where you belong and stop playing these games in these streets Romeo" She continued as she grabbed hold of the front of his pants.

Without much effort she pulled him closer and he kissed her on her forehead.

"Thank you," she said softly.

She started to say something else, instead, decided to just keep quiet.

"Whass' up?" asked Romeo.

"Nothing . . . never mind"

"Girl what"

Romeo held her gently by shoulders. She looked up deep into his eyes.

"Well I . . . no . . . we want you to go to church with us Sunday"

Little Romeo chimed in right on cue. "Pleeeeeaaaaase Daddy"

Romeo laughed at the way he was being double-teamed. He returned the same deep look into Renee's eyes. That's when he felt the sparks and realized that he still truly loved his chocolate star.

"Boy ya'll sho'll know how to butta' a nigga' up huh"

Renee' slid her body in a little closer and rested one of her hands on Romeo's chest.

"It's not like that baby . . . sometimes I just get a little scared and we don't want anything to happen to you in these streets . . . and plus little

Romeo just wants to spend a little more time with his dad"

After that spill form Renee', Romeo's tone softened all the way up, like medicated cotton.

"Damn girl . . . you know how long it's been since you called me baby?"

"Hush up," she said softly, slapping him gently on his chest. "If you just wise up and come home you might be called sweeter things than that".

Renee' pulled away from Romeo's embrace slowly and walked back around to her side to get in the car. Romeo got him another close-up look at that ass then leaned in the window and gave his little one a kiss.

"Daddy loves you little man" He stated.

"I love you too Daddy, said Little Romeo.

Romeo then trotted around the car catching up to Renee' before she got in the car. He gently popped her on the ass making her jump in surprise. He didn't want this moment to end. Every thug, despite the way life goes, just wanted to be wanted, needed, respected and loved. And this was the moment for Romeo, where he truly felt it all.

"Call me if you need anything baby girl . . . hell . . . just call me"

"Okay . . . I will. You just be careful . . . bye"

"Bye daddy," yelled Little Romeo.

Romeo stood there at the curb for a few second while Renee' and little Romeo drove away. He stared at the car leaving as little Romeo continued to wave out the rear window. A surge of pain shot through his heart making him grimace. It was the same pain that shot through him the first time he lost her. Romeo continued to stand there staring off into the empty space Renee and his son had already disappeared into the distance. C-loc and D-Kay was walking up the driveway and saw how Romeo was staring down the block.

"Com'on back big homey" Shouted C-loc.

Romeo snapped out of his trance without a word. D-Kay passed him a blunt.

"Here big homey . . . get yo' head back in the game cuz" Stated D-Kay.

Romeo took the blunt from D-Kay and pulled on it with a long breath. He held the smoke in and began smacking on his lips like he'd just tasted a new tropical flavored now

&later candy. When he released the smoke, he also let out the pain he had just endured a few seconds ago. Romeo dug in his pocket and retrieved his car keys and hit his own button. It not only shut off the alarm, but also turned the motor on, rolled the windows down halfway, and turned on the music.

"Ay loc's . . . I'm gone to holla' at my boy cuz . . . when I get back it's on so be ready cuz"

BG and D-Sac joined the fella's in the front. Romeo got in his wagon to leave.

"Ay BG cuz . . . you need to take the little one to his moms or something loc" Stated Romeo

"Fuck that bitch cuz . . . I got my nigga" BG responded.

"Com'on homey . . . he don't need to be around this shit love one" Expressed Romeo.

"I told'em big homey," said D-Kay.

"Shet' that shit up cuz . . . you ain't told me shit!"

"Ay . . . you nigga's cut that shit out loc . . . on tha' real, kill that bullshit . . . look cuz . . . go holla' at Kia and tell her I said I need her to watch yo' little one tonight and I owe her one"

"Aright cuz," agreed BG

He was kind of fired up about the situation. He has mad love for D-ay but speaking on his son will get your shirt wet up, thought BG. BG maintained his anger and didn't trip because he knew the fella's was just looking out for his little ones' best interest. Anything goes in this game, and everybody near it is fair game, so BG understood that Romeo was telling him some real shit.

"Aright I'm out loc's"

He slowly backed out of the driveway and pulled off. By the time he hit the end of the block, an unmarked police unit turned onto the block from the other end. Romeo turned right at the corner. D-kay, C-loc, D-sac, BG, and lil Flash headed back to the rear. They didn't notice the police cruising by slowly in their direction, but the cops noticed them for sure as they disappeared into the rear area. When the officers reached the corner, they turned opposite of Romeo and continued cruising.

◄○►

Romeo was hitting a few corners as well as hitting on a blunt and bumping his theme music, "Paper Chase", by UGK, in his CD deck. Romeo wasn't really a fan of rap music but certain occasions warranted certain songs. This was one of them, a moment of big opportunity for a thug. Everyone raised in these streets, that's involved in the game, years for this moment . . . to get plugged. With Romero, Romeo was now definitely plugged. Whatever he felt he could move Romero was willing to supply him with, with no hesitations. They were hand and glove in this game . . . a solid team. And on these streets, in this game, you ain't shit without a team. Most thugs didn't really understand the necessity of loyalty. However, Romero and Romeo were bred this way . . . same meaning but different cultures.

Romeo turned left, off of Wardlow and onto Long Beach Boulevard. There was a large warehouse-like building almost a block and half long, with a huge sign that read, "Nice & Wet". This was Romero's paint shop. Romeo pulled into the parking lot and drove up to a large garage door. He flipped open his cell phone and made brief phone call.

"I'm here my nig," he said and hung up his phone.

Immediately the giant door began to open slowly. Romeo then pulled into the shop area and parked. He was greeted by Sneaks with a handshake and some admiration of his whip as he got out of his car.

"Damn gee . . . this motherfuckers bad ay!" exclaimed Sneaks.

"Good looking homey . . . I'm Romeo cuz . . . I'm here to see Romero loc"

"Yeah holmes . . . He's in the office"

Sneaks pointed Romeo towards the office as Romero was exiting it. Sneaks stayed by the wagon and continued to admire its fashion.

"What it do fool!" Romero yelled as he approached Romeo.

Pelon was still inside the game room in the cut, watching everything that was going on in the shop. It was killing him to see this nigga in the shop getting all this love from his big homey. Although it was some homies from his neighborhood that were black, to Pelon they were exceptions because there from the neighborhood. In other words, there was an exception to the rule in fucking with blacks . . . as long as there from the neighborhood. In this case Romeo is a crip. And Pelon didn't understand for the life of him why Romero was stuck on dealing with this black crip, or was it that he just didn't want to understand. To Pelon, Romeo was not considered an exception to the rule. Romero and Romeo embraced one another with a hug as if they were family. This boiled under Pelon's skin as he watched. Sneaks really didn't trip off of what was going on, he was just a youngster with still a lot to learn. So all he does for now is take orders and roll with the flow. Monster on the other hand kept it gangster. He understood one thing, it didn't matter who or what, but how you deal with whoever that truly counted. So Monster never expressed any feeling either way. His only concern was maintaining his position.

Romero led Romeo into the office to conduct the business.

"Damn you tensed fool" Romeo stated.

Romeo just smiled a Romero's statement. He was anxious to do the damn thang and get the hell out of there. Pelon walked into the office quietly. Romero asked him to grab the weed box out of the other office real quick as he wrapped one arm around Romeo's neck.

"I know what you need homeboy" Stated Romero

"What box esse'" Interrupted Pelon.

"Ay fool . . . you act liked you got a prollem' or somptin' ay . . . You got a prollem' esse?" exclaimed Romero.

Sneaks stepped into the office, and was surprised at the way Romero was talking to Pelon. He kept his mouth shut and just observed.

"Ay homes . . . whass' up ay . . . . who is this vato ay?" Pelon snapped.

Romero immediately became aggressive towards Pelon's comments. "No!" He snapped back. "Who the fuck are you questioning me fool . . . this my shit motherfucker . . . like I say ay, you got a prollem' ay?!"

Sneaks touched Pelon's shoulder, and Pelon let up before the heat turned to flames inside the office.

"Naw esse'" He replied.

Monster stood right outside the door and was observing everything going on inside. Pelon left the office in silence returning moments later with the weed box. He set it on the desk and again left.

Monster stepped in and threw an arm around Sneaks.

"Ay fool . . . its some blunts in that top drawer," said Monster.

He and Romero exchanged head nods. This was the most thugs did to greet on another on occasions. Monster didn't wait for an introduction, he gave a little slight tug at Sneaks neck and the too left the office. Romero turned and watched them leave to go and join Pelon, disgusted at the way they were acting.

"Punk ass motherfuckers!" Romero expressed, "Com'on fool . . . twist one of them thangs boy . . . and lossen up ess'" He continued.

Romeo scooted one of the chairs up to the desk and began breaking down some of the the weed from the box. The box was sexy, it was cherry wood with a silky looking fluorescent-green bud leaf engraved in its lid. The weed inside was even sexier. When Romeo opened the lid, he was once again mesmerized by the K.G.B. mermaid. After about eight minutes Romeo finally had a blunt rolled. At last . . . the ritual was over, thought Romero; Romeo took a long look at the perfection of his rolling. Romero then slid a lighter across the desk.

"Damn homey . . . you take that shit to serious ay" Stated Romero.

Romeo tossed the blunt on the table next to the lighter.

"Oh . . . you can't smoke one with yo' boy or what ay?" asked Romero.

"I'm cool my knott . . . it ain't like that, I'm just ready to handle this biz loc . . . and plus yo' boyz bout to catch somethin' if they keep looking crazy cuz . . . feel me" Stated Romeo

Romero laughedvand remembered why he liked Romeo. Although they were different, they're so much alike. To Romero, it really didn't matter who he dealt with because at any given time a real gangster is going to handle business no matter what. And that's the first thing he loved about Romeo is that he's with the business . . . however, whatever, whoever, whenever.

They started smoking on the blunt. Both of them were damn near coughing up their insides as they toked and choked. It seemed as if their eyes turned blood shot red as soon as they exhaled the first cloud of smoke from their lungs.

"Ay Monster . . . . check it out ay" Yelled Romero.

When Monster came into the office, Pelon and Sneaks was behind him. When Romero saw this he reached and grabbed the blunt from Romeo, took a long toke, looked directly into the faces of his three so-called comrades, and spoke very calmly but serious.

"Ay homes . . . this my comrade ay . . . he's a part of my family from this point on ay"

Romero paused his words, and went over and stood next to Romeo and threw an arm around his shoulders, then continued.

"He's good people ay . . . that's on my palabra, (my word) . . . I excpect respect for him the same as I do for me ay . . . and again, on my palabra esse' it will be retuned in full . . . now we need to handle this biz ay"

He still had his arm around Romeo as to engrave the love he had for him into his homies heads. Then he sent Pelon to retrieve the load they had prepared for Romeo.

"Com'on fool . . . lets go the lab ay . . . I wanna sho' you somethin'" Romero rugged at Romeo's neck lightly.

"Ay esse' . . . grab a barrel of that cut ay and bring it ay," he ordered Sneaks.

Sneaks immediately peeled off in the opposite direction. Within minutes they all reconvened in the lab. This was large room located upstairs in the far back of the second level. It was very spacious with large tables, no windows or chairs. Romeo recognized immediately that this is where it all went down. Pelon came in and chunked the gigantic duffle bag onto one of the tables, and unzipped it. He pulled two big baggies of weed out and set them off to the side. Then he started unloading the bricks of cocaine onto the table. One by one he sat them on the table as Sneaks slid the small barrel of the procaine closer. Romero went to the table and Romeo followed. He began to show and explain to Romeo how to properly cut and rebrick the cocaine step by step.

"Check it out ay" Romero said to Romeo. "Most motherfuckers want they shit on the brick homes . . . this way they can half ass tell that the shit might be decent just by looking ay . . . so peep . . . . what chu' do is . . . take two bricks ay"

He took two of the bricks and set them side by side in separate shoe boxes. He handed Romeo a respirator so none of the powered poof into this nose. Then he took a meat tenderizer hammer and began busting one of the bricks down inside the box.

"When you bust them down homes . . . you take twelve ounces out of each one ay . . . put it in another shoe box. Now you got three boxes with twenty-four zones a piece. Then you take twelve zones of this pro and added it to each box ay then you mix it real good ay. Rebrick it and bam fool . . . you got three kilo's from two ay"

Romeo saw the finished product and immediately began calculating the dollars in his head. If for every two kilo's he make three, which would give him a total of thirty bricks, and he would only owe for twenty. Now twenty bricks cost him ten thousand apiece, which totaled two-hundred-thousand. That number made him shake a little but just knowing that he would have ten free bricks made him smile.

He showed no emotion, however he just stuck his fist out and gave Romero a pound-pounds, then helped him rebrick the other two.

"So where can I get the pro?" asked Romeo.

"Don't trip ay . . . you ain't got to buy shit . . . . if I got it you got it homey"

Romeo smiled and they embraced to seal the deal. They both packed the drugs back into the duffle. Monster and Pelon left the lab and Sneaks helped Romero and Romeo load the dope in the wagon. Romeo was set. All was left od was get the crack cracking.

"Ay fool . . . lets smoke another one before you go ay" Romero suggested.

Romeo shut the door to the wagon. They stood at the hood of the car, twisted and smoked another blunt together. Pelon couldn't stand how Romero was treating this outsider, as he and Monster watched from one of the offices upstairs.

"Ay homes . . . the homey letting' this vato in too quick ay" Stated Pelon

Monster closed the blind to the window.

"We got to do somethin' esse" Continued Pelon.

"Hold yo' tongue fool . . . the time will come" Concluded Monster

CHAPTER SEVEN

This was a gorgeous Sunday morning. Little Romeo was already awake when he heard the knock at the front door. He was sitting in front of the gigantic T.V. set located In the den of this mom's home watching cartoons.

"Who is it?" He yelled.

Renee had just gotten out of bed when she heard her little one yelling, who is it. She grabbed her robe and threw it on to go and answer the door.

"Who is it?" she asked sleepishly.

"Open the doe' and see sexy"

Immediately she recognized the voice, and so did little Romeo. He jumped up and ran to his mother's side quickly.

"Ooh mommy . . . its daddy!" he shouted

The little one was super excited as if its been a long time since he's last seen his hero, when it was only yesterday.

"Open the door mommy" Little Romeo demanded.

Romeo stood outside the door patiently, laughing at his son's anxiousness.

"Okay . . . Okay . . . My god . . . yall too much alike" Renee' said.

When she finally opened the door she had to catch her breath. Romeo was standing there looking as sturdy as an old Oak Tree. Only this Oak tree had on a two-piece linen suit. It was cream-white with blue attributes. Romeo held in his hand a godfathers hat that was also cream-white with a blue band. His shoes match as well. Blue Stacey Adams with a few cream touches.

"Daddddyyyy!" screamed Little Romeo.

Even little Romeo recognized his dads shiness and refrained from jumping into his arms. Renee' stood there stunned and starin into Romeo's eyes in a lustful daze.

"Damn girl you gon' let me in or what?" he asked.

"Oh I'm sorry . . . but . . . but this is a surprise"

"What'chu mean surprise girl . . . you the one who asked me to go to church with ya'll"

"And here you are Mr. Jackson" Renee stated in amazement.

Romeo smiled and walked in, he passed by Renee, following his son into the T.V. room. As he did so Renee' shut her yes, tooka adeep whiff of the air through her nostrils, and marinated on his scent. It was definitely her favorite, "Versace Green Jeans" for men. She opened her eyes and was refreshed to see this was no dream. The love of her life had just walked back through her front door . . . and damn he smelled so good.

"Baby girl, what time we gotta be at church?" he asked.

"Daddy the church don't open this early" Replied Little Romeo.

"Well what chu' doing up so early fo' homeboy"

"Watching cartoons daddy . . . you know that's my favorite"

Romeo took a seat on one of the couches and Renee stood in the doorway absorbing all the love being shared between the two special men in her life.

"Okay little fella' . . . My bad fo' asking . . . Well let me ask you this then . . . What time are we going to church?"

Renee' saw that little Romeo was back into his cartoon trance as she answered.

"We don't need to be there until ten-thirty babe"

"Mmm . . . that means I got enough time to cook us some breakfast huh?"

At that, Romeo stood up and peeled off his shirt. Renee' licked her lips, swallowed, and then blinked a couple of times. She was beginning to realize that the more she stared the more she became enamored by the thought of him being home for good.

"Com'on little one, come help pops cook some breakfast" Romeo said.

Renee' continued to stare. Little Romeo jumped out his trance to his dads request.

When they made into the kitchen they began pulling everything out of the refrigerator. Eggs, sausages, bell peppers, onions, cheese, milk, and everything else that was needed for Romeo's master omelet. They all sat at the table to eat together. Little Romeo said grace and gave thanks of having his dad here to share breakfast with him. When the little one finished blessing the food and this rare moment, Renee' dug in her omelet and retrieved a nice healthy bite.

"Mmm" She said, releasing a long sound of deliciousness

Little Romeo laughed aloud

"Oooh babe this soooooooo good . . . can you do this more often?" She asked with a sly smile.

Little Romeo and his dad exchanged a look and then burst out laughing.

"What ya'll laughing at?!" shouted Renee'.

"Nothing baby girl" Romeo responded quickly.

"What he laughing at lil Romeo . . . I know you're gonna tell mommy

"Mommy, daddy told me in the kitchen exactly what you was goin to say and you did it"

Little Romeo went on to mimic his mom

"You said, ooh babe . . . this is gooood"

They all laughed aloud and enjoyed the rest of the morning and breakfast together. Romeo finished first and got up from the table. Without saying a word he left the kitchen and went into the bathroom where he then ran Renee' some bath water. She walked in while he was sitting on the edge of the tub adding some bubbles.

"What's all this about?" she asked.

"Well I figured I help out a bit to kinda' speed up the getting dressed process is that okay with you beautiful"

"Sure . . . I don't have a problem with any of that"

With that being said, Renee' untied her rob and allowed it to drop to the floor. Damn, thought Romeo as he stared at some of Victoria Secret's sexiest panties and bra on the heavenliest angel ever existed. She swiftly wrapped her arms around Romeo's neck and gently fed him her tongue. She kissed him like never before and he really felt it like never when they pulled apart, they looked at one another like someone had done something wrong, or maybe, something right.

"Hey . . . you better take your bath so we can get to church" Romeo stated.

"Kay . . . if you insist handsome"

Renee' replied in the sexiest voice Romeo had ever heard her speak. He leaned in and kissed her again.

"Hold that thought" He whispered.

As he left the bathroom, Renee' just stared, she took a deep breath then whispered to herself, "be patient Renee'". She stepped into the tub as she came out of her underwear. As she sat down in the nice hot bubble bath she shut her eyes and imagined the water as his love her protection. She smiled at the thought of having Romeo as her husband . . . or just in her life permanently.

Back in the kitchen, little Romeo has pulled a chair up to the kitchen sink and started doing the dies. When Romeo walked in the laugh in silence.

"What it do little one?"

"I'm doing the dishes before we go to church daddy . . . I try to help out because its only me and her."

"Well since I'm here today . . . you want me to help out a little?

"Yeah . . . we can do it?" he answered.

"As a matter of fact baby boy . . . let me handle this and you go get dressed for church . . . how about that one?"

"Okay" said little Romeo

He jumped off the chair and sprinted out of the kitchen. Romeo paused for a brief second and looked around the kitchen. For that moment he really began feeling like he belonged to something worth belonging to.

After about forty-five minutes, Renee' was in her bedroom putting the finishing touches on her beautiful sexiness. Her two men were outside warming up their car, which was a Chrysler 300C, Romeo had purchased for her last year for her birthday. He went through hell just getting her to accept it. Little Romeo was sitting inside the car flipping through the radio stations with remote, searching for his mom's favorite gospel station. Renee' was headed out the front door. She had on a sleek, shiny, creamlike evening gown that accented her dark complexion perfectly. It was as if she was on her way to the White House for a presidential dinner with the president, the first lady, and of course Oprah Winphrey opposed to just going to church. Romeo hadn't noticed her until his little one raised his awareness.

"Daddy!! Daddy!! Look at mommy . . . dannng"

It sounded like he himself was falling in love with his own mother. Romeo turned and was stuck on what he saw. The dress was fitting her like skin, and the way her hair laid over her shoulders and down her back rendered him speechless.

"What ya'll staring at" Renee' asked.

She stopped in front of Romeo who was sitting in the driver's seat of the car. He stood up out of the car, looked her up and down, and the led her around to the passenger side, still without a word. He opened the door to let her in waving of his hand and bowing as a servant would do for a beautiful princess.

"Your Highness' He said.

"Why thank you kind sir" She replied going along with the skit being played out while little Romeo laughed in the background.

"Mommy . . . you look like a black Pocahontas without the braids . . . you just got the long pretty hair"

Renee' and Romeo fell out laughing at their sons comment. It sounded to Romeo, like something he would've said at little Romeo's age. As she enjoyed the ride over to the church, Renee' sat quietly and listened to Mary Mary sing praises on the radio. Every now and then she would sneak glances at her Romeo admiring how sweet and at peace he was when he was with her and their son. This is where he needs to be all the time, she thought. Love lingered in the air as they arrived at the church. Renee' reached for knob to turn down the music inadvertently touching Romeo's hand as he was doing the same. They both smiled.

Romeo then parked and got out quickly so that he could hurry and get around to the other side to open the door for his Queen. However, there was no need to rush. Renee' had realized his motives for the day and waited patiently and allowed him to be her gentleman. Little Romeo let himself out, closed his door, and gave himself a look-over to his satisfaction. He was wearing his off-white double breasted three-piece suit he'd gotten for Easter Last year. He headed for the front doors of the church where he then held them open so that his mom and dad could enter first. When inside, Romeo and Renee' sat in the middle pews next to each other. Little Romeo on the other hand went straight to the front and sat with the rest of the Deacons. Today was a blessed day for the little man and his mom and dad. They received a beautiful message from Pastor Blake and really enjoyed the choirs singing. Little Romeo walked around with the offering tray for the offering and was proud when his dad put five hundred dollar bills in. As the church services came to a close, Romeo made his way back to the car and waited for Renee' and Romeo Jr. He was no stranger to church but he was new to this one in particular. He knew that the sister had a few questions for Renee', so he waited patiently. Little Romeo popped up first, opened his door, took his suit coat off, and climbed in.

"You ready to go home and smoke daddy?"

Naw I ain't trippin' little one . . . daddy just enjoying the day"

"You spendin' the night with me and mommy tonight?" he asked

"I don't know . . . . Why? You want me to?"

Just as Romeo was finishing his question to his son, Renee' walked up. Romeo immediately got out and went around to her side to let her in, as he was doing his gentlemanly thing he noticed a small group of Renee's church sista's standing by the side door of the church staring. He politely smiled and waved as he strolled back around to his side and got behind the wheel. He released some of his funny ass sarcasm.

"Well . . . did the jury approve or what?"

He caught Renee', off-guard with that one. She stumbled over her words when she attempted to respond.

"Ahhh . . . Whaaat . . . huh? What are you talking about?" She managed to ask.

It was written all over her face in big bold letters. She was definitely in love again. She quickly brushed Romeo's last comment off by changing the subject.

"What was ya'll talking about?"

"Who," Romeo asked.

"You and your twin back there" She said/

"Mommy I asked daddy if he was spending the night tonight."

"Uhh . . . I don't know baby . . . your daddy may have some unfinished business to tend to . . . so maybe next time okay" Stated Renee'. "Ummmm . . . daddy . . . you got to finish your business first" Little Romeo said sadly.

Romeo noticed the change in his son's tone and felt the hurt himself, from Renee's sweet way of saying no to him spending the night.

"Look champ . . . this what daddy gon' do . . . I'm 'a fix din' din' for you, me, and mom's tonight right . . . . then we gon' say our prayers

together. That way we can pray for daddy to get all his business handled
. . . cool?"

"Alright . . . is it cool mommy?"

"Yeah that's cool baby"

Renee' looked at Romeo proudly. She admired the way he'd just handled
that situation. She too felt the hurt in her little man's voice when she
said no to his spending the night.

The finally made it home, got situated, and Romeo made some simple
soul food taste gourmet. He smothered some pork chops in homemade
gravy, with buttered baked potatoes, some broccoli with cheese sauce,
and homemade biscuits. Renee' had bought a strawberry cheesecake the
last time she went shopping so that's what they had for desert. Little
Romeo was full in every sense of the word. This day he'd remember for
a long time. He and Romeo ended up playing Madden Football for the
rest of the evening until Renee' requested for the little one to get ready
for bed, Romeo offered to do the tucking in of his little fella'. Little put
on his pajamas then they all got down on their knees at the foot of the
bed. Sounding like a tiny angel, little began leading them in prayer.
"Our Father which art in Heaven" He began.

A tear came to Romeo's eyes as he began to reminisce on the trips to
church and the times he'd spent on his knees with his grandmother. He
kept the tears hidden with the help of the darkness of the room. His
reminiscing blocked out some of the little fella's prayer but he did hear
the best where the little one said, "oh Lord . . . please keep my daddy safe
for me and mommy while he handle his business with the little homies
. . . Amen" Renee' quickly got up and left the room. Little Romeo
opened his eyes, brightened up the room with a big smile, and gave his
dad a huge hug. Romeo returned the squeeze and secretly wiped away
tear, he then put his little one in bed, kissed him and whispered, "boy
you something' else" Little Romeo closed his eyes still smiling. He knew
he had impressed his hero in a real way. Romeo left the room quietly.
Renee' was waiting for him at the doorway with a warm towel.

"Here," she said softly.

Romeo laughed, accepted the towel, and wiped his face. He went into the front room to sit on the couch and Renee' followed. They sat here quietly and just stared into one another's eyes for a few seconds and Romeo sighed.

"Damn baby girl . . . he sharper than I thought"

"Yes he is" Stated Renee'.

They sat there until almost two in the morning talking about little Romeo. Several times Renee' reached out and grabbed hold of Romeo's hand. He didn't react, although he wanted to He knew what Renee' was referring to when she made the statement in the car about business and decisions. She was second to none and definitely nobody's other woman. Romeo understood exactly what she meant. He loved Renee' in a real way. He also knew why he was with a hoochie and not Renee'. To Romeo, there's two kinds of woman. One's a bitch, who'll do what she's told, and don't really give flying fuck about nothing or what happens to nobody, as long as she's being taken care of. Then there's the woman . . . . she's a lady who adores being loved as well as loving someone. She'll put her all into loving her man and she'll do what's right as well as what's neccassary and still maintain her dignity as a woman. She'll accept her position as his backbone and in return all she'll expect is his love, loyalty, honesty, and security. Knowing this, Romeo could not and would not subject her to the bullshit in these streets. Finally, Romeo left Renee's and headed home. When he arrived at the house he calls home, Nisha was nowhere to be found. Neither was D.J. He rolled himself a blunt and slapped his Sade CD in the player and listened to her sing, "Hold on to Your Love", until he fell asleep on the couch.

◄○►

Renee's still sat awake in her bed contemplating picking up the phone and calling Romeo. He wasn't just in her thoughts he was once again engraved in her heart. Only the Lord knows how much she wanted Romeo to stay the night. It's been quite some time since she's been touched or loved by a man. Not that she hasn't wanted to be loved but Renee' has always managed to put little Romeo's needs before any of her wants. She sighed to herself and just stared at the phone, as her heart pounded and temptation teased. Through all the tempting thoughts she persevered and never broke. She believed very strongly that if it were meant to be, it will be, and that if Romeo makes the decision to change his lifestyle for his family then it will also be better. Although she worried about Romeo's well being, she didn't want to put her heart through the pain of losing him to these streets. She vowed to herself that she would stand strong and do whatever it takes to get him out that street life. Furthermore she knew she at the least had to try, if nothing she felt she owed that to little Romeo. Renee' got out of bed and dropped to her knees at the foot of her bed and began to pray again.

CHAPTER EIGHT

Romeo was rollin' in his wagon on his way to the safe house. He flipped his cell phone opened and chirped BG.

"Whass' up big homey?" BG answered.

"Ay love one I'm on my way cuz . . . call the loc's and have everybody meet there"

"I'm on it cuz" Stated BG before hanging.

By the time Romeo arrived, the Squad was there and had already assembled some blunts. Soon as Romeo walked through the door DK lit one up.

"Thass' my nigga'" Romeo said.

DK sucked long and hard on the blunt until he felt his lungs couldn't hold any more smoke. The cherry got so red on the blunt's tip you probably could've welded together two pieces of metal. The smoke overwhelmed his lungs causing his insides to explode outwards. Everybody fell-out laughing. C-loc grabbed the blunt from DK and took a couple of short tokes to prime his lungs for what's to come. They continued to smoke while Romeo discussed business.

"Who still got dope left cuz?" asked Romeo.

Nobody answered.

"So everybody sold out? Romeo asked. "Damn cuz . . . this just turned from a meeting to a celebration," he continued.

The weed was so potent everyone was already on their way to being high, that they just laughed and started the celebration with some more smoking. Romeo was surprised that they all sold out . . . surprised, but pleased.

"Ay loc . . . how much you cook off them fo' bricks?" Romeo asked C-loc.

"I sold it all in Q-P's big homey so my cash count is eighty-five Gee's . . . . I would've made mo' but a nigga' gotta' eat while he grindin"

"Good shit cuz . . . . where the rest of ya'll at?" complimented Romeo.

BG chimed in with his count first. The DK, D-Sac, and Lil Flash. Everybody's total together came up to be three-hundred seventy-thousand and some change. They all got quiet when all the money was counted. Romeo Then tossed each one of his loc's a ten stack

Ya'll straight with that . . . let me know cuz . . . cause this gon be the payroll every month . . . thass' how long it took us to flip this shit"

"Thass' straighter then straight big homey . . . we making mo' money then some of them politicians cuz" Stated Lil Flash.

They all laughed is agreeiance and C-loc lit another blunt.

"Fo'sho' cuz . . . thass' love loc . . . like you always say, we fam cuz . . . so we straight if you straight" Said C-loc

"And we know it's mo' to come cuz" interjected D-Sac.

"You damn skippy cuz . . . let me call m and let him know I'm on my way . . . ay BG count me out two-hundred kay cuz . . . thass' what we owe him and I'll get us a fresh load"

"Fo'sho' . . . puff puff pass cuz" Stated DK

They were all satisfied on the business so far. Romeo's satisfaction came through the loyalty of his squad. He thrived on the bond that held them together through whatever. He felt that trust and love amongst them could never be broken by anyone . . . at least that's what he had hoped.

"What it do boy!" he stated on the phone.

"Ay fool . . . whas' up" Romero answered.

They were only on the phone for a brief moment before hanging up. None of their phone calls lasted long, and their meetings were more like smoke sessions. Romeo hung up the phone and got back with his young loc's, on their own smoke session.

"What cho' Mexican say big homey?" asked DK.

"We on my nig' . . . he waiting on me . . . ay you ready love one"

BG quickly loaded a large paper bag with loot and handed it to Romeo. Instead of grabbing the bag Romeo grabbed the blunt BG was smoking on.

"It's all there cuz' BG stated

"Yeah . . . I feel ya' but right now this got priority" Romeo said jokingly as he held up the blunt.

He joked to ease some of the tension within himself. Toting this kind of money around in the streets of Los Angeles just ain't safe at all. They all shared a good laugh and enjoyed a couple of more blunts. About forty minutes passed, Romeo made another quick call, and he was on his way out the door. While getting in his car Kay Kay was lurking in a window, watching his every move. She noticed he was carrying a brown paper bag, and knew it was one of two things . . . dope or dope money, She had gotten suspicious of all the extra movement going on around here for the past couple of weeks, now she knew why. Kay Kay had been trying for a long time to fuck Romeo. Not that she was in love with him, but she knew he was about getting his money and she wanted to be a part of that. And any bitch would want to be papered by a nigga' like this. At least this bitch did, she thought.

—◄◦►—

Soon as Romeo got in his car he lit up a blunt then headed out for the paint shop. He picked up his cell phone and called Kia's number.

"What it do baby girl?"

"Hey daddy" She answered.

"Like what?" she asked.

"Like you ain't got no friends"

"Well . . . I'm lonely . . . and you always talk to me like I'm just one of the homies and you know how I feel about you Romeo"

"Girl I don' told yo' crazy ass whass up . . . look . . . I'm 'a try and slide through there tonight aright"

"Should I wait up?" she asked

"Yeah . . . wait up baby girl . . . I'll be there"

Romeo hung up the phone and turned up the music. He knew Kia was crazy about him, however, the only bitch he felt he would ever really love is Renee'. He knew that Renee's love for him was genuine. Romeo figured, how can a bitch love a nigga the way Kia claimed and she hadn't even been fucked yet . . . so how would she know what she was getting? It really didn't matter one way or another to Romeo. Kia was just another notch in his belt . . . . another piece of pussy whenever he needed it . . . . just another pawn in his chess game. He finally made it to the paint shop and pulled up it's huge garage door. When it opened enough he drove in, parked, and got out with the paper bag in-hand. Remero came out of the office and met him with smiles and a tight handshake as Romeo was sitting the bag down on the hood of his car.

"Whass' up fool?" stated Romero as they shook on it. "Two-hunnett-kay love one" Reponded Romeo.

"Damn boy . . . you drive around L.A. like that fool"

Romeo didn't respond to that statement with words, he raised his shirt and allowed Romero to get a good look at the pistol-grip handle of his new fifity-caliber desert eagle.

"Oh shit . . . boy I need one of them . . . what tha" fuck is that fool?" asked Romero.

"This that new fifty boy . . . what it do tho! Let's count this shit homey I got a lot of shit to do cuz" Romeo said.

Romeo looked at Romeo like whoa.

"Awe shit . . . my boy don' turned into a shrewd businessman" Joked Romero.

They both started laughing.

"You got time to smoke one with yo' boy or what ay?"

"Always my knott" answered Romeo

Before they smoked, Romeo yelled out to Monster to get Romeo's next batch reay. Monster didn't like this at all, but he did it anyway. Of course Romeo or Romero didn't give a fuck about what was or wasn't liked by whom ever. The two of them, without second thought, ventured on into the office and smoked not one but two blunts with one another.

This wasn't the fact that you had two bud-heads; the fact was that you had two businessmen who understood the importance of interacting, and the growth of trust, loyalty, and respect that stems from interacting. Anything that had no direct bearing on the business, occupied no space in these two chronicized minds. They kicked back in the office smoking maybe forty to forty-five minutes give or take a few. Romeo sighed, stood to his feet, and stretched.

"Damn love one . . . I'm fuuuuuuuucked uuup" Romeo dragged out.

"Naw you burnt out wit cho' big head ass fool . . . . damn boy I just now realized yo' shit is so big esse" Joked Romero.

They laughed at that one as if someone was tickling them. The effects of the chronic began to overwhelm their funny bones. Romero talked Romeo into the game room where they ended up playing Madden Football on the Playstation2, this lasted about another hour, maybe more.

"Damn boy . . . . you kicked my ass ay" Stated Romero

"Thass' what nigga's do love one . . . kick ass" Replied Romeo

"Oh like that esse"

Romeo grabbed Romero around the neck like a little brother. This was in appreciation of his hospitality and all the love. They shared another laugh together as Pelon and Monster were lurking in the cut, watching all this love transpire between the two, and didn't like it a bit. Monster kept it together, whereas Pelon was cursing under his breath in extreme anger. When monster stepped out the shadows, Pelon followed like his little puppy. There sudden presence didn't affect the atmosphere around Remo and Romero at all.

"Ay homey I'm 'a head out cuz" Stated Romeo

He noticed Monster and Pelon's dissatisfaction as they approached.

"Whass' up esse?" asked Romero

"That shit is ready ay" Stated Pelon. "And Freddie called ay . . . . he want to know if you're ready for him yet" He continued.

Romero ignored Pelon, knowing his motives. Romeo walked over to his car where the duffle bag was sitting atop his hood. He grabbed hold of it and chunked it through the rear window onto the backseat of the wagon, turned and walked back over to Romero, and gave him a pound pound.

"Good lookin' out love one" He said.

"All the time fool . . . don't trip ay its nothin'"

"I'll get back as soon as this ones done homey"

Romeo hopped in the wagon and turned on the motor. It purred like a two ton cat ready to roar on the open road. The music was low, yet it can be heard and felt. He had that old cut, "Get Yo Money While You Bullshittin'", by Sugar Free, playing, Romeo immediately started to boogieing in his seat as he began backing out of the shop. When the wagon was all the way out he pumped up the volume. Romero also boogied to Romeo's music as he strolled back to his office.

The decision to do business with Romeo was solely based on just that . . . . business. These two were hooked up through a mutual acquaintance, who respected and spoke highly of the both of them, and his acquaintances credibility is A-1.

Big Joe is a Hispanic O'Gee. He was Romeo's pop; Big C's connect before he was killed. Big Joe and Big C were like brothers, just as Romero and Romeo are today. When Joe gave his word to Romero about Romeo, any and all doubt he might have had about Romeo was out the window. Because of this their relationship was bonded from the beginning.

Neither of them, Romero or Romeo, paid any attention to, however they were yet aware of the disfavor of Monster, Pelon, and Sneaks. They were two well trained thugs in "STREETANOLOGY" and very aware of the consequences of getting caught slipping.

———————————————◄○►———————————————

When Romeo made it back to the safe house with the new load, only BG and his son was there. He took the duffle bag inside with him when he entered unit C. BG greeted him as he came through the front door.

"Whass' up Big homey?" said BG.

"Hey hey . . . what it do love one" Romeo responded.

"Damn cuz . . . you high as heaven . . . smoke somptin' wit' cho lil homey cuz" Stated BG.

Romeo unzipped the duffle bag and tossed BG one of the large baggies of the chronic weed that was inside.

"Twist us up a few loc . . . who here with you cuz?" asked Romeo.

"Ahhh just me and my little one Big homey"

"Cuzz . . . what I tell you loc' Stated Romeo.

"I know Big homey . . . but his mama trippin' cuz . . . and yo' snow bunny just got home, so I posted my lil cuz here with me"

"Lil homey check this out loc . . . this ain't no game fo' kids cuz . . . . if the feds kick in the doe' yo' lil one can be a casualty cuz or property of the state loc . . . and that's bad biz . . . . feel me . . . I aint trying to see that or have that on my conscious cuz . . . so what I need you to do is find lil BG a babysitter and I'll pay fo' it loc"

"I'm on it Big homey"

BG handed Romeo one of the blunts' he just rolled. As he lit it he attempted to further explain to BG some of the downsides to having to having his son around this havoc prone lifestyle. BG say and listened attentively, however, it still went through one ear and out the other. BG couldn't and wouldn't allow anyone to baby-sit his little one under no circumstances. It was as if they were attached at the hip. Romeo chirped the rest of his little homies while he and BG smoked. The first to show was C-loc. He came into the unit prepared, pulling a blunt from behind his ear and setting fire to it. C-loc took a long pull the greeted Romeo with it.

"Ay . . . What it do big homey . . . here this shit from Compton cuz . . . . I got it from my Damu nigga's" stated C-loc.

Soon as Remeo began smoking on that blunt, DK and D-Sac walked through the door followed by Lil Flash. D-Sac got a whiff of the smoke and immediately started reaching for it.

"Oooh wee . . . pass the dutchie cuz . . . damn that shit smell good" Squealed D-Sac.

"The homey got this shit from Compton cuz," stated Romeo.

"Yeah . . . I heard them Hollyhood nigga's got bomb cuz" DK said. "Thass' where it came from too" responded C-loc.

Everybody's attention was now focused on getting high. They all sat and smoked. After a few minutes Romeo flipped his phone open and called Kia.

"Hey boo," she said in a hopeful tone as she answered Romeo's call. She was hoping he would have some time for her today.

"Whass' up baby girl . . . look sexy . . . I'm bout to straighten out the homies . . . . then I'll be over there . . . but in thirty minutes I need you to come through the back way and grab this shit fo' me"

"Okay" She said.

She quickly hung up after hearing that. He told her that he'll be over and that's all she needed to hear. Kia thought to herself, should she beautify now or after she finished the task he instructed her to do. She decided on after. She figured that if she does it now, he would see what she had planned. So she waited, to keep her plan a surpise for him. She was very cautious of Romeo letting her hold his dope. It wasn't that she was scared, because she'll the devil for him. It was the thought of Romeo giving her just enough room to fail him, whereas this will remove any chance of her being his Juilet and this was not going to happen on her watch, she thought. She would do any and everything in her power to please him.

Above thirty minutes later, as she was instructed, Kia stepped out onto her front porch and surveyed the area. Just as she thought, she spotted that nosey bitch Kay Kay peeking through the cracks in her blinds.

Kia had studied her blinds when she knew Kay Kay wasn't home so she'd know when she was, because the bitch couldn't help being nosey. Without alerting Kay Kay that she's been spotted, Kia nonchalantly went back inside her unit. She then exited her unit through her backdoor and headed over to unit C. Kay Kay's view was blocked by a tall thick green hedge across the rear of unit's A, B, and C. this made it possible for her to pass through from her unit to unit C without being seen by anyone, especially nosey bitches. Kia knocked softly on the backdoor of unit C when she got there, before entering. As she then made her way into the front room where Romeo and the fella's were indulging in another one of tier smoke sessions, she took a long whiff of the bud's sweet aroma. Kia strutted pass everybody with a soft and sweet, "Whass' up fella's", and went straight to Romeo and took her seat, which was in his lap. She was sporting some sexy blue and gold boy-shorts that fitted perfectly. Her scent was soft and sweet, her legs freshly shaven smooth with the prettiest little feet connected to their bottoms with some comfortable looking summer sandal on them. After sitting in Romeo's lap she threw an arm around his neck and accepted the blunt that Romeo offered. She briefly puffed and passed then she and Romeo made their way towards the backdoor where he handed her the duffle bag.

"Stack that shit in the safe for me baby girl" He stated.

She didn't say a word, just grabbed the duffle, threw its strap over her shoulder and left the same way she came. Romeo headed back to the session still holding half of a blunt in his hand, and as soon as he reappeared in the front room BG was reaching for it.

"Pass that Big homey" BG said.

"Here cuz . . . I'm fucked up loc" responded Romeo.

C-loc stood up and announced his departure. He had already stashed his issue of the drugs in his car and was now ready to go get his grind on.

"Aright cuz . . . I'm out loc's . . . I'll holla"

Everybody gave him an "Aright Mafia . . . stay up", and he was out the door. DK and D-Sac was the next to leave with their sacks ready for the streets. Flash posted up with BG for a little hit playing Madden Football and Double-O-Seven on the video game.

"Ay BG cuz" Stated Romeo.

"Whass' up loc"

"Don't forget what I told you cuz" Said Romeo.

"I got'chu Big homey/

Romeo headed out the door and went next door to Kia's spot. He walked right in without knocking. Kay Kay was still being the nosey bitch she is, peeking out the back bedroom window. She hated herself for looking this time because what she saw broke her heart and had her steaming. She knew Kia had an extreme thing for Romeo but she never figured him to fuck with a white bitch. Kay Kay cursed at herself for several seconds before devious thoughts took over her mentals. She left the window and let her mentals take control.

<hr>

Meanwhile inside Kia's unit, Romeo sat on the coach. It had a nice glass coffee table in front of it with wooden base. Kia had some of the weed and a few blunts already rolled and layed out on the table for Romeo. Of course he took one end lit it up immediately. As usual he took a long and hard toke and blew it out with a loud and hard breath as if he were exhausted from a long and hard days' work. When the smoke cleared from Romeo's view, Kia appeared from her bedroom wearing a hot-pink Teddy that spelled out, "come fuck me", to any man. Romeo continued to sit and smoke, as he admired her sexiness as she pranced around the apartment. Her hair was down her back, in no particular style, just laying and silky with blond streaks. Everything about her was clean, as if she'd just stepped out the shower. Even her scent was new and more vibrant. She floated into the kitchen and poured her and Romeo a drink of Hennessy and Alize`. She then returned and sat the two drinks on top of two coasters that were placed on the table. Romeo couldn't take eyes off of her. He observed her every move as she briefly disappeared into her bathroom. The jacket of her Teddy rode just above the bottom of her ass cheeks. Romeo was in such a trance, she caught him staring in her direction when she returned to the front room.

"You like what you see Mister Man" She asked

She spoke in her very soft and "please come fuck the shit out of me," voice. Romeo just laughed and continued to smoke and sip on his drink. Kia floated over to the stereo and popped in a CD, during which she had to pose right in front of Romeo's view. She then hit the play button and went over to the window, shut the blinds, and then dimmed the lights. The CD was mixed with a variety of slow jams. When it finally began to play . . . so did Kia.

Romeo allowed her to remove his shirt, exposing his muscular upper body. When kia saw that she had been given a green light to continue, she did. She softly pushed Romeo into a parallel position on the coach to where he was laying on his back to length of the coach. He softly tossed the blunt he was smoking on in the ashtray as he willingly obliged her request. Kia moved gracefully towards his lips and passionately began feeding him her tongue while one of her soft palms explored his bulging torso. Romeo laid there stiffened by his reluctance to return such passion. Then he thought to himself how hard Kia try's to please him and what she willing to go through to do so, as well as the risk she takes for him. He gently returned the kiss causing her to squeeze him in passion. Surprised by his enthusiasm she suddenly had to gasp for air. No words were exchanged from this moment on. Kia quickly regained her composure and continued her mission to please. They were sucking on each others' tongues aggressively as Kia made her way down to the floor whereas now she was on her knees. Romeo remained in the position he was in. Kia's kisses left Romeo's lips wet with passion as a rainy day abandons the streets. She kissed a path down his neck, across his chest, and around his navel, pampering his body attentively all the while undoing his pants. She wasted no time pulling his pants, underwear, shoes, and socks off all in one piece. She then attacked Romeo's nut sack. Sucking and moaning, sending vicious flood of vibrating sensations through his erogenous zone. Romeo grabbed hold of one of her couch pillows and squeezed. Kia took full advantage of this opportunity to show her stuff. She finally had Romeo all to herself and she vowed to make every second worth his while. She drove up the side of his dick with her soft and wet lips as her tongue left its hot streak of wetness behind. She began bobbing her head swallowing the head of Romeo's dick attempting to suck all the life out of him through his penis. Romeo stared down at her and watched as her hungry ass mouth performed some sensual feats on his dick. One being the way her head rose to the tip of his penis and bobbed his helmet with short, wet, and hot strokes of her wet lips. Romeo closed his eyes for a brief moment, then reopened them and again staring. This bitch knows what she's doing, he thought. He sat up on the couch completely naked. Kia remained on the floor in between his legs. Romeo the gently pulled her up towards him gesturing that she stand. As she did so in front of him, be began removing her garments. Kia's flat stomach was exposed displaying her sexy pierced belly button at Romeo's face level. He started kissing her bronzed flesh and slowly teasing her navel with hot spurts of breath and his wet tongue. The scent of her wetness made Romeo's mouth waster. He lightly ran his fingertips down the sides of her body, from her breast to her protruding hips, lie raindrops falling from the Heavens. Kia latched on to his shoulders as Romeo anxiously relieved her wetness from the confines of her sexy panties. She was now completely naked, as was Romeo. He stood to his feet in front of her staring deeply into her eyes as if he were in love. He launched his tongue into Kia's mouth, again surprising her. Her reaction was to wrap her arms around his neck. He then wrapped his around her waist, gently lifting her off the floor, and securing her in his grasp. Kia felt his hardness against her stomach then she wrapped her legs around his waist and allowed Romeo to carry her into the bedroom as they continued to feed off of each others' lust. He stood aside as Kia released her leg-lock. She sat on the edge of the bed and Romeo slowly dropped to one knee as if he were to propose her hand in marriage. Instead he maneuvered his body in between her legs and began teasing her nipples. He gently pushed Kia backwards in a laying position as he continued kissing and sucking on her torso until he finally came upon her perfectly shaven pussy. It had golden hair that glistened with a wet sweet scent, and was the prettiest shade of hot-creamy-pink Romeo had ever seen. He raised both of her legs into the air bringing them down to rest on his shoulders. He positioned himself while staring sensually into her eyes. Romeo started to softly kiss Kia's inner thighs sending spurts of hot breath across her clitoris every time he crossed over to kiss the other. She gasped at every kiss. Finally, she had her Romeo, she thought. Still she couldn't believe what was happening. One of her thighs trembled. This was Romeo's cue to dive in, he dove into her throbbing pussy with the full length of his tongue sucking and licking passionately, causing Kia to claw at the bed coverings with both hands. Romeo then took one of his hands and pushed down gently at the top of her pussy causing her pearl-tongue to reveal itself. Romeo eagerly attacked it as if it were his last chance at a meal, sucking furiously, yet remaining gentle. Both thighs trembled and she gave in, quickly releasing her thick creamy juices. As it flowed from Kia's pussy, Romeo was like a puppy lapping milk from a bowl. He then stood over her while she pushed with her feet to position herself in the center of the bed. Romeo climbed on top of the bed on all fours like a dog and stared deeply into her eyes as she so eagerly inserted his dick inside her. With his first thrust she came again instantly, squeezing his shoulders to brace herself for the next. His strokes were slow and full of passion, as he was in no rush with this session. He felt her warmth lock on to his hardness as she began to fuck him back. She squirmed, and grinded under his thrusting. They were moving to their own slow music now, meeting each other with every stroke. Kia felt her passion reach its peak again. She tensed her body and Romeo began fucking her furiously hard, pounding his body against hers. Thrusting in and out of her at a rapid speed. Suddenly they stop and began panting and kissing. One last climaxing thrust brought them both to exhaustion. Romeo locked himself inside of Kia as she continued to nibble at his neck and claw at back. She squeezed his dick with her inner muscles, milking every drop of his cum as if it all belonged to her. Romeo took a deep breath, pulled out slowly, went into the living-room, lit a blunt, got dressed, and left. On his way out, he paid no attention, but Kay Kay was back at her post . . . the cracks in the blinds of her bedroom window . . . pissed off!

CHAPTER NINE

It was six in the morning, Romeo found himself sitting at his kitchen table by himself having a cup of coffee. He knew that he would hear it from Nisha, being out all night. One thing was peculiar to Romeo and that was the fact that she didn't blow his phone up last night with calls. His thoughts briefly switched back to last night with Kia. He smiled to himself. The smile quickly faded when his thoughts switched back to Nisha. He thought to himself that she had to have smelled Kia all over him because she was in fact all over him literally.

Nisha was getting out of bed as Romeo sat in the kitchen sorting through his thoughts. She went and handled her morning beauty ritual in the bathroom before joining him in the front room. Romeo had done the same before his cup of coffee.

"Hey Mr. Man . . . how you doing this morning?" Nisha asked,

Her choice of words as well as her sweetness caught Romeo off guard. He was expecting more of a hoochie approach, which contained more vulgar language.

"Whass' hattnin' sexy" Romeo responded, as usual being quick on his feet. "What's on yo' agenda today?" he added.

"Nothing . . . I call myself getting dressed so that I can be ready for whatever . . . like you always tell me to be"

"That's right . . . where DJ at?" he asked

"She spent the night at one of her friend's house"

"Which one baby girl?" Romeo asked

"I don't remember the little girl name boo . . . why? . . . that girl knows how to handle herself"

"What da' fuck you mean she know how to handle herself . . . nigga do you even the girl mother or father . . . . or if she even go one . . . or are you just letting DJ park her fass-ass whereva' she want to like a little hood-rat!"

Romeo was yelling at the top of his lungs. But even he didn't understand why. He got up and walked outside into the backyard for some fresh air and some brief alone time. He thought to himself, why am I trippin' . . . DJ don' spent many a nights at several friends, then, it could be this white bitch he just fucked because he knew his heart belonged to Renee' . . . . the love of his life . . . the mother his pride and joy. All kinds of thoughts were scurrying through Romeo's head when Nisha stepped outside.

"Romeo" She said.

When he turned around and faced her, she had a tall glass of juice and a blunt handing it to him. She sensed something wasn't right, so instead of pouring gas on the fire, attempted to calm him down and try and understand where this fury was stemming from.

"You alright babe?" she asked with sweetness in her voice.

Romeo took the blunt and turned down the juice.

"I'm straight baby girl," he said. "look man . . . I didn't mean to blow like that but babe you better start worrying where and with who yo' daughter is" He continued.

Nisha didn't respond, she just wrapped her arms Romeo's waist and laid her head in his chest. Romeo took a pull on his blunt then exhaled.

"C'mon baby girl let's go"

He pulled away from Nisha and headed back into the house pulling her along.

"Where we going?" she asked.

"Stop asking questions . . . just c'mon"

They moved quickly though the house, gathering keys, money, and of course more weed and blunts. When they reached the car Romeo was still smoking on the same blunt Nisha had given him in the back yard. He got in the car, started it up, adjusted the music, and the changed the CD. Nisha took her time getting in. She was looking at Romeo strange as she made her way around to the passenger side. Something about the way he was acting wasn't sitting right with Nisha, including the fact that he didn't open her door for her like he usually does. She finally got in the car anyway and yet Romeo paid her no attention. He had that blunt sticking out from his lips as he still fumbled around with the CD player's knobs, which was now out of their driveway and hit freeway a short time later. Rome had finally finished the blunt he was smoking.

"Baby girl . . . you got some gum or a piece of candy or something somewhere down in yo' purse?" he yelled over the music.

She didn't answer him right away, but she did start digging in her purse.

"Here", she said handing him a stick of gum keeping her eyes straight ahead as if she were the driver. Romeo traveled the freeway about thirty to forty-five minutes before he exited it and pulled into a car dealership. Romeo noticed the curious look Nisha's face. He parked and got out, again failing to perform his gentleman's courtesy by opening her door. He headed straight for the front door of the dealership with a small paper bag in his hand and entered one of the offices located off the main corridor. Inside the office a beautiful plus-sized white girl was sitting at the desk typing. It was something about her demeanor and the way she was dressed gave Romeo the impression that she was much more than just a secretary. Romeo immediately turned on the charm. He reminded her that he was the gentleman that phoned earlier inquiring about the BMW 735i.

"Yes I remember you sir" She stated accompanied by a flirtatious smile.

"Mmm . . . you're even more-prettier in person than you sounded on the phone" He said.

"Are you flirting for a better deal or just flirting?" she asked sweetly. Romeo just smiled and thought to himself, fuck the deal. It as if she read his very thought, as she returned his smile and thought to herself . . . . no, fuck me. Still smiling and staring Romeo deeply in the eyes, she stood up from her desk, turned to her fine cabinet, and pulled out a file folder, displaying to Romeo what she was Heavenly blessed with. Romeo noticed off the back that she wasn't fat at all, just luscious in all the right ways. The skirt she was sporting let it be known that she had a gang of ass too. It rode right above her knees, showing off a sexy pair of muscular calves, and a hint of smooth-creamy-strong thighs

"Well Mr. Romeo I've already started your paperwork" She said

Turning back to Romeo with a brighter smile, she noticed that by the look and smile on his face, he enjoyed the show she had just purposely put on for him. They both made eye contact and smiled.

"Mm . . . Mm . . . Mm" he said, shaking his head in amazement.

"My I ask what that is for?"

"What?" Romeo asked.

"That little mm . . . mm . . . mm" she said.

"Oh . . . . that was nothing . . . just me admiring your sexiness"

He turned up the charm to his bedroom tone, making her blush so hard that Nisha must have sensed it from the car. She burst through office door with an obvious attitude.

"I hope you having fun!" she exclaimed

"Girl, knock it off, all she doing is getting the paperwork done for yo' car" Romeo said.

"Yeah . . . but what else is the bitch trying to do"

"Umm . . . excuse me Ms, but my name is Ellisa, not Bitch" "Bitch ain't nobody asked you yo' damn name!" screamed Nisha

Romeo quickly got out of his seat and in between the two women.

"I said knock it off!!! Yo' car is ready" He spoke in a stern tone to Nisha

Ellis picked up her desk-phone and made a quick call. Seconds later a salesperson showed up at the door and escorted Nisha to her new car. As she left the office her attitude kind of changed. It was as if a cloud of excitement came upon her. Romeo remained inside the office and continued to pour on his charm even thicker while he signed the sales papers and paid cash for the car.

"Look aaahhh"

"Ellisa," she said reminding him of her name.

Romeo looked up from the papers and was pleased to see that her bright smile had returned.

"Ellisa look . . . . don't let that bitch ruin your day, and thank you kindly for you kindness"

"No problem handsome . . . and if you have any problems with that car or anything, give me a call" She said handing him one of her business cards.

As he reached to grab it, she flipped it over exposing two more handwritten numbers.

"Or just give me a call anyway, when you have some free time" She continued in a light whisper.

Romeo smiled, took the card as he left the office and headed out to his car. When he got there, he got it, started the motor, and grabbed a blunt. Before he lit it, he quickly glanced down the lot in Nisha's direction and noticed a man hanging in the window of the car he had just purchased for her. He then quickly pulled out and drove down to where she is. This character was so into his conversation with Nisha that he didn't even notice Romeo pulling along-side of him. Romeo threw his car in park with aggression, got out, and walked around his car to approach them.

"Is it a prollem' with the motor or something cuz!" Romeo asked, gritting his teeth.

"Naw . . . naw . . . homey I was"

Romeo cut through his words viciously, like a brand new razor.

"Do it look I'm talking to you loc!?" said Romeo.

His body language told Nisha that shit was about to get hectic.

"Baby you trippin' for nothing boo" She said in attempts to calm Romeo down.

He half-ass ignored her comment and locked eyes with he perceived to be a fat ass wannabe baller, until he heard that sweet "boo" at the end of her comment. Nisha called his name a couple more times.

"Romeo . . . Romeo" She said softly.

When the fat-ass heard Romeo's name, he kind of just backed away.

"Ay homey . . . I didn't know the lady was spoken for . . . my bad gee"
He said, throwing his hands in the air in a peaceful gesture. He then
quickly turned and walked away, got into a white Cadillac truck and
drove off.

Romeo paid no attention, nor spoke a word to Nisha. He jumped back
into his car and peeled out. When he reached the freeway he lit his
blunt and pumped up the volume on his music. At this time Romeo
had no destination in mind.

◄○►

Romeo pushed in and out of traffic for an hour before pulling into a
gas station. He got out and stuck the pump in his tank to fill it up. In
the meantime he sat inside the wagon and lit another blunt. As he was
smoking, Renee' and little Romeo pulled into the station.

"Mommy, that's my daddy's car"

"it sure is . . . I wonder where he's on his way to"

Little Romeo got out his moms car and walked over to his dads car on
the drivers' side.

"Daddy!" he shouted. "What are you doing in the gas station?"

"Heeey! Little one"

"Daddy you gon' blow us up smoking in here"

Romeo didn't respond with words. He put the blunt in the ash tray and
closed it. He then reached and scooped little Romeo up into his arms
and drowned him with his love.

"DDDAAAADDDYY!!!" he screamed in laughter.

By this time Renee' had walked up to the car.

"Thass' a shame . . . ya'll more like brother's . . . I guess why my mom call ya'll twins huh?" she stated.

"Hey beautiful, whass' up," Romeo said as he sat up and released his grip on the little one.

"Hey," she replied softly.

She stood right in front of Romeo, posing her sexiness. She was wearing some low-cut jeans with a fitted DKNY blouse and some Nike tennis.

"Daddy, what you finna' do today . . . you wanna' come with me and mommy?"

"What ya'll bout to get into?" asked Romeo, looking up to Renee' for a response.

"Too much of nothing" she said, "Little Romeo wants to go to I-Hop so that's where we're on our way right now"

"Aright I'm with that . . . . so you ridin' with me or what little dude?"

Lilttle Romeo climbed over his dads lap to get in. He buckled himself into the seat and started fumbling around for the remote to the stereo. As he raised the middle armrest, and located the remote, he also saw his dads forty-five.

"D-A-D-D-Y . . . Yo gunnn" He sung.

Renee' immediately jumped down Romeo's throat.

"What the heck! Junior, get out!" she exclaimed.

"Naw he cool babe . . . . I'll put that up baby girl . . . please don't start trippin'" Romeo pled.

"Trippin' . . . . look, we'll just meet you at the food place" stated Renee'

She rushed around to little Romeo's side of the car, got her baby out, and headed back to her car. She then strapped him in his seatbelt, finished pumping her gas, and left. Romeo followed right behind them in the wagon. By the time they reached I-Hop, Romeo's understanding of Renee's tongue lashing about the gun had changed. They all went inside and was seated. Romeo immediately apologized for his stupidity and his awareness being low.

"Baby girl . . . thass' my bad . . . I wasn't thinking, and I know I don't have no room for not thinking or mistakes with him" he said, nodding his head towards his son.

He reached and grabbed her hand, looking her in the eyes. His charm even brought a smile to her face.

"It won't happen again boo" he said.

They enjoyed the rest of their morning eating pancakes and crepes, with strawberries and whipped cream, and bagels with fruited cream-cheese. Little Romeo enjoyed himself the most. Having his mom and dad together in harmony was always a joy for him. Romeo got a call on his cell phone, stayed a little while longer enjoying his son and his moms company, then left. Shortly thereafter Renee' and little Romeo left.

All kinds of thoughts were racing through Renee's head as she was driving. So much so, that she didn't hear little Romeo when he thanked her for taking him and his dad to breakfast. She continued thinking and driving as the little man enjoyed the rest of the ride.

◄○►

Later that evening, after handling a few errands and chilling with his little homies, Romeo finally headed home for the night. It's been a couple of days since he and Nisah been in the same room with one another, aside from this morning. The lack of trust had already evolved in Romeo from his knowledge of Nisha's promiscuous past. However, Romeo was man enough to give everyone a clean slate from the beginning. As he pulled up to his home, he set his mind on going inside and making up for lost time with Nisha. He notice her car parked in the driveway. He parked next to it, got out and went into the house. However, no one was home. At that particular moment this didn't bother Romeo, but he did wonder why the house was empty. He threw his keys on the counter and went straight to his weed box. He rolled and lit up a blunt and chilled in the living-room for about fifteen minutes before Nisha walked through the door with a both hands full of bags.

"Hey boo" She said.

"Hey hey . . . whass' hattnin" he responded. "Where you been?" he added.

"At the mall shoppin' . . . where you been?"

She had a slightly suspicious attitude in her tone, yet she didn't wait for response. She strolled to the bedroom with her bags. When she returned, she was wearing a very sexy and provocative, royal-blue negligee. She posed against the living-room doorway and cleared her throat to get Romeo's attention.

"How this look baby?" she asked/

Romeo was laying across the couch still smoking on the remnants of his blunt.

"Mmm . . . thass' niccccee" He sang.

"What's wrong with Romeo . . . . you tired or something?" Nisha asked.

"Naw . . . I ain't tired, but I am trying to get some sleep . . . . me and the little homey got to go handle some business O-T (out of town) tomorrow"

Just that quick, he lied without even trying. Damn, he thought, could it be this white bitch is still on his mind like that. He jumped up, grabbed his car keys and cell off the counter and headed out the door.

"Where you going?" Nisha yelled out.

"I don't know" he responded

This was true. Romeo didn't know where he was going. He just wanted to get out of there, so he just left. As he was rolling in the wagon, smoking and listening to some oldies, he got his thoughts together. This was what he needed first and foremost, to get his thoughts back on track. He came to a stop light as the song on the CD was changing. In that instance he noticed his cell ringing. He reached and turned down the volume before the song came on, then answered the call.

"Hello" he said

"Hi handsome . . . are you busy?"

Romeo immediately noticed the voice of that chunky white girl from the car lot. Just what he needed to help clear up some of his thoughts, he thought.

"Naw, I'm just out and about, whass' up" he said.

"Well . . . I was just wondering if you had a little time, could you stop by . . . . I'm off work today and I could use some company"

"Where you at?" asked Romeo.

"At home" Ellisa said.

"And where's that sexy"

"Oh . . . I'm sorry . . . my address is2344 Daisy . . . . it's right off Willow Street.

"2344?" checked Romeo.

"Yes," said Ellisa.

"I'm on my way"

"Okay sweetie . . . see you when you get here"

Romeo hung up the line and dialed BG.

"What it do big homey?" asked BG when he answered the phone.

"Ay loc . . . I'm finna' swing through, I need you to run a ounce of that good out to me when you hear me pull up cuz" Romeo said.

"Got'cha' love one . . . but whass' up?"

"You know me cuz . . . I'm bout to go fuck sumptin'"

Moments later Romeo pulled in front of the safe house. BG was already headed up the driveway. He trotted up to the wagon and threw the ounce of chronic through the window, turned and went back to the back. Once again Kay Kay's nosey ass was peeking out through the blinds as Romeo pulled off the continued his fuck mission.

◄○►

Romeo finally made it over to Ellisa's about 2:30 in the afternoon. She was anxiously awaiting his arrival. When Romeo knocked softly at the door, Ellisa quickly answered wearing absolutely nothing at all. Romeo stood there until she invited him in, he didn't want to seem too anxious himself. Her invite was aggressive. She grabbed him by his shirt, pulled him inside, and literally attacked him. Rome just went with the flow and assisted her in undressing him. It seemed as if they were dancing. Spinning and twirling in circles as Romeo's garments were being torn away from his body. They finally reached the bedroom where Ellisa's king sized waterbed laced with all the finest trimmings awaited them. She pulled away from Romeo's grip and climbed onto the bed, giving Romeo a birds-eye-view of her mountain of an ass. She rolled over onto that ass of hers, sat up leaning back on her palms, and cocked open her legs inviting Romeo to do whatever. And he did just that.

No foreplay was needed. He had smoked several blunts throughout the day and plus this bitch was already anxious and wet as he recognized her glistening juices. He too was more anxious than he believed, as his "Big Dog" rose to the occasion quickly as he climbed on top the bed. He heard Ellisa take a deep breath and then open her legs even wider as he entered her. He started off with slow short strokes while flooding her mouth with his exploratious tongue. Ellisa was moaning and groaning fiercely with every stroke as Romeo pumped harder with every moan. Sweat began to roll off his forehead and she lapped up every drop like a thirsty pink poodle. A desiring feeling overwhelmed Romeo as he started to pump harder and faster. She started panting as if she had just run a marathon at full speed. All of a sudden she wrapped her arms around Romeo as tight as she could, squeezed and shivered. He continued to pump while locked in her grips. She released another load of her juices, this one hotter than the last, and flexed her pussy muscles around Romeo's dick causing him to burst. Hot cum spurted into Ellisas' pussy making her cum again and again. It was as if one triggered the other. Romeo didn't realize he had so much to give; however, he just kept on giving. This passionate quarrel went on for about another two hours. Finally Romeo got up and jumped in the shower and rinsed himself off. When he returned to the bedroom, Ellisa was passed out naked across the bed. She looked peaceful and happy as she slept, thought Romeo as he stood over her and stared, admiring the completion of this mission. As he continued to stare he also admired Ellisa's thickness. Her thighs were chunky and muscular like she lived in the gym. She didn't have a stomach pouch or no sign that her gut was ever out of shape. A big butt, big boned white girl is how Romeo summed it up. He quietly got dressed, kissed Ellisa's forehead, and left.

On the way home he reminisced about Ellisa and smiled to himself as he enjoyed another blunt of the good. When he hit the corner to his block he say that Nisha's car was in the driveway. As he pulled in next to it he noticed a bright red and black Chrysler 300 parked on the street and admired its paint job. He didn't make anything of the car, for all he knew it might of just been one of the neighbors guest. He parked, got out, and headed on up to the front door of his house. He would've usually yelled out or knocked so someone inside could open the door for him. This particular time he didn't for two reasons . . . . One, the house was dark . . . And two, it was getting late so he didn't want to do any yelling to possibly wake the neighbors, so he just fumbled around for his house key then quietly opened the door and let himself in. As soon as he was inside he smelled sex. Immediately he thought of jumping in the shower again this time using soap. Then he heard sounds coming from one of the bedrooms, like somebody was fucking in his house. Right away he thought about Nisha's daughter DJ, and went straight to her room under the impression that it would more than likely be her fast ass. Romeo figured it to be DJ because he really didn't believe Nisha to be that stupid. He approached DJ's door and reached for the knob, when his own bedroom door flung open. There Nisha stood . . . butt ass naked and surprised

"You punk bitch!" Romeo yelled, as he pulled a blue-steel forty-five under his shirt. He swiftly pushed passed Nisha to get further inside his bedroom where there was fat butter-ball ass nigga jumping around trying to put on his clothes. Romeo paused and flashed back as he recognized the face. He remembered being at the car lot, inside the office flirting with the luscious white girl, at which time Nisha was outside being flirted with by this fat ass wannabe baller ass nigga. Romeo snapped back to the present when he heard Nisha screaming in his car.

"Baby please . . . . Noooo! Please no baby!"

"Baby my ass bitch!" Romeo exclaimed.

"Baby I'm sorry . . . I love you . . . baby I promise I'm sorry" cried Nisha.

Romeo just stood there with his pistol in his tight grip, contemplating and staring at this fat ass nigga.

"Get the fuck out my house nigga befo' I do somptin to yo' punk ass . . . and take this punk bitch wit'cha' nigga . . . you can have'er!"

Romeo returned to leave and Nisha jumped in front of him begging and pleading for his forgiveness. He just pushed past her, grabbed his car keys, went to his car, got in, lit a blunt, and left. In his mind as he pulled away from his home, he could see the fire burst from the barrel of his forty-five and disintegrate Nisha's head. He wasn't really tripping on the fat boy, knowing that he himself have fucked a lot of niggas's bitches and wives. Also the thought of life in prison flashed through his head along with being away from little Romeo. And he just couldn't live with that. Let alone having to deal with Renee'.

While Romeo was being harassed by his thoughts, he phoned Renee'. She answered the phone still half-asleep, so he didn't speak a word. He hung up and let her rest.

◄○►

In the meantime . . .

A bunch of L.A.'s finest was at the safe house. Half the block was taped off with yellow tape it seemed. Kia was shook up as she was being questioned by a detective.

"Ms . . . I'm Detective Caldwell . . . I'm with the L.A. Gang Task Force . . . may I speak with you a bit? He asked Kia

She shook like someone was physically shaking her. "Yes" she squeaked out.

"Did you see who did this?"

"No sir . . . well . . . . not exactly" Kia said.

"What do you mean, not exactly Ms.?"

Kia started crying again. Tears all at once began pouring from her face as she tried to explain to the cop.

"I mean all I heard was a lot of shots . . . and when I looked through my bar-door, I saw two people wearing ski-masks running up the driveway"

"Can you give me a description of the two people?"

"No!" she screamed, frustrated at the questioning. "I told you they were wearing masks."

The detective noticed her frustrations and fear. He handed her one of his business cards from his inner pocket.

"Here Ms . . . . Please . . . in case you remember anything else; give me a call . . . please"

He turned and walked away but hesitated.

"Oh . . . . Ms . . . . Did you know the victims?" asked Caldwell.

Kia's attention was beamed in on Kay Kay's window where she notices somebody is peeking out through the cracks.

"Ms . . . Ms" said the detective.

"Huh . . . yes?" Kia said.

"Did you know the victims?" Detective Caldwell asked again.

"No" Kia said softly

She turned and walked back inside her unit, immediately scoops up her cell phone off the table and tries to contact Romeo for the twentieth time, still to no avail. Kia hung up the cell in frustration and just sat there in the darkness of her living-room trying to piece together what the hell was going on.

CHAPTER TEN

Romeo woke up in his car parked outside of Renee's house. He looked at his clock and saw that little time had passed. So he lit a blunt, flipped his cell phone open, and got out of the car. He leaned against the hood pissed at himself for allowing for allowing himself to be played by a dirty bitch like Nisha. He couldn't shake the anger so he dialed Renee's number again.

Renee' was in bed when she answered her phone. The time on her clock read fifteen minutes past midnight.

"Hello . . . who is this?" she asked.

"Hey baby girl . . . . it's me" Romeo said softly.

She quickly rose in her bed to alert when she recognized the voice and who it was.

"What is it . . . What's wrong . . . Where are you . . . Are you okay?" she asked all at once.

Renee' couldn't help but wonder why the hell would Romeo be calling her at this time of the night . . . or better yet this early in the morning. He laughed at her moment of hysteria.

"Damn girl . . . calm down . . . I'm cool, just tired"

"Where are you?" she asked again.

"I'm on the front porch" He said.

"Whose porch . . . mine?" she asked.

Before he could say anything else to Renee', she was opening her front door. Romeo stood up from the chair he was sitting in and Renee' welcomed him inside with loving and open arms. Renee' had on her bath robe with nothing underneath, however she held it closed with her free hand until she opened the door and seen it was really her Romeo. She relieved her hands of their duties by dropping her phone and letting her robe just hang open. Underneath she was completely naked. From head to toe Renee' was one tone, and that was pure chocolate. She quickly wrapped herself around the one man that she truly loved for so long. Sensing his hurt she began to ease his pain with everything she's got, with no reservations or prolonging questions. Although Romeo had just endured a flurry of sexual releases he always had a reserve for the right woman, and the right in Romeo's life has always been Renee'.

When she kissed him, he felt like his whole life had just changed in that instant. She was kissing him and walking backwards, drawing him to her touch. He followed her lips with his, like a little puppy being drawn by a once in a lifetime treat. As she lead him, Renee' reached and grabbed his forty-five she knew was in his waist. She placed it on the counter as they gracefully made their way to the bedroom. All of her attention was on lifting some of the burdens she knew Romeo was carrying tonight. He completely fell into her trance. Stuck like metal to a magnet, the two of them floated to the bed and intertwined their bodies together as one massive body of genuine unconditional love. Every movement that was made, they made together as one. She spoke to Romeo through her eyes and Romeo understood every word her loving eyes said. His responded with tears as they both came to a long deserving climax simultaneously. Together they soared into their own world of bliss, full of ecstasy, again . . . finally.

The light of morning came and little Romeo was up bright and early. When he made it to the kitchen to fix a bowl of cereal, he noticed his dads gun sitting atop the counter. He curiously stared at it for a long time, considering. Little Romeo knew the dangers of guns and he really knew the dangers of getting caught playing with his dad's gun, yet he was briefly fascinated. The little one took off from this enticing scene, darted to his mom's bedroom door, and began banging on the door furiously.

"Daddy!!! Daddy!" he shouted. "its me daddy . . . open the door"

"Its open sweetie" Renee' said sweetly.

Little Romeo turned the knob and pushed his way in on soon as he realized that it was really his dad his eyes lit up. He then ran, jumped up into the bed, and landed right on top of his dad.

"Thass' a shame" Renee' once again expressed.

Romeo began tickling the little one, and his laughter filled the house.

"How'd you know I was here smarty?" Romeo asked.

Little Romeo looked at his mother and then back to his dad with cautious eyes.

"I saw your gun on the counter daddy" He said.

Renee' immediately left the room to retrieve the pistol and put it away. When she returned to the room, Romeo had taken little Romeo's mind off the gun. He had hooked the Playstation game up to the T.V. in Renee's room. She then returned and put the pistol up in her closet without little Romeo seeing her. She and Romeo made eye contact and she just winked at him, giving him the heads up on the coast is clear . . . now that's team work, she thought. Romeo blew her a silent kiss that caused her to smile. Inside, Renee was truly scared. She barely understood what exactly was going on, but she knew she truly loved this man, therefore, she believed in her heart that her position was at his side. As she watched her two men bond, her mind scrambled and her heart continued to race. She vowed that whatever was going on here at this moment, she would never let him slip away again.

"Romeo," she said in a very sweet voice.

They both answered at the same time.

"Oh yeah . . . I forgot I got two of you"

"You're a lucky lady then, mommy" the little one said.

Renee' and Romeo were thrown by that remark from their son, and burst into laughter.

"I'm talking to the big one baby" She said.

"Whass' up baby girl?"

"I need to talk to you for a minute . . . please" she requested.

The two Romeo's looked at one another briefly, and together they both let out a fearful,

"Uh Ohh"

"Oh stop it, nobody's in any trouble little Romeo" said Renee'.

Little Romeo laughed and continued to play the video game. Renee' led Romeo out into the living-room and sat on the couch. Romeo followed quietly and sat next to her. She then grabbed both of his hands and caressed them gently in hers, looked deeply into his eyes, and began to explain how much she loved him. Before she really got started, Romeo cut into her words.

"Look baby girl . . . I know how much you love me . . . and believe me, I'm crazy about you. But baby the way I'm living just ain't fo' you and my little man . . . I know shit gotta' change baby girl . . . its just right now I'm stuck in da' game paper chasin'"

"No . . . you look . . . I'm not letting you get off that easy this time mister man . . . . you're not stuck nowhere and we need you here . . . now you listen . . . you do what you have to do, but her is where you belong, and here is where we want you . . . . so you just make sure you come home every night" she stated.

Romeo always admired the way she takes control, in her gentle way, over him. He's always loved her and his son dearly. It was pure fear that broke up his family, the fear of something happening to them because of him and these street games. Renee' kissed him and got up from the couch.

"So that's it?" Romeo asked sarcastically.

"That's it that's all baby . . . why . . . . you got something else you wanted to say?"

Romeo just laughed.

"Alrighty then . . . oh your phone has been ringing off the hook all night . . . it maybe one of your little hoochies" Renee' said as she strutted away smiling.

He once again laughed along with her sexy sarcasm then calls for little

Romeo.

"Hey little man," he yelled.

"Huh?"

"Ay homey would you grab daddy's phone off the dresser and slide it to me real quick?"

Without another word, little Romeo showed up seconds later with the phone in hand. The glow in little Romeo's eyes was obvious. He was very happy his daddy was home again, at least that's what he hoped.

When Romeo got the phone, he scrolled his missed calls list. There were twelve missed calls from Kia and four from Romero. He figured Kia was just being sprung, and Romero just wanted to smoke something, but none of this was more important than what he was doing now so he didn't answer any of the messages right away. At this moment he just wanted to enjoy the rest of the morning with Renee' and his son.

"Daddy," yelled Little Romeo as he was carrying a tray with juice and napkins to his pops. "Me and mommy made you some breakfast," he continued.

"Yeah . . . we trying to get daddy to come home where he belong . . . ain't that right baby," stated Renee.

"That's right mommy"

"Shiiiittt . . . you keep keeding me like you did last night . . . how can

I not wanna' come home" Romeo said

Renee' playfully popped him across his head. "Boy stop being mannish," she said, "And F.Y.I. (for you information), that ain't nothing compared to what momma got in store."

Romeo smiled and sat at the coffee table to eat his breakfast with little Romeo and Renee'. She had questions about the messages on his phone, however she refrained from asking. Romeo could almost feel exactly what she was thinking. He knew she was curious about the messages. That was the real reason he didn't check them right away. He also knew how good it felt to be home and surrounded by love, and he didn't want to fuck that up in any kind of way . . . for nothing in the world . . . . at least not this morning.

CHAPTER ELEVEN

Romeo was at St. Mary's hospital awaiting the status of his son's injuries. He had made several calls to Romeo however he's yet to receive any responses to any of them. Romeo was quickly becoming very antsy and frustrated from just standing in a crowed waiting-room not knowing what exactly was happening or has happened to his junior. Ma'Ma", Romero's mother, as well as Monster, known to Romero Jr. as Uncle Tony, also shared in Romero's suffering the fear of the unknown. They all waited against their civilized will impatiently to see if Junior was alright. No one knew the extent of the little fella's injuries, but everyone worried.

While playing in the front yard of Ma'Ma's house yesterday around six-thirty in the evening, Little Romeo was struck by a stray bullet as someone drove by the house and fired multiple shots.

The waiting was now driving everyone in the room ballistic. Even those who were there for themselves were worried of what might be the outcome for the Ramirez family. Romero was etching towards the edge in his pacing the floor of the waiting-room which only made everything the much worst.

"Romeo! Cientate!" Ma'Ma' yelled. Telling him to sit in spanish.

She scared the shit out of everyone in the room, especially Romeo. He immediately stopped in his tracks and sat as she requested. A doctor was entering the waiting-room as Romero's ass was almost relaxed on the hard plastic. He had on all white garments and was carrying a clipboard with a chart attached to it, which he was flipping through.

"Is there a Mr. Ramirez here," he asked looking up at the crowded room.

"Yeah . . . Yeah . . . That's us . . . I, I, I, mean that's me." Romero answered anxious and fearfully.

Romeo was scared as fuck and really didn't know what to expect.

"Sir . . . calm down," the doctor said. "Take it easy . . . the bullet barely grazed your sons arm . . . he's just a little shaken up . . . Awash right he's asking for his uncle."

Romero was still antsy and frightened. His mind wasn't registering what the doctor was saying, right off.

"Aaaaaaahhhhhhhh, yeah, yeah this is his uncle Tony right here." Romero managed to mumble out as he grabbed hold of Monster's shoulder.

The doctor quickly held up one of his hands as to say stop.

"No sir . . . He's asking for a uncle Romeo"

Romero immediately took out his cell phone and frantically attempted to call Romeo's number. Still he got no answer, yet he left another message.

MESSAGE:

"Ay fool . . . Lil Romero is in the hospital ay . . . he got shot last night. We at St. Mary's . . . get here ay . . . he's asking for you."

———————————◄○►———————————

Romeo and his junior was still doing their bonding thang back at Renee's, while she just simply stood in the harmony of their atmosphere. Romeo's phone was posted on the coffee-table when Renee' noticed it was vibrating. She started to answer it but decided not to, however as she reached to grab it, it stopped vibrating. Still she took it in to Romeo.

"Hey sweetie . . . this message is from Romero, and it has a 911 code attached."

Romeo took the phone from Renee', looked at its screen, and then pushed in a sequence of numbers to listen to that one message, although he had several other missed calls. The urgency in Romero's voice immediately raised red flags in Romeo's head. He held the cell phone to his ear tightly, as if to erase the present words that were so clearly being relayed to him. After listening to the message several times, Romeo was finally able to jump to his feet.

"Awe shit!" He yelled.

He quickly began moving about the house. Grabbing his keys, wallet, and slipping his arms back into the shirt he wore yesterday almost simultaneously. As he then headed for the front door, Renee' called out to him unsuccessfully. Finally she was able to catch up to him, and stop him before he got out the door by grabbing him by one of his back pockets. She noticed the puddle of tear building up in his eyes which immediately sent her own fears to it's peak.

"What's wrong Romeo?" she asked.

Right off Romeo had difficulty speaking. The cat had his tongue. His mouth was moving but no words were escaping with sound. He took a few deep breaths, shook his head vigorously, and managed to repeat the words, "awe shit," several more times. This created hysteria in Renee'. Little Romeo looked on from his bedroom doorway in confusion. That's when Romeo realized the static he was causing, so he took a couple of more deep breaths. Finally he was able to calm himself down and speak clearly.

"Lil Romero was shot . . . that was his pops on the message . . . I gotta'
. . . I gotta' go to the hospital now!"

The little one wasn't dressed for the day yet. He still had on his pajamas.
Despite how young he was, he still heard and understood the urgency
of this situation. He quickly turned inside his room, threw on a pair of
tennis, and was the first one out the door.

"Naw baby girl . . . I got this . . ."

Renee' swiftly cut Romeo off mid sentence with her own flurry of words.

"Naw nothing Romeo . . . at you side is where we belong and that's
where we're gonna' be . . . end of discussion . . . now let's go."

Romeo raised an eyebrow In surprise, yet he realized that, that was in
fact, definitely the end of that discussion.

—◄◦►—

Meanwhile . . . at the Hospital.

Romero and Ma'Ma' were waiting for the paper-work to release little
Romero.

They were standing at the reception's desk when they heard little Romeo
yell out to Romero.

"Uncle Romero!"

He ran and leaped into Romero's arms, and they hugged one another
tightly.

"It's cool lil homey," Romero stated in hopes to ease any worries or fear
the little fella" may have had.

Tears began building up in Renee's eyes as she stood at a strengthened
attention next to her big Romeo.

"He's alright ay," Romero reassured them. "The bullet barely touched him ay."

Renee covered her mouth with one hand as the other planted on her chest as if to push back an oncoming heart-attack. She was clearly frightened, yet relieved to hear that the little on would be fine.

One of the nurses walked up to Ma'Ma' and handed her some paperwork to fill out. Afterwards they all walked to the room where little Romero was being cared for. Romero carried little Romeo in his arms. Although he felt secure in his uncles' arms, he yet didn't know what to expect walking into his best friends' hospital room. They pass through a set of double doors then continue down a long and busy corridor. After turning a few unexpected corners, and passing several other rooms, Renee' noticed that one of the other rooms was being occupied by another gunshot victim, by the sign posted on the door next to a chart. When they all entered Lil Romero's room, he lit up with joy.

"Hey champ!" exclaimed Romeo with a big smile. "You okay?"

Romero Jr. was excited to see everyone.

"Look . . . I got shot right here . . . my Pappa say I'muh soildier ay."

"A soldier huh . . . boy com'ere." Romeo said as he gently snatch the little one up into his embrace without disturbing his injury. His eyes were still kind of watery from the earlier scare.

"Let me tell you somptin' . . . me an yo Pappa don't want ya'll being no soldiers okay . . ." Romeo looked away and deeply onto Romero's eyes, and then again refocusing his thoughts back to the little fella'. "you and little Romeo gon' grow up and be something' betta'," he continued.

"Yeah mijo." Ma' Ma' interjected. "You can be better."

She couldn't hold back her tear any longer. She quickly popped the shit out of Romero and Romero before heading out the door and bursting into tears.

"Ahhh Shit Ma'Ma' . . . why you hit me?" Romeo asked.

"Because he's silly but you know better . . . and you should teach him better . . . AYE!" she exclaimed.

The two ones laughed at the way Ma'Ma' bullied their dad's, as they always do whenever their dads get into trouble with Ma'Ma' or Renee'.

Romeo's cell began vibrating as they gathered together Little Romero's things, preparing him to be released. He seemed to be ignoring the vibrating phone on his hip, however, Renee' noticed it right away from the flashing screen. The fact that Romeo wasn't answering it bothered her, so she took it upon herself to unclip it and answered it. Romeo reached for it as Renee' took it, but she was persistent enough to push his hand away and answer it.

"Hello,' she said respectfully.

"Yes . . . it Romeo available" a voice just as sweet asked.

Renee's tone changed immediately when she heard this sweet voice on the other end of her Romeo's phone.

"May I asked who's calling" Renee' said with an attitude.

"It's Kia."

"Well Kia, Romeo is kind of busy at this moment so can I give him a message for you or something."

"Yes . . . pleae tell him that BG's is in the hospital and lil BG got killed last night . . . . look just have him call me as soon possible . . . . I'm at St. Mary's hospital in room 221."

"What!" exclaimed Renee'.

Her mouth dropped to the floor and she straightened up her attitude quickly.

"Sweetie I'm so sorry . . . what room did you say?"

"221." Kia repeated.

"Oh My GOD! . . . we're in room 224 at St . . . . umm hold on . . . . umm Kia."

Romeo's attention immediately focused on Renee' when she mentioned a room number and Kia's name.

"What's up baby girl," he asked.

Renee' looked spooked. She was in spontaneous shock, and wondering how much worst can this day get for her Romeo.

"Baby . . . Baby . . . . it's B'G." stuttered Renee'.

"What . . . Girl who is that . . . What the hell you talking bout . . . Give me tha' phone." He shouted.

Renee remained in a petrified trance as Romeo snatched the phone from her grip. Before he got the chance to put the receiver to his ear, Renee managed to get out what she was trying to say.

"Lil B'G is dead." She said pointing towards the door to the room they were in. "B'G is in room 221," she continued.

Romeo sat little Romero back down atop his bed and stormed out of the room. Seconds later he burst through the doors of room 221 to the sight of B'G laying extremely still in a hospital bed. Romeo had tears and a furious look in his eyes.

"What'tha fuck happened!" he yelled as if B'G could hear him.

All he heard in response was beeping from the machines that were now assisting B'G in staying alive. There were several tubes running in and out Romeo's little homey, and they didn't look like they were helping B'G in any way. All Romeo could do was grab his head with both hands as if to struggle to hold himself together. Renee noticed Romeo's mere breakdown. She reached out and wrapped her arms around him in hopes to comfort him.

"Baby, calm down . . . baby . . . calm down." She repeated as her Romeo bawled in her arms like a child.

"Thass' my lil nigga' . . . Thass' my lil nigga cuz!!!" he cried.

Kia was standing next to B'G's bed crying her eyes out. However, she wasn't only crying for B'G's misfortune, but also and mainly because of the pain It was causing Romeo, and plus the fact that he was now being comforted by another woman.

The eerie sound of the machines flat line-beep caught everyone's attention. They all looked up at B'G as several medical staff rushed into the room and attempted to revive him. Romeo, Kia, and Renee' were told to leave the room, in which they stepped right outside the door and stood there in silence. Several minutes had passed before Romeo broke the silence.

"What tha' fuck happened, Kia," he asked harshly.

Renee' took her place at Romeo's side like she so adamantly vowed to be. Kia recognized Romeo's acceptance to Renee's proclaimed position and held back her feelings. She knew that now was not the time for two bitches to go to war over territory or claim staking, so instead Kia maintained her composure and began telling him what she saw that night.

Renee' handed her some tissue from her purse as she noticed Kia's eyes began to water.

"Thank you" Kia said. "I heard a bunch of shots . . . . so I looked out through my bar door an saw the two dudes running up the driveway." Kia went on to say.

"You don't know who it was . . . you didn't recognize nothing about them" drilled Romeo.

"No . . . . no . . . . not right off . . . but when the police left I did see that bitch in the front peeking out her blinds again . . . that's when it dawned on me . . . . when them dudes was running out she was fumbling with her blinds and closed them all the way . . . . and the bitch never do no shit like that. So if you ask me Romeo that bitch know something . . . and one of those nigga's did kind of remind me of her brother."

Renee' closed her eyes and midly shook her head. Why the hell this bitch, just tell him that . . . thought Renee'. She tightened her grip on Romeo as she felt his entire body tense up. She softly rubbed his stomach with her free hand in attempts to keep him calm like he was some kind of alligator or croc-like monster.

"Bay com'on . . . I need to get you home", Renee' insisted.

Romeo was dazed. Renee' gave a light tug on his arm and they headed back into the room with Romero and his son. Everybody said their goodbye's and I love you's.

Romeo was dazed. Renee' gave a light tug on his arm and they headed back into the room with Romero and his son. Everybody said their goodbye's and I love you's.

Romeo gave a soft kiss to Ma'Ma', and lil Romero, then he and Romero embraced as brothers would in times like these, then they all departed.

Romeo, his son, and Renee' made it home. The entire trip was in silence. They were all heartfully exhausted from the days' events. Romeo got into the house and sat right down the couch with a look of obvious pain on his face. Even lil Romeo saw that this dad was hurting as he sat on the couch next to him.

"You feel like playing the game daddy?" he asked sympathetically.

Romeo attempted to smile as he threw an arm around his son.

"Naw . . . not right now son, okay . . . . daddy need to think for a minute." He said in a very low and sad-like tone.

Renee' stood in the kitchen thinking to herself. She wondered what could she possibly do to help her Romeo get through this.

"Lil Romeo" she yelled out.

"Yes" he answered.

"It's bout that time for your bath baby . . . don't you think?"

Okay mommy . . . but can you please do something to cheer my daddy up . . . he sad right now."

Romeo looked into his son's eyes and tried to smile again. He felt worst when he heard his little man's plea to his mom on his behalf.

"Daddy cool lil one," he lied.

"No you not daddy . . . it look like you wanna' cry," responded lil Romeo.

As the little one stood up in front of his dad, Romeo leaned in and pulled him up into his arms and reassured him.

"Daddy alright lil one . . . I'm just thinking bout the lil homey and his lil man . . . . I'm gon' miss'em . . ." Romeo then looked to the ceiling for more words to share with his son to ease any worries he may have for him.

". . . listen little man . . . . know that I love you and daddy really want you to be good and listen to mommy okay . . . don't be no fool, learn all you can in school. Daddy don't want nothing to happen to you and mommy. You're a good little man and daddy loves you a helleva' lot man . . . daddy loves you a whole bunch . . . . and . . . . and . . . . if something happens to me I need you to take care of yourself and mommy and become a better man okay . . . I love you son . . . I . . .

I . . . I love . . ."

Before Romeo started bawling in front of the little one, Renee' came over, holding her own tears back, and grabbed Lil Romeo by the hand and led him away.

"Com'on baby . . . . daddy's gonna' be alright okay . . . me and you gonna' make sure of that . . . let's go get that bath now okay."

Before Renee' pulled Little Romeo away from his dad's embrace completely. The little dude leaned in and gave his pop's a strengthening peck.

"We'll always love daddy . . . remember that." He said

The both of them, Renee' and Lil Romeo, left the living room hold back their own pool of tears. Romeo got up and went over to the stereo, popped in some slow jams, and returned to his grieving post. The pain of losing love one's will take the gangster out of any gangsta' . . . . exactly what Romeo was thinking . . . at least for the moment.

CHAPTER TWELVE

Ma'Ma' was in the kitchen when Romero arrived home. He did usual thing, kissing her on the cheek to greet and remind her of how much she's loved. He was doing fine until he opened his mouth and asked how little Romero was doing. That's when Ma'Ma' went the fuck off!

"What the hells' the matter with you!!!" she screamed.

Romero was stunned by the way his mother blew up on him out of the blue.

"Ma' . . . wha' . . ."

"Shut up!" she yelled, cutting his words. "You just be quiet, and listen . . . and you listen good boy!"

Romero submitted by pulling one of the chairs from under the kitchen table and sitting down. He knew he was in for it, seeing Ma'Ma' in this rage . . . and walking out wasn't an option.

"Ma' . . ." he tested.

"Shuush!" . . . . I didn't say you can say nothing . . . you just sit and listen!"

She stared and Romero with daggers in her eyes as she held onto her head with both hands as if to hold back a migraine headache from exploding in her head.

"Aye! . . . your father has life in prison."

Romero was again stunned. His mother and the rest of his family had been lying to him all his life. Yet and still he sat there in a trance and respectfully listened.

"He committed a murder when you were just a boy . . . . he was a street thug mijo . . . a thug!" she screamed through her overflowing tears . . . "I asked him not to go . . . I begged and begged, and begged and begged, and ye he went anyway."

Ma'Ma' was now crying heavily, as her emotions began to overwhelm her.

"I lost him . . . he's always been here in my heart, but I lost him . . . I don't want to lose you son . . . Romero . . . . I Can't-Go-Through-ThisAgain! . . . . and my grandson . . . OH MY GOD!!!! My grandbaby!" Ma'Ma' threw her hands up in the air, fed up of all the pain.

"Romero you can't see that he's trying to be just like you!" she screamed. "Can't you see that mijo' . . . are you blind . . . or just too damn dumb to look . . . you're just like your father . . . AYE CAVRRON!" she yelled

She went into a furious Spanish frenzy, screaming obscenities at Romero like she was throwing darts at him. This glued Romero's ass in his seat, his eyes on Ma'Ma', and his ears on her every word. He reached and tried to grab a hold of her hands in an attempt to calm her.

"NO!!!" she said as she viciously snatched away. "Don't you touch me . . . if you want to be like you father, you go right on ahead . . . but I'll damned if I let you take my grandson with you . . . I'll be damned!!! Do you hear me . . . I'll be damned!"

If looks could kill, Romero would be a dead motherfucker from the looks Ma'Ma' was giving him as she stormed out the kitchen. Romero remained in his seat and continued to allow those stabbing words from his mother, brutally poke holes through his heart.

After soaking up all the hurt, he went into the garage where he could be alone, and rolled him a fat blunt. While sitting alone In the dark smoking, he allowed every single harsh word she spoke penetrate deeper, and register in his every thought. He also dwelled on the fact that everybody he knew had been lying to him about his father all this time. How could Ma'Ma' do this to me, he thought. After a couple of blunts and a few hours he called Monster and informed him that he wanted to have a meeting with him and the homies. He need to know who in the fuck had enough balls to do a punk-ass-drive-by on his house. He sounded furious on the phone, and Monster felt it. He sat in the garage for a little while longer smoking and trying to calm down. This method wasn't working by itself so he flipped his cell-phone and made a much needed call to Sabrina.

"Hello," she answered.

"Whass' up with you ay?" he responded

"I'm at home by myself . . . lonely pappi," she said.

"Well look ay . . . . I'm gonna' come by and kick it with you for a little while . . . I need to get away ay . . . you whit' that baby girl?"

"Baby how long before you get here?" she asked.

"Why . . . you got company or something' ay?"

"No . . . Crazy . . . I just wanna' straighten up the house and myself before you get here . . . is that okay daddy?"

"Awe my bad baby girl . . . . give me bout a hour ay . . . . is that cool?"

"Sure pappi . . . I'll be waiting."

After that call, Romero felt a little better. Now all that was left to do was make this get-away last long enough to clear his head. He took a deep breath, got up an left. When he got into his truck, he made sure the music was turned all the way down before he started it up, so that Ma'Ma' and his little one wont hear him leaving. However, little Romero was already posted in his bedroom window. He saw and heard everything that was going on.

Romero hit a few corners before he pulled into a liquor store. He went inside and purchased a pint of Jose' Quervo Tequila, some limes, and a box of blunts.

When he reached Sabrina's house he had to call her so that she could inform the security at the front gate, that she was having a guest.

Sabrina lived in a private community in the city of Cypress. The security here was "white tight", and Romero knew that it was peaceful, and that was just what he needed. No one would know where Romero would be, so he know that he wouldn't be disturbed if he turned his cell-phone off. After the security buzzed him through the gate, he did just that, hitting the off button.

Sabrina answered the door looking like one of them sexy ass Hispanic models from a Smooth Magazine. She'll make you wonder, what the hell motherfucka's see in Vida Guerra. This was one fine ass chicana.

Romero stepped inside feeling luckier than a Las Vegas jackpot winner. She quickly grabbed him by the hand and they floated to the bedroom. Sabrina possessed the gracefulness of a dance. The way she moved, mesmerized Romeo. He stood in the doorway of her bedroom and watched her undress, and he continued to smoke his chronic to mentally boost his performance. He continued to watch her every move as each piece of clothing hit the floor finally revealing a creamy, smooth, five-foot-one-inch petite body of this Mexican goddess.

Romero quickly peeled out of every piece of his own clothing. Within seconds they were indulging in a horizontal tango. Within minutes they were done. Romero was sleep soon thereafter, Sabrina, however, got out of bed and hit the shower. Her pussy still throbbed for passion. She laid down in the dub with her throbbing pussy positioned right under the faucet, and her legs in the forming a giant vee. She let the thrusting warm water beat against her pussy sending a pulsing sensation through her body. Still she yearned for more. Her hand slowly began to make its way to her hot passion pool. Soon as she felt her finger slide inside, her pussy muscles tightened around it like a constrictor. One finger . . . then two. Suddenly she started pounding a loveable sensation between her legs thrusting faster and faster. With the help of the pounding hot water, Sabrina reached a surprising orgasm. She continued to vigorously thrust her fingers in and out until she drained her pussy of every drop of yearning-for-dick it had left. Satisfied for the moment, Sabrina rinsed herself off, got out the tub, remained naked, and continued on with her mission.

Romero was laid out across the bed sound asleep. Sabrina went straight to the pile of clothes Romero had peeled off. She snatched up the pants, dug into his pocket, and retrieved his car key's she had a big devious grin across her grill as she quickly grabbed her robe from the back of her bedroom door, and threw it on headed out to Romero's truck, moving swift and very methodically. She went right for the money. There were rolls of it tucked inside of the middle console. Sabrina grabbed two of the rolls then locked the truck back up. She returned the key's to his pocket, stashed her stash, and got back into the bed Romero.

She began kissing him around his neck area, then down his chest. As she straddled and kissed, she felt his nature rise beneath her. She continued to slide down further until she reached his rod, and swallowed it. Romero jerked to life from her hot ferocious sucking. He rose and propped himself up in sitting position.

"Damn Bitch!" he exclaimed.

Sabrina continued as if she were trying to win the contest of bobbing the life out of a man through his dick. Suddenly she snatched her lips away and slammed herself on top of him, surrounding his dick with her ravenous pussy. Sabrina then bounced her way to satisfaction, stealing an orgasm from him . . . just as she had his money. Again Romero was put to sleep. Sabrina go up, smiled her devious smile, and thought . . . the least she could do was give him his money's worth.

The next time Romero opened his eyes, it was late in the evening. He got up and noticed that Sabrina was gone by the note she had left.

"Had to go pappi . . . mom needed me . . . see you later," she wrote.

He jumped in and out the shower, smoked some more bud, and watched a little T.V. After a while he decided to hit the streets. As Soon as he got into his truck he noticed someone has been inside. When he had parked earlier, he left his cell phone sitting on the middle console and now it was in between the seat. Romero opened the consoles compartment and knew it was the bitch Sabrina. He'd noticed that she had clipped him for a couple of stacks. He laughed to himself.

"Stupid Bitch . . . . you was supposed to take it all . . . . it was for you, you dumb ass tramp." He said himself.

He shook his head, laughed again to himself, and left. He thought, I could leave the dumb-bitch a note . . . "ay you bitch, you left the rest of yo' money stupid!" . . . . He took a long pull on his blunt, picked up his cell phone and left her a message instead. She'll feel dumb as fuck when she hear that, he thought as he headed out.

—◇—

Kay Kay was as usual being a nosey bitch, always peeking out her windows at something like she was the neighborhood-watch captain. Little did she realize fate was closing in on her nosey ass. Like now, she was sitting at the back door in her kitchen looking through the blinds, spying on Kia's unit, as somebody was knocking on her own front door. The entire house was blackened from the darkness of her not having on any lights. Too busy at being nosey, without asking who it is, she just opens her door. BOOM! She hit the floor hard as she drifted into a painful daze. She heard a deep voice speak, however she was unable to make out what the voice was saying. Neither could she make out the face that was hovering through her blurred sight.

"Where yo' brotha' at bitch!"

Kay Kay was unconsciously reaching for her head, still dazed. She attempted to put together some words but all she could do was grunt from the pain throbbing in her head.

"Where yo' punk ass brotha' at Bitch?" the voice repeated.

"Ugh . . . I don't know . . . what's going on . . . . why you in my house?" she finally managed to asked.

Suddenly she felt a kick to her ribs. Feeling surrounded, she tried to scream, but the agony silenced her. Romeo told one of his little homey's to hand him the phone.

"Look bitch . . . I don't care what you have to do but you betta' get that nigga' on the phone and get him over here! . . . matter of fact, tell'em you found the rest of my stash so he need to come get like pronto . . . you hear me you punk bitch!" stated Romeo.

He grabbed Kay Kay by the throat causing her to gag and choke. Finally she was able to put a face to the voice she was hearing. Now she was really spooked. She had never seen this side of Romeo before and she had no idea what he was capable of or what he had planned for her future.

"Okay . . . Okay." She pled through her choking. "Please Romeo . . . I didn't have shit to do with it." She continued.

Again she felt a boom. This time a fist crossed her mouth like a wrecking ball condemning an old building. On top of that, Romeo slapped the shit out of her with her own phone.

"Bitch shet the fuck up and get that nigga on the phone now!" he shouted.

D-Kay pulled out his gun and chambered a slug. When Kay Kay heard that "click and clack", she quickly got the program.

"Okay" she cried reaching for the phone.

She cleared her throat and sniffled to get herself ready to talk and sound convincing. Her life depended on it.

—◄○►—

Big Fred was at the Century Club living it up with a few of his homies when he got the call. The club was poppin', the music was loud and bangin', and the hoochies was slangin' ass all over the place. When his phone vibrated, he immediately answered it. As he put it to his ear, he had to plug his other ear up with his finger to block some of the club's noises out.

"Hello . . . Hello! He yelled into his phone.

Unsuccessful at hearing any response, he yelled into his phone again.

"Hello . . . Hello . . . . Who dis' . . . speak up I can't hear you."

Kay Kay was still surrounded by nigga's with guns as she tried to talk, which made her nervous as hell. However, the frustration from her fears sat in and she managed to yell out.

"Man it's me!"

Fred recognized her voice and told her to hold on. He made his way into the restroom of the club.

"Damn sis . . . I couldn't hear shit . . . I'm in the bathroom now . . . whass' up?" he asked.

"Man you ain't gon' believe this shit." said Kay Kay.

"What."

"You gotta' get over here man."

"Why . . . what it do blood?"

"I found the rest of O'boy's stash in the back man . . . so come get this shit . . . Fred . . . it's a whole bunch of this shit too, and I'm getting nervous and paranoid as fuck . . . plus I think that white bitch saw me back there."

Fred lit up like a Christmas tree listening to what his sister was telling him.

"Whaaaaaat . . . . you bullshittin' sis."

"Fool . . . . I ain't got no time to be playing . . . you betta' hurry up and get yo' ass over here cause I'm finna' leave man."

"No . . . No . . . don't move sis . . . I'm on my way."

They both hung up the phones. Kay Kay had a pleading look on her face as she was looking up at Romeo. He redirected her attention towards D-kay by nodding to him. That's when Lil Flash quickly grabbed a hand-full of her hair, pulled her head back, and slashed her throat from ear-to-ear with his hunting knife.

"Throw that bitch in the tub befo' she bleed on everything cuz' stated Romeo.

Flash and C'Loc did just as Romeo requested. Before they returned to the front room, Flash turned on the shower and just let it run over Kay Kay's body.

"Ay D-Kay . . . go make sure all the vehicles is out of sight loc," requested Romeo.

<hr>

Romero was pulling into the parking lot of his paint shop. This was where he conducted most of his business and had his meetings with his homies and associates. As he got out of his truck he flipped his phone open and made a quick call to Monster.

"Ay holmes . . . I'm at the warehouse ay . . . call the homies and meet me there ay."

Romero didn't wait for a response from Monster. He hung the phone up immediately after making his request. Full of rage once again, he entered the shop, locked the door behind him, headed straight for his office, fired up another blunt, and went off into somewhat of a scarface-rage. He started yelling and knocking shit all over the office. Tears ran down his face from the thought of nearly losing his son. He kept flashing over the events of the past few days in his mind.

"Muthafucka's wanna' shoot at my boy . . . shoot at me punk ass . . . . shoot at me ay!!!" he pounded on his chest like a mad ape. "What . . .

What Ma'Ma' . . . why you bitchin' at me ay . . . it ain't my fuckin' fault . . . I ain't did shit to nobody ay . . . fuck everybody . . . fuck everything ay . . . I try to help muthafucka's and this the thanks I get ay . . . you blame me when shit go wrong . . . fuck that shit ay . . . . it ain't my fucking fault, I ain't the blame ay . . . I didn't do shit to nobody ay . . . fuck this shit ay!"

Romero was in a rage for what seemed to be hours. He had only smoked half of the blunt he fired up. The rest of it just burned in the ash tray. When Monster had entered the shop he noticed Romero in the office pounding on the walls. Instead of just walking in, he tapped on the window until he got Romero's attention. Romero quickly gathered himself and opened the door. However, Monster was reluctant on entering, so he remained outside the door.

"Ay esse' . . . what tha fuck ay . . . you straight esse' . . . what you trippin' out on ay?" Monster asked.

Romero walked around the desk and sat down in his chair and put his head down in his arms.

"I'm tired homey . . . . I'm tired of this life ay . . . I'm tired of Ma'Ma' blaming me for every fuckin' thang ay . . . she act like I inveted this fucking game ay . . . I'm just fucking tired ay."

"Look holmes the homies are on their way ay . . . but you don't look too hot ess' and the young homies don't need to see you like this ay . . . so you want me to cancel this meeting ay?" stated Monster.

"No . . . don't cancel shit fool . . . I want to know who tha' fuck had the balls to shoot them fucking bullets at my son . . . at my familia ay . . . and I need to know now ay!"

"Ay holmes we told you ay . . . . fucking with them blacks esse' . . . its bound to be some foul play ay . . . I wouldn't put it pass'em ay."

"What fool!!! Who da' fuck is we ay!" demanded Romero.

He didn't mean for it to be a question. He spoke to Monster in a demanding tone. After he made that, "we told you", statement, Romero had a cautious smirk on his face.

"Me and the homies," Monster said, "Ay fool . . . we just trying to look out for the familia ay . . . ain't no need to jump all crazy esse'."

"Tell'em I said I'll get back later ay . . . I gotta' handle something fool."

"I'ma roll with you holmes."

"Naw I'm cool esse' . . . I got this one ay."

Romero quickly grabbed his cell phone and keys off of his desk and immediately left the warehouse heading towards his truck while making a call at the same time.

◄○►

Romeo was still posted with his squad inside Kay Kay's house waiting for her brother. D-Kay had just returned from moving the cars out of sight.

"Ay loc . . . you moved the whips cuz?" asked Romeo.

"Yeah big homey . . . I moved your's around the co'na' . . . them nigga's don't know our cars but I still parked'em down the street." Stated C-Loc.

"Cool . . . now all we do is wait."

Romeo pulled out a blunt and lit it. D-Sac joined him in the kitchen to hive him some assistance in smoking it. C-Loc sat in the living-room with Lil Flash, in the dark, sharing a blunt of their own. They were all extremely pissed at the lost of their loved one as they awaited the arrival of Kay Kay's brother. Romeo's phone vibrated and broke the silence.

"Hello", he answered.

"Whass' up homey?" asked Romero.

"Whass' cracking love one?" asked Romeo.

"Ay fool I need you ay . . . it's a emergency ay."

"Where you at homey?"

Romero was flying in his truck on the 710 freeway heading home.

"Ay fool . . . meet me at the house ay . . . I'll be in the garage . . . and ay carnal . . . try to keep it quiet when you pull up ay."

"Whass' up homey . . . you straight?" asked Romeo

"I need you holmes . . . hell naw I ain't straight ay!" exclaimed Romero.

"Damn loco . . . . I'm trying to handle something right now cuz."

"I need you ay . . . meet me in the garage."

Romeo hung up the phone on that note. He sensed the urgency in the drop of Romero's tone. Something was up.

"Hey lil homies . . . I gotta' make a real quick run cuz . . . when this nigga get here tie his punk-ass up loc . . . and if his homey is with him put his bitch ass in the tub with sis . . . I'll be back cuz."

Romeo left Kay Kay's spot in a speedy fashion. He ran all the way to the end of the block to get his car. As he was approaching it, he got an uneasy feeling that he was being watched, so he quickly surveyed his surroundings. He paused briefly, looking at the black sedan creeping up the block in his direction. All of a sudden gun shots rang out from the window of the dark. Romeo quickly ducked behind one of the near-by parked cars. He reached down in his waist and pulled his pistol to return fire. The car sped to the end of the block and turned right. Romeo hurried to his car, got in, and got gone before them or the cops come back. It ain't never been no shooting on this block, he thought . . . . . what the fuck was going on . . . nigga's knew better.

CHAPTER THIRTEEN

t took forty minutes for Romeo to arrive at Ma Ma's house. He pulled up quietly like Romero had requested. When he got out his car he was extra cautious, due to what he had just encountered about forty-five minutes ago on the other side of town. He stepped out of the wagon gun in hand ready to squeeze at anything that moves wrong. He made it to the side door of the garage and tapped on it real lightly. Nobody answered. Romeo then slowly turned the knob and cautiously walked inside. He was startled by the sound of Romero's voice.

"I'm here fool." whispered Romero from the darkness.

"Damn Cuz . . . cut some damn lights on in this mutha fucka' homey . . . why you in the dark cuz?" Romeo asked.

Romero got up and hit the light hanging over the pool-table so it won't be that bright.

"Ay Romeo . . . shit is bout to hit the fan homey . . . I need you to be real with me ay."

Romero stood opposite Romeo, on the other side of the pool-table. He still held his pistol in-hand.

"What tha' fuck you talking bout cuz . . . wha'd up homey . . . . whass' going on with you?"

"Look esse' . . . shit bout to hit the fan ay."

"You damn right shit bout to hit the fan muthafucka . . . some of yo' lil homies just tried to have my head loc."

"What . . . who! . . . did you see'em ay?"

"I'm pretty sure the one that was driving was Pelon homey . . . matter of fact I'm positive."

Romero grabbed his head in disgust. He was sure of what he was thinking now. Romeo had just confirmed it for him.

"Whass' up loc . . . something ain't right cuz . . . it's all over yo' face homey." Romeo stated.

"I think them vatos is tryng to start a way ay."

"What the fuck is you talking bout . . . we already got a war cuz . . . that ain't nothing new."

"Naw big dawg . . . . I'm talking about a war between me and you esse'."

"Who?"

"Listen ay . . . . the didn't want me fucking with you from jump-street ay . . . . now that we don' bonded fool . . . fuck!" his words were cut short by his thoughts and memory. "That fucker Monster tried to convince me several times that you had something to do with the shooting at the house ay."

"And you think . . . naw homey . . . I don't think yo' homies would shoot at yo son cuz."

"What you think esse'?"

"Go get yo' little one loc."

"Naw . . . I don't want . . ."

"Naw my ass cuz . . . you wanna know or not . . . . look if anybody saw who . . . it's the little one. Other than that we gon' be assuming cuz . . . and you know how that shit gon turn out . . . so go get the little fella' and tell'em his uncle Romeo is here to check in on him."

"But Ma'Ma' . . ."

"But Ma'Ma,' what!" she exclaimed . . . "What are you two up to this time?"

Romeo and Romero, was spooked for a brief second by Ma'Ma's sudden appearance in the garage.

"Hi Ma'Ma'. Romeo said. "Where's my little dude at?"

"He's . . ."

"Uncle Romeo!" Romero Jr. shouted.

Romeo discretely tucked his pistol, and let his T-shirt conceal the handle as everyone's attention was focused on the little one's excitement.

"Right here . . . . now what's going on?" Ma'Ma' continued.

Romeo scooped little Romero up into his arms and flooded him with hugs and kisses.

"How's that arm champ?"

"It don't even hurt uncle Romeo."

"Thass' my little man . . . look little one uncle just came by to check in on you real

Quick . . . and little Romeo sends his love too."

"Tell'em I love him too uncle Romeo . . . . can little Romeo come spend the night tonight uncle Romeo?" he asked.

"Yah lil one . . . as long as Ma'Ma' says it's okay. Hey listen . . . unc glad you okay, but I need to ask you something okay."

Ma'Ma' and Romero remained silent, and allowed Romeo to work his magic. This charm he possessed attracted everyone to him. It was a rare that a person wouldn't like him. Kids loved him.

"Did you see who shot you that night?" he asked Jr.

"No . . ." the little one replied.

There was a brief pause that filled the room with a chilling silence. Romeo and Romero looked at one another and let out a sigh of relief.

". . . But my uncle Sneaks was driving." The little one added.

"Huhh!" Ma'Ma' gasped.

It was like everything in the room stopped, even time. Romero's heart dropped to the bottom of his feet, ricocheted back up and blew up his tear shed. His eyes erupted into a steady flow of salty tears from his anger. All he could do was stare with fiery tears in his eyes.

"Hey champ . . . good looking out . . . your're a real champ . . . . uncle's big boy. I'm real proud of you and papa is too. And I'll tell little Romeo what you said okay."

"Okay . . . I love you too uncle Romeo, and you too papa."

Romeo let him down out of his arms and gave him a few more kisses. Little Romero then ran over to his dad and hugged him too. Romero returned the hug and looked up to Ma'Ma' with those same fiery tears.

"You do what you had to do mijo." She said.

She took her grandson back inside with her. Romero and Romeo remained inside the garage for a little while longer discussing the business at hand.

"What you think now esse'?" Romero asked.

"I think this shit is fucked up homey . . . what'chu' wanna do?" asked Romeo.

"Naw I got this ay . . . you go handle yo' business homey . . . don't worry out me ay . . . I got this holmes."

"You sho'?" asked Romeo.

"I'm positive holmes." Romero answered deviously.

"Holla' if you need me, my nig' . . . I'll be here pronto feel me."

"All the time holmes."

They embraced and Romeo left the garage on his way back to Kay Kay's house. He pulled off leaving the music down low. He was pushing faster than usual due to the events of the day. As he pulled up to a red light, he sensed some hard stares coming from the Mexicans in the blue Impala to his right. Romeo quickly noticed it was three of them in the car. When he looked in their direction, he and the driver locked eyes on one another viciously. Romeo pulled his forty-five glock from under the middle armrest, took a deep breath, and focused on their movements while waiting on the light to change. When he light finally turned green, they took off fast, showing off the power of the Impala's motor. Romeo let off a light sigh, released his grip on his pistol, grabbed his cell phone, and slowly pulled ff.

◄◦►

At Kay Kay's house the fella's waited patiently. Finally, someone knocked at the door. It was Fred, Kay Kay's brother, knocking and calling her name. He was with his homeboy, G-Red who was standing behind Fred, looking around suspiciously.

Lil Flash answered the door in a low tone.

"Who is it?"

"Fred."

Lil Flash opened the door to let him in. The house was dark and the music was on low.

"Who da' Fuck is you homey?" Fred asked aggressively.

Fred was a big heavy-set man with an aggressive voice. He stepped inside in an intimidating fashion followed by G-Red. Lil Flash had a happy look on his face like he just got a two-for-one deal on some Jordan's.

"I'm Lil Flash homey." He whispered.

"Where my sista' at blood?" asked Fred.

"She in the tub big homey . . . she told me to open the doe' fo' you when you showed up."

"Ay sis . . . get yo' stankin, ass out tha' tub my nigga." He yelled. "Ay Red close the doe homey . . . and damn blood . . . cut some lights on in this bitch."

When G-red turned and reached for the door knob, D-Kay met his head with the butt of his pistol. The thump was so loud it drew Fred's attention immediately. The light's flicked on and Fred was knocked to floor by C-Loc and D-Sac. They all had their pistols drawn now.

"Is that enough light fo' ya' chump-ass nigga." stated Lil Flash.

Fred was tremendously dazed by the blows he'd just endured. He looked up from the floor confused and unable to recognize any of the faces looking down on him.

"Man . . . what's goin' on . . . . and where my sista at?" he asked.

"I told yo' punk-ass that bitch in tha' tub . . . CUZZ!"

The squad laughed at Lil Flash's sarcasm.

"Ay check that nigga' for heat." Stated C-Loc'

"Man . . . what'chall' need homey . . . some money?" Fred asked nervously.

He attempted to dig in his pocket as if to retrieve some cash to offer for his life, but before he was able to, D-Sac stomped his head into the floor and chambered a slug.

"Look like this nigga wanna join his sista' fo' a bubble bath cuz." joked D-Kay.

"Ay somebody need to call the big homey and let him know we got these bitch-ass niggas." suggested D-Sac.

C-Loc made the call but didn't get through. He figured that Romeo had the music up loud so he chirped him.

Romeo noticed the screen-light on his phone was blinking.

"Whad'up . . . who'dis." He said answering the call.

"It's "C" mafia." C-Loc answered.

"What it do loc?"

"Ay we got them fools cuz."

"Both of em?" Romeo asked.

"Yah nig homey . . . this other nigga's name is G-red . . . these nigga's offered us some money cuz."

"oh yeah . . . I'm on my way loc . . . don't do shit till I get there cuz."

Romeo hung up his phone and put a little bit more foot to the accelerator. C-Loc had also hung up on the other end of the call.

"Ay the big homey said chill . . . he on his way . . . hold on till he get here."

"Oooh wee cuz . . . we gon' have some fun with these busta's." stated D-kay.

G-red was coming around from being knocked out. When he was able to open his eyes, Lil Flash was right in his face smiling.

"Remember me bitch!" Flash said.

He slid across his chin with the butt of his gun again before Red had a chance to answer. And again, G-Red was out like a light.

Fred watched fearfully. He knew that shit was all bad. They were being hovered over by a hungry pack of young, crippin,' wolves.

It was no more than fifteen minutes later, Romeo was turning the corner onto Temple Street, where the safe house was located. He pulled right into the driveway. There was no need to stash the car anymore. As he was getting out of the wagon, Lil flash was cracking the front door open.

"What up big homey." He stated

"Whass' crackin' love one." Responded Romeo.

"M-business." Flash said with his signature devious grin.

"Good shit loc."

Romeo and lil Flash re-entered the house. Romeo greeted the rest of his squad with a simple head-nod. They all responded with the same.

Big Fred was sitting in a chair bound by ripped sheets and D-Sac's shotgun pointed to the back of his head. Romeo approached him with an angry and vicious look on his face.

"Nigga' did you actually think you was gon' get away with this shit." Romeo asked through his gritting teeth.

Fred was already in tremendous pain as well as bleeding from his face. Romeo still reached back, Flash put a forty-glcok in his hand, he took it and wacked Fred across the nose with it's handle, breaking his nose across the bridge. Fred yelled out in agony.

"Ay gee . . . I didn't know it was yo' shit homey . . . sis just called and told me she had a lick for us." Fred pleaded.

He was slapped across the face so hard and swift, he didn't even see who did it.

"Shet tha' fuck up snitch-ass nigga' . . . now you wanna put it all on sis huh!!! You's a bitch nigga. My lil homies mad chump . . . you killed the homey and his son nigga . . . you thru' you punk-ass piece of shit!" yelled Romeo.

"Ay big homey . . . what we gon' do wit hthis other busta'-ass nigga?" asked Flash.

"I don't give a fuck cuz . . . ya'll have yo' way with both of these nigga's."

Romeo head-nodded to his squad and they all commenced to beating G-red to a bloody pulp, giving Fred a close-up preview of what he can look forward to. Romeo turned and walked out, leaving the squad to handle them two busta's.

On the drive home he lit up the other half of the blunt he had left in his ash-tray. He gazed ahead at the red lights on the back of the cars ahead of him as well as concentrated his peripheral on the flashing yellow lines zooming by as he drove. Anything to keep his thoughts off of BG, and his little one.

CHAPTER FOURTEEN

Today will be dooms-day for Pelon, Sneaks, and Monster's punk-ass, thought Romero. Their little mutiny scheme had backfired. He had been sitting in his office of the paint shop all morning since four-thirty, bothered by the fact that these three muthafucka's would go to the extent of shooting at his son to break up a business relationship that they don't approve of. Romero was really in the mood to do some killin'. As he sat in his office thinking, he came to the realization that he would need some help so he phoned Big Joe. This was one of the five Generals that ultimately called the shots over all the Hispanic gangs in Southern California, the main one. When Big Joe got the call, Romero explained to him what was going on, and he too was furious. He ended up sending five of his best henchmen over to assist Romero in his cleanup.

When these men arrived at the paint shop, only one of them did the talking with Romero as he stood out in front of the office with them all.

"Whass' up esse'?"

"Que Vo' holmes . . . I'm Romero ay." He stated, introducing himself and reaching for a handshake.

"Names ain't important esse' . . . we here for the demolition then we out ay."

"Orale." Romero responded, which means, Okay in Spanish.

Romero was looking hurt, betrayed, and disgusted. However, he was reassured to see that Big Joe had sent some real killa's to assist him with his problem. They wont know what hit'em.

"Ay esse' I'm gon' need ya'll out of sight when these fools get here ay . . . I want to talk to these fools first and then I want to see the look on their faces when they find out I know everything ay." stated Romero.

"No prollem' esse' . . . whatever you need ay."

"Orale . . . when ya'll come out the cuts ay be ready to blast these fools holmes . . . they stay heated ay . . . and I really do appreciate this holmes . . . sedio ay, my palabra ay . . . anything yawl need esse' just holla' ay . . . . anything fool."

Romero shook hands with the one. The rest of them just stood there like trained military soldiers, only with khakis and T-shirts instead of army fatigues. After the handshake they dispersed in separate directions into the shadows of the shop. Romero went into his office and waited for Monster, and the other two pieces-of-shit to show.

It was going on eight-o-clock when Romero went into the shop area to check on Joe's boys. When he stepped out of the office he didn't hear or see anything. He knew that they were still there because Joe had ordered them to be, and leaving without handling what they came here to handle would be defying Big Joe, and everybody knew that defying Big Joe is a wrong decision for anyone. It's like the next thing to defying God.

While Romero stood there peeping out the scenery, Monster walked in the shop smoking on a blunt.

"Damn esse' . . . how long you been here ay?" he asked.

"I just pulled in about twenty minutes ago ay . . . where the homies fool."

Before Monster could answer, Pelon and Sneaks walked through the door horse-playing with one another like adolescents.

"Whass' up esse'?" asked Romero/

He greeted and embraced them as usual to avoid any suspicion.

"What's this meeting fo' big homjey?" asked Sneaks.

"We need to get to the bottom of this shootin' shit ay . . . I need to know who shot my boy ay."

"I been keeping my ears to the streets ay . . . and if you ask me ay it was them black fools ay." Stated Pelon.

"Oh yea . . . what the streets been saying to you holmes?" asked Romero sarcastically.

"What'chu' mean esse'."

"You say you been keepin yo' ears to the streets . . . . so what the streets been sayin ay."

"Naw esse' . . . what the homey mean is we been asking around ay

and . . . ."

"I know what this fool is saying ay . . . I ain't stupid fool . . . do I look stupid to you ay . . ."

"Ay esse . . . what up with that shit ay . . . . why you getting' crazy with us fool . . . it was them black putos ay not . . ."

"Naw esse' . . . them black putos ain't did shit ay!!!" shouted Romero, cutting deep into Monster's words.

As Romero shouted, Big Joe's boys seeped out from the darkness like smoke through the cracks of a burning building. No one noticed them until one of them jacked a round off into the chamber of his A-K. Pelon turned and was shocked at the arsenal pointed at his life. Everyone was frozen in their place until Monster went for his piece. Before he could get his hand on the butt of his pistol, one of Joe's boys whacked him across his head with the stock of his rifle. Pelon's eyes opened as wide as a silver dollar is round, as the fear set deep in his chest.

"What the fuck holmes." Screamed Pelon.

Monster hit the floor hard from that blow across the head. The one that clocked him across the head reached down and snatched the pistol Monster was reaching for out of his pants.

"Ay homey . . . . what the fuck is this all about ay?" Pelon asked again.

"Shet da'fuck up you piece of shit!" Romero grunted out. "Meet a few of my real comrades ay."

As Romero was tormenting Pelon with fear, a loud boom silenced him. The side door of the warehouse was blown off it's hinges. This brought Monster back to his feet.

"FREEZE!! L.A.P.D.!" yelled an officer.

Everybody scrambled for cover except Monster. When he finally came out of his daze and made a move for cover, his body was viciously riddled with bullets from several of the officers that was now flooding the shop. Gunshots rang out from all over the shop in every direction. Romero and one of Joe's boys managed to get to the office and barricade themselves inside.

"Sneaks was the first to be captured alive by officers. Before they were able to put Sneaks into one of the police cruisers, Pelon had given himself up. Both were immediately escorted out of the paint shop and put into separate cop cars. Shots continued to sound off for several more minutes inside the shop. Outside, the chief Task Force Officer of the Gang Unit received a call over his radio.

"Ahh chief . . . over."

"Yeah . . . this is the chief . . . what do you got?" asked the chief.

"We got five cold sir . . . and ahhh, two barricaded in a corner office sir . . . over."

"Is the entrance clear?" asked the chief.

"That's affirmative sir . . . the entrance is clear . . . over."

"Hold position . . . I'm coming in." he said.

The chief entered cautiously with his team as coroners removed the bodies of Monster, and four of Joe's boys. The chief gathered with his team and methodically discussed the current situation.

"How many we got in there?" asked the chief.

"It's only two inside the office sir."

"Any hostages?"

"No sir."

"Do we know any of the suspects?" asked the Chief.

"Sir . . . one of the suspects is our primary target sir . . . . Romero Ramirez . . . the other subject is unknown at this time.

"Okay . . . get me some tear-gas in here pronto." Demanded the chief.

He and his Unit Sergeant eased closer to the office. The chief noticed that the two suspects were ducked down behind a desk.

"Post my two snipers . . . tell them if anybody raises their head . . . knock it off." The chief ordered.

"Sir we have Ramirez's mother on the phone."

"GET ME MY FUCKING TEAR-GAS!" was his response.

An officer immediately came in an handed the chief a tear-gas gun, loaded and ready. Another one of the officers brought him in the bullhorn.

"Alright now Mr. Ramirez . . . I'm going to shoot some strong shit in that office in about three seconds, unless you and your accomplice comply with my commands . . . now throw out any and all weapons and come out with your hands held high where I can see them."

"Fuck you ay!" yelled the last one of Joe's boys.

He stood up and squeezed, getting off a few rounds through the office window before one officers of the chief's snipers knocked him off his feet with one of the deadly rounds from the sniper-rifle. Before his body hit the ground a spooky silence filled the shop, then a loud thud form the body hitting the concrete. Romero was now clinched in a fetal position full of fear and mentally as well as physically dodging death.

"Ay Romero . . . you still with us?" asked the chief.

"Ay holmes . . . I didn't do shit ay . . . I didn't do shit!" yelled Romero.

"Listen." Said the chief. "why don't you just throw your weapons out the window for me and stick your hands as high in the air as you can."

"I don't have no fucking weapon man!"

"How about your partners gun Mr. Ramirez . . . do you have it?"

"Naw man . . . I ain't got shit . . . I don't have nothing ay."

"Ay Romero . . . I'm about to send two of my officers in to get you . . . I need to see your hands now!" demanded the chief.

Romero immediately complied with the chief's orders, as officers merged on the office to subdue Romero Ramirez. They had him cuffed and were walking him out within seconds while reading him his rights and then stuffing him into one of the police cruisers.

Romero noticed that the cops has already had Sneaks and Pelon in their custody, along with the five bodies of Big Joe's boys and the one of Monster. His mind was racing over the recent events of the week. He was unable to gather his thoughts. It was as if his head was going to explode. All he did was stare out of the car window at the crowd of onlookers staring at him.

While scanning the crowd, Romero noticed Big Joe camouflaged within. They made eye contact, Romero blinked, and Joe disappeared. There was nothing left to do. Romero hung his head, closed his eyes, took a deep breath, and awaited his fate. After the Gang Task Unit gathered all they needed to shut Romero's entire, operation down, they locked up the shop and carted Romero Ramirez off to jail.

It was ten-thirty P.M. when Romero was finally booked into L.A. Men's County Jain. All that was flowing through his head at this time was what his mother thought of him now. All Ma'Ma' wanted was a good son, nothing more, just a good son. Now, everything that Ma'Ma' had ever told him about his dark life . . . his destructive lifestyle . . . is blatantly coming to the light.

This is a whole other world, thought Romero as he leaned against the wall and silently cried. His mind began to journey all the way back to his adolescence where heard his thoughts scream, "I want my Ma'Ma'!" he shut his eyes tightly to try and make his memory disappear. When he reopened his eyes he couldn't believe the reality of where he was. It was like being in a filthy waiting-room to see a sorry-ass doctor that's prescribes aspirin for everything. Only this was no ordinary waiting-room, although it was very filthy, filed wall to wall with the scum-of-the-earth, some may say. The doctor was a Judge and his prescription was time.

The tank was cold and dense. There was no room to sit or lay down so Romero had no choice but to lean against one of the walls. This tank continued only Hispanic gang members, or those of other races belonging to a Hispanic gang. Everyone in this tank, either knew, knew of, or at least heard of the name Romero.

"Ay holmes . . . whass' up . . . I'm Rusty ay from El Monte ay."

"Ay fool . . . do it look like I feel like talking ay!" Romero exclaimed.

"Orale fool . . . it's just a intro esse' . . . nobody asking for a conversation ay,"

Romero struck Rusty in the throat with a hard chopping blow, that sent him stumbling backwards, unable to keep his feet. Three other Mexicans then met his body with their feet and fist as he hit the floor. They stomped him into the ground viciously. By the time they were finished, so was Rusty. When the jailer approached the holding tank, Rusty's mangled body was left laying on the floor at the front of the cell.

"What the hell happened here?" asked one of the Deputies.

"He slipped and hit his head." One of the inmates responded.

The jailer took a few steps back from the bars and radioed for assistance. Several officers and medical staff responded quickly. When they got there, all they could do was remove the body, and ask everyone, did you see who did it. Of course everyone's response was "No". Then all the inmates were relocated to another holding tank to wait for permanent housing.

As he waited, Romero sighed, and whispered to himself . . . "Welcome back to hell, stupid".

Each day seemed worst than the last to Romero. One good thing about this predicament to Romero was the fact that the blacks and Hispanic's were now separated in the county jails. He remembered how chaotic those days were cursed his self, realizing that those days wold haunt him once again once he's sent to the State Penitentiary.

By the time Romero began his court appearances, he was extremely exhausted of being away from home. He jumped on the first deal the D.A. offered, which was seven years with eighty-five percent. Ma'Ma' had already cut all his ties to Romero Jr. He was left with only Romeo to relay his messages to his son. The only real message he had was, "Tell'em I love'em homey."

Pelon didn't last long at all. The day that Romero caught the chain from the county to the state, Romero put a hit out on his head.

◄○►

Pelon was housed in Wayside Super-max. He knew he had gotten on Romero's bad side. He also knew that it was only a matter-of-time before he'd send somebody for his head. He maintained a low-profile and stayed away from the other Mexicans he felt knew the business between he and Romero. Every situation had it's own level of intensity. But this one, for Pelon, was sticky. He had known that Romero had taken a deal, so his testimony was no longer needed. What he was hoping now was that the cops won't leak the fact that he was going to testify against Romero.

Pelon had been sitting on the shelf for almost town months now awaiting his fate. He wanted to snitch and ditch this hell hole, however, that remedy fell through. The courts did offer him five years with eighty-five percent for possession of a controlled substance and gang affiliation, now we was hoping he would still be able to jump on that deal.

On the other hand, everything had been calm and smooth for Pelon so far as for the prison politics. Yet he still maintained his full awareness and stayed on his P's and Q's.

It was nine a.m. and Pelon and some paisas were playing dominoes in the day-room of the dorm. An announcement came via the P.A. system for Rafael Ruiz to report to the visiting room. Pelon paid no attention to the page, and no one in the dorm knew him as such. He continued to play dominoes unfazed by the loud announcement, until it came again . . . five minutes later.

"Ruiz . . . Rafael Ruiz . . . number 633-26-up . . . report to visiting."

Pelon stopped playing dominoes and looked up at the P.A. speaker like it was going to repeat what it had just spit out twice already.

"Who did they just call . . . what bunk was it esse'?" he asked.

The paisas who were sitting with him just looked. They didn't understand exactly what he was asking so they just shrugged their shoulders. "Ay esse' . . . ehy said bunk 26-up ay . . . . what's your name ay?"

"Ruiz." Pelon said.

"That's you esse' . . . they called you for a visit ay.'

"What! . . . awe shit ay."

Pelon scrambled away from the table. One of the other things there offered him some decent clothes. He rushed in putting them on, grabbed his pass from the cops, and headed to the visiting area. When he hit the main corridor he had to walk along a yellow line painted along the wall. This led him straight to visiting check-in. He showed an officer his pass in which he then directed Pelon to be seated at window five. He sat patiently, and was antsy at the same time, anticipating the happiness when he found out who it was visiting him. Several more inmates were seated on his row before the visitors were allowed to come in. To his surprise, it was Brown Eyes, one of the veteran home-girls from his neighborhood. Pelon got nervous, his palms got sweaty, and his eyes got a burning sensation which made them itch. Brown Eyes picked up the receiver on her side of the window. Pelon hesitated for a second or two then grabbed his.

"Whass' up esse'?" he asked cautiously.

"How you holding up in there fool?" asked Brown Eyes.

"I'm fine holmes . . . to what do I owe this visita' ay?"

"Awe what fool . . . a bitch can't come visit or what ay . . . you scared yo' bitch might get mad or something' esse', she clowned.

"Naw homey . . . whass' up tho' ay . . . what brings you this way girl?"

"Well fool . . . the homies was a little concerned about you ay . . . they wanted to make sure you were okay esse'."

"Tell'em I'm good ay."

"You sure esse'?"

"I'm positive holmes . . . ay you heard anything on Romero ay?"

"Si'mon esse' . . . . he took a deal ay . . . home-boys chained up as we speak ay . . . headin' to la' penta . . . thanks to you esse'."

Pelon was sent into shock with Brown Eye's last statement. She smiled at his response. His eyes bucked wide open and his entire body tightened up. Before he was able to gather his thoughts and say anything. Brown Eyes winked and hung up the receiver. Pelon was stuck in a trance as the two inmates on each side of him commenced to stabbing him until all the life leaked out of his body. The other inmates paid no attention to these activities, neither did any of the visitors.

When the visits were over, everybody walked out as if nothing happened. By the time officers noticed Pelon's body, he was surely dead. The jail was locked down for the rest of the day. And the officers report read; Inmate found dead at O-nine-forty-hours . . . no details.

◀◦▶

Romero was shackled hands and feet and wearing an orange jumpsuit on the transportation bus taking the long and lonely ride to the State

Penitentiary. He laid his head back against the hard seat, closed his eyes, and thought about something good in his life . . . . Romero Jr.

CHAPTER FIFTEEN

Romeo pulled to Renee's house exhausted from the day. He parked his car, got out, and went inside straight to the bedroom where he saw that she was laying there peacefully sleeping. He stood there briefly and stared at the beautiful chocolate woman, whom he knows, love him truly.

"You coming to bed or are you gonna' just stand there and stare all-night?" she asked in her sexiest bedroom voice.

"I thought you was sleep baby girl . . . I didn't mean to wake you."

"I couldn't sleep . . . I . . . I . . ."

"Shhhhhh."

Romeo approached her and cut off her words with a soft touch of his finger tips to her soft lips. He began to remove all of his clothing until he was wearing nothing but a pair of diamond earrings. He climbed into bed with her clenching one fist closed and looking deeply into her eyes.

"I love you beautiful." He whispered.

"I love you too Romeo,"

"Baby I need you . . . . all the time baby . . . I need you in my life . . . you the best thang that's happened to me in a long time baby . . . . will you marry me?" proposed Romeo.

He opened his fist revealing a beautiful diamond surprise fit only for a Queen . . . his Queen . . . Renee'. Tears began to swell in her eyes. Love was definitely in the air. She reached past the ring that was glistening in the center of his palm and embraced her diamond in the rough, her true jewel. She wrapped her arms around his neck and pulled herself closer to him and then slowly composed a silent melody with their bodies in a bundle of love' sharing spurts of air through kisses weighed down by passion. She yearned for him to be inside of her and her heard her body cry out for him. Romeo slowly slid his dick inside her throbbing pussy. Together they blew pass lust on their journey into real love. Thighs rubbed together, lips locked, tongues tangled, and passion roared until they were both asleep in one another's protective stronghold safely locked away in each others' heart.

Renee' was awakened that morning by some banging. She rose in her bed and was relieved to see that she wasn't dreaming. The love her life was in fact in the bed with her. She sighed and got out of bed then proceeded to the front room where the banging was coming from. "Open up! . . . Long Beach Police!" several voices was yelling/

"Romeo!" shouted Renee'.

Romeo sprung up to life at Renee's scream. Before he could get out of bed, several officers were already inside the bedroom with guns pointed at him. One officer threw him his pants after checking the pockets.

"Put these on Mr. Jackson." He ordered.

Romeo stood up out of bed and slid into his boxers and then the pants.

"Whass' all this about?" he asked.

"You are Romeo Jackson . . . right?"

"yeah man . . . thass' me."

"Sir you're being arrested for unlawfully discharging a weapon in a residential area . . . you have the right to remain silent . . . you have the . . ."

Romeo cut the officer off by smacking his lips and requesting that he be taken away form the house before little Romeo wakes up. The officer understood and immediately took Romeo out. One stopped him at the bedroom door and cuffed him. As they were escorting him to the awaiting police car. Renee' and little Romeo stood on the porch crying as the love of both of their lives was being taken away.

Seeing Renee' go through this painful event was more than enough to bare. But when Romeo saw his little one clinging on to his mother with tears streaming from his eyes, he felt like snatching his own from his chest. He couldn't stand to see them go through this hurting. He dropped his head and cried . . . the only thing he could do.

The Long Beach Police held on to Romeo for forty-eight hours with no bail while he awaited his arraignment. The morning of, he was very scared and extremely nervous. With his history they may have the tools needed to strike him out. His prior convictions, consists of shootings, attempted murders, drug dealing, and a whole lot of gang banging. He'd been committed to the Youth Authority once for five years, and two Prison commitments for a total of seven years. Now this, he was now in court sitting at the defense table with his attorney, Ed Sutton.

"Don't worry dude . . . I got this taken care of," said Ed.

"What they talking bout . . . how much I gotta' do?" aske Romeo.

"Three with eighty-five . . . you cool with that?"

"Where do I sign." stated Romeo.

"All rise!" shouted the baliff.

The judge walked in looking like mix between the grim-reaper without the hood and a prince from Zamunda. Romeo looked, shook his head, then thought, why a black man always go to be the one that help string the nigga's up.

"Your Honor we don't need to wasted any of the courts time with this case. We've offered the defendant, Romeo Jackson, a term of three-years with eighty-five-percent. The defendant is being charged with unlawful discharge of a firearm in public domain. No enhancements will be assessed to the charges Your Hono." stated the district attorney.

"Very well . . . how do the defendant plead counselor?" asked the judge.

"Your Honor my client has agreed to the terms of the court. He pleads no contest to the charges."

"So be it." stated the judge.

"Ah . . . Your Honor . . . my client has accepted the courts plea bargain in good faith. He has a current operating business and a family . . . we are asking the courts permissions for my client to surrender himself forty-eight hours from sentencing for the purpose of saying his goodbyes and business affairs . . . . my client Mr. Jackson is not a flight risk and do hereby promises the court to comply with all court orders and dates thereof."

"Well put counselor . . . any objections from the prosecution?"

"None Your Honor," said the D.A.

"Mr. Jackson I hereby order you to report in to Los Angeles Men's Central Jail, Thursday October nine, no later than four P.M. Do you understand these terms Mr. Jackson?" asked the judge.

"Yes sir, You Honor" The judge was stern when explaining the terms of his orders to report, to Romeo. After, he pounded his gavel two times then adjourned his court.

"Hold it!" the judge shouted, "Before we all leave for the day . . . . Mr. Jackson . . . I strongly advise you to clean up your act for your family's sake . . . . no more brakes Mr. Jackson . . . . I can assure you of that."

Romeo walked out a free man for the next forty-eight hours. He, Renee', and Lil Romeo walked down the corridor and met up with Romeo's lawyer, Ed. He and Romeo shook hands and parted ways.

The next couple of days was spent the way Renee' and Lil Romeo wanted . . . . at home as a family.

◄◊►

They were in the front yard throwing around a Frisbee, playing keep-away from Bootsy. Renee, was sitting on the porch watching over the three of them like an angel.

"Daddy why you have to go to jail?" asked little Romeo.

Romeo lost his concentration at the surprise question from the little one. However, he was still able to catch the Frisbee before it hit the ground. Then he fell silent. He couldn't focus or hear anything but that question echoing in his thoughts. He stared into his son's eyes mentally asking him, why did you ask me that. He quickly turned and made eye contact with Renee'. Silently asking her for help. Still silence overwhelmed the moment. Renee' buried her face down in her palms, realizing her heart was pondering the same thought as little Romeo. Romeo dropped his shoulders and released a long sigh. He went over and sat on the step below Renee', then called his little man over to join him.

"Check it out little one." He said.

Little Romeo trotted over to his dad with joy, but the words he spoke when he got there reflected sadness in his heart.

"Daddy I don't want you to go to jail." He said softly.

"I know little one . . . but daddy was bad and I have to pay the price."
"How much it cost?" he asked.

"Wayyy to much." Romeo responded. "Look . . . this what I need you to do . . . you have to be strong just like daddy . . . because I need you to be a big little man and take of mommy for me. Make sure you always remind mommy that daddy loves her okay . . ."

He had an abundance of tears pooling in his eyes where did all his gangsterism disappear to, he thought. He mustered up every bit of strength he could to hold back his emotions. He wanted to wanted to strangle the stupid muthafucka' who said that gangsta's don't cry.

". . . . Look little man . . . . I'll be inside in a minute okay and we'll play the game . . . so go get it set up while daddy holla' at moms real quick."

Little Romeo jumped out of his dad's lap instantly filled with excitement.

"Oooh daddy I'm bout to take you down." He shouted.

Romeo stood and laughed at his son's playful aggression, and hoped that hit remains playful. He walked over to Renee' and sat next to her. Romeo softly laid a hand on her back and began rubbing a feeling of comfort into her emotions.

"Don't trip baby girl," he said softly "It'll all be over in a minute baby . . . look at me"

"What!" she asked, looking up at him and then quickly turning away.

"Look at me baby girl, please."

"What Romeo . . . I can't do this no more . . . I'm scared . . . I don't know what's happening . . . anything could happen . . . I . . . I . . ."

Renee' burst into tears. Her eyes ran like the falls of Niagara. All Romeo could do was wrap her in his embrace. He held on tightly until she fell asleep in his arms, tucked and secure.

It seemed like blink of an eye and the forty-eight hours was over. The last couple of days with Renee' and his mini-me was the epiphany of his life. Now all he had to do was stay true to his new beliefs and live for it. Even if he didn't deserve it . . . they did.

◆◦◆

The bus rolling down a very lonely highway, Romeo felt like he was literally being pulled away from the world. One thing he was cool with, and that was the fact that he was transferring out of that County jail quick. After turning himself in, he was on the chain and on his way to the State within forty-eight hours. He pretty much slept those away. Everyone on the bus was quiet with a look on their faces drained of life. Romeo was sitting in a rear seat alone, shackled hands and feet. He kept dozing off like a baby to the sound of the bus' roaring motor. However, the bounces from the rigid highway woke him every five seconds. It was a long ride.

The bus had three officers, two in front and one riding inside the rear cage. They were all heavily armed with assault rifles and sidearm's, hoping somebody did something stupid. The driver of the bus hooked a hard right and headed down another long road. Romeo stared out through the tinted window off into the distance. He watched the heat waves float upwards from the sizzling pavement, and noticed the prison towers moving closer and closer. "Welcome to hell stupid ass," he whispered to himself. He dozed off again before the bus actually pulled into the prison. When it finally came to a stop it was in front R&R . . . . Receiving and Release. Romeo was suddenly wide awake. He took a deep breath then let out a long and exhausting sigh. His chest tightened up and his eyes swelled with tears from missing home already, and he's only been gone forty-eight hours, how the hell was he suppose to endure three years, he thought.

Six officers filed out of R&R like some kind of military special forces-unit or something. They all posted up along the side of the bus. An officer by the name of Williams stepped onto the bus and took charge.

"Gentlemen . . . . listen up . . . I'm only going to say this once!" he yelled. "When I call your name step off the bus, one of the officers will remove your restraints . . . give that officer the letter and last two numbers of your C.D.C. number. Proceed inside, line up along the wall and stand on the red line. There you will be told to strip down to your birthday suit and there you will be issued your new outfit . . . welcome to Delano ladies."

It was happening all over again, thought Romeo. Being degraded by a bunch of puss-ass muthafucka's who didn't give a fuck about who you are what color you are. All they know is that their suppose to hate you. To them, you're not even human . . . you're nobody.

It was only six inmates on the bus that were dropped off here so the humiliation was brief, even though mentally, its lasts a lifetime.

Romeo was feeling sick at the stomach when he was being broken down by a your rookie-ass white boy cop.

"Take off everything, throw it in the bin, and then face me." He demanded of Romeo. "now open your mouth . . . raise your tongue up . . . down . . . raise your lips with your fingers . . . raise your arms up . . . down . . . show me behind your ears . . . raise your nuts . . . . alright turn around . . . show me the bottom of your feet one by one . . . now I need for you to bend over, spread your buttocks aprart, and cough for me three times."

These muthafucka's had to be some kind of fags or something, Romeo thought.

The officer then threw him a pair of boxers, socks, pants, shoes, a T-shirt, and a blue hospital-like shirt. Romeo was also given a sack-lunch to eat while he waited to be housed. He had no appetite. He just sat in the back of the holding tank sulking in his pain and anger . . . the two emotions that should never be mixed.

There was no property to be passed out by the officers so Romeo and the others were housed pretty quickly. They escorted by three c/o's (correctional officers), to their assigned yard and housing unit. Every move they made, Romeo was being reminded of his past experiences.

"On the way to the yard . . . . it's a straight line and absolutely no talking!" yelled one of the c/o's.

Romeo stared straight ahead, trying his best not to give these superficial ass-holes a reason to fuck with him.

They finally reached the gate to the entrance of A-Yard. Other inmates were programming on the yard, enjoying their day-to-day activities; working out on the exercise bars, shooting some B-ball, while dominoes and other table games were being played at the cement tables placed around the yard.

Romeo swiftly scanned the yard, then shook and dropped his head noticing the blatant segregation between the races.

They proceeded through the gate. The c/o stopped the line when they got in front of the program office.

"Rodriguez T-63!" yelled c/o Coontz.

"Yeah . . . right here."

"You go to A-2 . . . the officers in there will tell you what cell." c/o Coontz said. "okay I gotta' ahh . . . . Phillips T-81, and Brown T-74 . . . A-3 . . . here's your I.D.'s . . . go . . . Conway T-90."

"Yeah."

"Here . . . your in building A-I . . . and Jackson T-94, and Smith T-98 you two are in building A-4

Everybody was given their I.D.'s and told where they would be sleeping from here until only God knows when.

As he was walking towards his assigned building, Romeo felt all the hard stares from the other inmates.

"Ay holmes . . . where you vatos comin' from ay . . . country?" asked a mexican named Shorty.

"Yah holmes." answered Rodriguez.

Everybody else stayed in stride and continued on to the buildings. Romeo paid no attention to nothing and nobody. He just wanted to lay-down, and gather his thoughts. When he got inside his building he reported to the podium where he handed the floor officers his I.D. While the cop was figuring out where to put him, Romeo just stood and looked around. Everything was just as he had left it years ago.

One inmate was using the iron, others' was enjoying the penitentiary comfort of television, and the rest were utilizing the indoor tables for their own chosen activities. Even the units were segregated. White's and Mexicans shared one side of the building, while the Black's, Northern Mexicans, and others' such as Asians, and Islander's shared the other side.

"You're in two-o-one Mr. Jackson." aid the floor c/o.

Romeo grabbed his I.D. respectfully from the c/o, then headed to his cell. As he reached the door it slid right open. The tower guard hit the button as he was approaching it. His cell-mate was an older gentleman by the name of Marshall. He was looking out the door as Romeo was approaching. By the time Romeo got inside the cell and shut the door, Marshall had resumed his position on his bunk, reading his book. Romeo turned, reached out his hand, and introduced himself.

"Whass' up homey . . . I'm Romeo." He said.

"Hey there youngsta' I'm Mr. Marshall . . . but the youngsta's round here just call me Marshall," he said, removing his book and shaking Romeo's hand.

"So where ya'll getting' in from?" Marshall asked.

"L.A. County."

"Whew . . . long ride huh?"

"Hell yeah O/G . . . . And I'm glad it's over.

Romeo threw his bed covering on top of the back desk and began making his bed. Marshall laid back and gave him the respect to do so.

"So how much time you come with youngsta?" Marshall asked.

"I ain't got too much . . . nothing I can't handle." Romeo said.

"Well if you got any gang enhancements, you goin' to a level fo' yard."

"Whereva' they put me O/G is cool . . . as long as my time don't stop . . . . feel me."

Romeo hopped up on his bunk, laid his head back on a folded blanket, and closed his eyes.

"If you've already been classified youngsta', you should be outta' here in a few days or so."

"Good." Romeo said

He took another deep breath then attempted to get some rest like he intended. The stint of the solid cement structure gave him nightmares causing him to toss and turn in his sleep. By the time he really began to doze off into his own la'la' land, it was count time. He was awakened by the loud ass announcement. His cellie, Marshall, was already standing at the door.

"It's standing count youngsta'."

"Yeah . . . riiight." Romeo mumbled.

"You going to chow? It's right after count."

"Naw O/G . . . I got that punk ass lunch up there."

"Suit yo'self . . . I'm goin' to eat."

As soon as the cop walked by and took his count, Romeo was back out for the count. He didn't come back to life until the next morning for breakfast.

It was five-twenty-five in the morning and it seemed as if everything was moving in slow motion . . . all except Romeo.

"I see you got some good sleep huh youngsta'?"

"Hell Yeah O/G . . . I'm ready fo' whateva' . . . I know a lot of muthfucka's so I had to be ready fo' all the handshaking' and huggin' and shit O/G . . . feel me."

The doors were racked open for Romeo's section to walk to chow. He and Marshall strolled out together.

"Ay Romeo!" someone yelled.

He turned around and saw that it was one of Madd Doggs' son. The kid quickly caught up to Romeo and Marshall.

Whass' up big homey?" he asked excitedly.

"Hey . . . what's goin' on young one?" said Romeo.

"I'm chillin' cuz . . . how long you been here big homey?"

"Cuz? . . . Boy where you from?" Romeo asked surprisingly.

"Awe big homey . . . I'm Tiny Ken Dogg from the Bunch!"

"What . . . what tha' fuck is that cuz?" asked Romeo

"Thass' yo' tiny loc's big homey . . . it's the click that BG started cuz."

Romeo went blank for a few seconds. He was the man for the East Side Mafia Crips. Then there's his little homies from the East Side Young Mafia Squad. What the fuck is a bunch he thought.

"We unda' the Squad big homey . . . East Side Mafia's Tiny Bunch." Stated tiny Ken Dogg.

"Where yo' daddy at love one?" asked Romeo.

"He up in Old Folsom . . . he got eight and I got five."

"Ya'll crimees'?" asked Romeo." Damn lil homey how old are you?"

"I just turned eighteen cuz."

"Looks like you got yo' hands full." Stated Marshall.

"You ain't lying O/G."

The three of them entered the chow hall, walked the line, and gathered their breakfast tray weighed with pancakes, grits, two sausages, some fruit cocktail, milk, and a juice. Romeo just shook his head as they sat sown to cat. When he read the menu, it sounded like he was on his way to I-Hops'. Seeing this shit up close and personal just made his stomach turn flips.

"Ay big homey."

"What'up loc?" stated Romeo.

"Ay cuz . . . . just to put a bug in yo' ear big homey . . . . them damn nigga's been getting into it real tuff with these esse's cuz."

"Oh yeah . . . so what it do?"

"I don't know but nigga's been groupin' a lot cuz."

"Who they man?" asked Romeo.

"Who?"

"The Damu's cuz."

"Oh . . . that'll be Big Scull from the Mob in Compton."

"What block he in loc?" Romeo asked.

"I don't know exactly . . . but he be on the yard every time it's open cuz."

"Alright . . . today when you see'em out there tell'em we need to holla . . . I need to get at the homies too."

"Fo'sho big homey."

They enjoyed the rest of their so-called breakfast. Afterwards the headed back to their cells.

It was somewhere around nine-o-clock when the yard was finally opened.

"Ay youngsta' . . . you watch yoself out there on that yard . . . them young ass boy's out there keep they self in a bunch of bullshit." Stated Marshall.

"yeah . . . I feel ya' O/G . . . this ain't my fist rodeo."

"You got one of these?" Marshall asked.

Romeo looked, and was shocked to see the old-timer handing him a proper homemade knife. This truly reminded him of what to expect . . . . . or better yet, what's to come.

"Naw O/G." Romeo responded.

"Here, take this one . . . and stop looking like it's the first time you don' rode this horse."

The announcement came over the loud speaker for the yard release. Inmates filed out of each of the buildings like kids being let out for recess.

As soon as Romeo stepped out into the sunlight, Tiny Ken Dogg was at the front door of his building to greet him, accompanied by two other babies claiming the Mafia's Tiny Bunch.

"What up big homey . . . this Tiny Blue Rag and Tiny B-G cuz." Introduced Tiny Ken Dogg.

Romeo swallowed so hard when he heard the name Tiny B-G, you heard it aloud.

"B-G", repeated Romeo.

"Yah big homey . . . my big brother from the Squad."

"Damn love one . . . B-G dead cuz." he stated sadly.

"What! . . . I just talked to cuz about two-three weeks ago."

"Yeah lil homey . . . the homey and his son got kilt in the spot about a week and a half ago loc . . . don't trip tho' . . . we got both tha' nigga's that did it and his sister cuz."

"Who was it cuz?" asked Tiny B-G.

"I said don't trip loc . . . not right now . . . I got something' else on my mind right now . . . ay where da' boy at Tiny Ken Dogg? Romeo asked.

Romeo felt weird calling this kid Tiny Ken Dogg. Big Ken Dogg is his daddy, and that made Romeo think about his Little Romeo. There was no way in hell, he thought.

"He over there with the rest of the Damu's cuz . . . . at they domino table."

"Com'on . . . mash over here with me loc." Stated Romeo.

When they made it over to the Damu's kick it area, there was no need for introduction. Everyone who needed to know, already knew who Romeo was, and the rest would find out one way or another, if it was important enough.

"Whass' up big dog." Spoke Big Scull.

"Awe damn." Romeo said, surprised. "How tha' hell you get locked up my nigga'? he asked.

"Dumb ass bitch got me in here . . . fo' a spousal." Stated Scull.

"Boyyy . . . I tell you nigga's bout them baby mama's . . . so whass' crackin' with these mahenda's love one?"

"They talking loud but ain't sayin' nothin' . . . . you know how that go."

Soon as Big Scull finished that sentence, every Mexican on the yard was headed their way. Before anyone knew what was actually about to go down, it was full-fledge race-riot in progress.

C/O's hit the yard quickly, wearing riot gear and toting rubber-bullet guns. The tower guards were blasting live rounds from mini-fourteen rifles, tear-gas bombs were exploding, and bodies were dropping everywhere.

Marshall said they'll be days like this, Romeo thought . . . just today.

It was as if they had heard what Big Scull said . . . "They talking loud-ain't sayin' a whole lot".

Chaos was everywhere, floating around like the gas from the tear-gas canisters. It took five dead, ninety-six seriously injured, and whole bunch of scared kids to surface, before this melee was under control. Everybody that was on the yard went to the hole, the hospital, or literally to hell, Romeo was one of the lucky ones. He made it to the hole.

In the hole it was single man cells. Romeo took this opportunity to really gather his thoughts. The last thought that ran across his mind before he went to sleep that night was . . . this gon' be a long journey.

CHAPTER SIXTEEN

Renee' was up early on this gloomy morning Friday morning. It was real obvious that something or someone was weighing heavy on her mind. Lately she had been feeling a little empty, like something was missing from her life.

This morning she called in sick for work. She had been contemplating going shopping but even that thought faded into just staying home. She sat on the couch for a few, figuring that something had to give before her little professor awakened. Somehow little Romeo always knew when something was bothering her, even when she tried to hide it. She had thought about taking the little one up to see his dad, but that thought quickly vanished. There was no way she'll take her baby to no jail-house, she thought to herself, although she knew that Lil Romeo wouldn't have cared where his dad was he'd want to see him.

Renee' stood up from sitting on the couch and took a deep breath. Still in her house robe she went out onto the front porch with a cup of coffee. Maybe what she needed was some fresh air to clear her thoughts, she thought. As she sat sipping on her coffee and taking long breaths of the morning's freshness, the mailman walked up and handed her a few pieces of mail.

"Good morning." He said.

"Good morning . . . thank you." Renee' responded.

She continued to stare off into the air, holding mail in one hand and her coffee in the other until she finally inside. Sitting her coffee down, Renee' slowly browsed through the mail. The one that was addressed to Romeo Jr. and Renee' caught her attention. She felt her heart began to pound at her chest.

"Romeo!" Renee' yelled.

Little Romeo was awake but still laying in bed next to Bootsy, watching cartoons. He heard his mom call out, however he was captivated by the cartoons on his T.V.

"Little Romeo!" she yelled again.

Bootsy jumped up to that call, and lil Romeo followed.

"Romeo Junior, you got a letter from . . ."

Before she could finished the sentence, lil Romeo appeared out of nowhere and startled her.

". . . . Oooh baby you scared me . . . . you got a letter from your dad." She continued.

"What! . . . My dadd?"

His face lit up with happiness. They both bounced onto the couch as Renee' opened the letter. Inside there was two letters. One for lil Romeo Jr. and the other for Renee'.

"Here" Renee' said. "This ones' for you."

Little Romeo swiftly unfolded his letter an began reading it aloud.

It read;

"Dear,

Little man'

I just wanted to let you know how much I'm missing you. I know you're getting bigger by the day. I wish I could see how big you've gotten so far. Son, I love you and I want you to continue to be a good little man and listen to mommy always. Always do your best in school and be a smart kid. Well little fella' daddy love's you and mommy a whole bunch.

Love Always.

Daddy."

After reading his letter he got up from the couch with a grand smile on his face and headed back into his room with his giant puppy following.

Renee covered her mouth with one hand to stop her gasp from escaping. She truly adored the way Romeo touched his son with his love. What she didn't understand, however, was this gangster façade he portrayed, but she still loved him. And she did understand that. She sat there on the couch by herself for a few, running some things through her thoughts. Finally, after about ten-minutes she gathered the courage to read the letter addressed to her.

"Hey-you," it read.

"It's been a long year and some change now, and I know your looking as beautiful as ever. Hopefully you and our junior are in the very best of health and definitely God's care, as well as good spirits by the time these heartfelt words of mine reaches your loving hands. Look . . . I know that this wasn't in your plan when we fell in love again with one another and I do deeply apologize for my stupidity as well as my mistakes and bad choices. Renee' I pray and hope that someday you'll find some compassion in your loving heart to understand that I truly adore you and my little dude more than my own life. Please forgive me baby . . . Baby I love you . . . I really do. And I hope you can still believe in me, and stay strong for all of us. Keep your head held high and remember I love you and lil Romeo.

Sincerely,

Your Romeo."

Tears poured from her eyes. She had them shut, visualizing her Romeo sitting next to her, saying those sweet words to her, face-to-face.

"Mommy why you crying . . . . my daddy said he love me and you . . . . did you read your letter yet?" Little Romeo asked.

Renee' grabbed hold of her little fella' and hugged him real tight, resting her head atop his.

"Mommy . . . you squeezing me . . . are you okay?" he continued.

"I'm just happy baby . . . mommy just sooo happy that daddy love's us so much . . . . hey . . . you wanna go pick up lil Romero and go to the mall?" she asked.

"Oooh yeah."

Renee' quickly picked up the phone and called Ma'Ma' to inform her of her plans to pick the little one up. She knew that she had to do something quick to get her little man off the subject of her tears. This worked successfully, causing him to take off to his room to get ready.

"Mommy what about Bootsy?" he yelled

"We'll just put some food out and he'll stay here and guard the house because I don't think they allow dogs in the mall baby."

"Bootsy . . . get over here puppy." He called out.

His overgrown pooch came running as he was commanded. He jumped all over lil Romeo licking away, while the little fella' just laughed. They played around for a little bit.

"Listen puppy . . . . you have to guard the home front for me and mommy . . . I'm gon' leave you some grub in the kitchen and you better not make a mess okay." Stated lil Romeo.

He gave his pup some orders to follow just like his dad use to. Renee' secretly listened outside his bedroom door. It must be gentetic . . . . he sounded just like his daddy, she thought. Her eyes began to puff up with another load of tears so she took off to her room. Taking her thoughts off Romeo, she occupied hersfelf with getting dressed and what to do to entertain the junior's.

Little Romeo did his part for the day, getting dressed and handling

Bootsy. Soon after, they were pulling into Ma'Ma's driveway. Little Romeo jumped out of the car almost before it stopped. As he made it to the door, little Romero was there to greet him.

"What took ya'll so long?" Romero Jr. asked.

"Me and mommy stopped to get some gas and we went to the store to get a few things for me and you."

"Where Bootsy at?"

"He still at home guarding the house . . . and my mom don't like dogs in her car."

"Romeo," called Renee'. "Are you guys going to grab the bags out of the car?" Renee' requested.

They both busted a quick U-turn and shot out the door as if a starter pistol had just started a race between them.

"Wow! . . . thank you," said Renee.

"Sorry mom . . . I forgot!" yelled Romeo as they ran out the door.

Displaying their manly-adolescent strengths, they grab as many bags as they could carry at once. When they made it back to the front door with the bags, the door was wide open for them to enter. They quickly dropped the bags in Ma'Ma's living room then headed to lil Romero's bedroom to play his video games.

"Ma'Ma' thanks for babysitting . . . my job called at the last minute just before we were leaving the house . . . I had told lil Romeo I would take them to the mall and maybe a movie," stated Renee.

"No problem mija . . . you know how much I love my two little gentlemen . . . . besides, I could use the company . . . they keep my heart pumping, and plus little Romero needs some company of his own age.

Renee was looking kind of sad as Ma'Ma' talked. Ma'Ma' recognized it right off. However she maintained a subtle approach into the subject.

"Yeah, well Ma'Ma' . . . we just don't want to be a burden," said Renee.

"Oh please child . . . it's no burden, we're family . . . and family is never a burden in this household," Ma'Ma said as she walked over to Renee' to give her a comforting hug.

"Now you tell me young lady . . . . what's on your mind?" Ma'Ma continued.

"Nothing," Renee' said quickly.

"Now that was just too quick . . . . And plus it's all over your face sweetie . . . now you tell Ma'Ma' what's going on."

Nothing Ma'Ma' . . . I'm alright," insisted Renee.

"Okay . . . if you say so but Ma'Ma' knows better . . . So how's my son doing?" she went on to ask.

"Who? . . . Romeo?"

"Yes sweetie."

"I guess he alright . . . . we got some letter from him."

"You did . . . I know that must have had that little fella' all excited."

"It sure did . . . he sat on the couch with me and read his letter like a big boy."

"Well did you write back or what?" asked Ma'Ma.

"No . . . not yet."

"Why?"

"Well I don't know what to say."

Renee's eyes were becoming watery. Ma'Ma' pulled up a chair and gestured to Renee' to sit.

"Ma'Ma . . . I love Romeo . . . I know I do . . . but I don't know how to do this jail thing . . . not with my son . . . . and I know that Romeo is going to expect me to do certain things Ma'Ma . . . and I just can't with my son . . . I can't."

"Mija listen . . . now I know one thing . . . and that's, I know just how much Romeo love's you and sure his son . . . I also know that he would never ask you to do anything to jeopardize the safety of you or his son. Now I know he's not my son but I do know his heart mija . . . and listen . . . I want you to understand something. I made a grave mistake of not keeping Romero in touch with his father when he was a young boy . . . . now look . . . he may now, one day, run into the man he never had a chance to know in that hell hole . . ."

"But I thought Romero's father was . . ."

". . . No sweetie . . . he's not dead . . . well somewhat . . . he's dead to the world because I let him die . . . . sweetie he's actually doing a life sentence in prison . . . Listen Renee' I won't lecture you on my mistakes . . . but I've always wondered "what if" . . . What if I had made it possible for Romero's father to be a part of his life even if he was in a jail, could he had said or written something that might have changed the course of his life today."

Ma'Ma began to get teary eyed herself, talking to Renee'. The pain was obvious, and Renee' recognized that it was genuinely sincere, so she listened attentively.

". . . Now I feel it's my fault," she continued. "I really don't know for sure . . . but I do feel at fault sometimes that I'm losing my son the same way I lost the love of my life . . . to these God forsaken streets . . . . Mija don't make the same mistake I did . . . . take you chance sweetie, cause life is only what you make it, and remember, Romeo loves you two . . . I'm sure of it."

Silence hit the moment like a heat wave in the summer. Renee' stared Ma'Ma' in the face as if she was offended by her wisdom. Her thoughts then faded over into a song that was playing loud in her head, "Lost Without You", by Robin Thicke. Yes she truly was, she thought . . . Lost without her Romeo. And she hoped he felt the same. She shook it off and went into Romero jr.'s room and said her goodbye's to the boy's. When she returned, Ma'Ma' was sitting out on the front porch. "Ma'Ma' thanks for the talk . . . I needed that . . . and I love you Ma'Ma'."

"Oh I love you too sweetie, and you tell my good son I love him and I also say that he'd better be good to you."

She kissed Ma'Ma' and then left. Ma'Ma' remained in her seat out on the porch as Renee' pulled off. She waved bye, then said a silent prayer.

Romero was her son. However, Romeo was how she wanted her son to be. Inside Ma'Ma' knew that Romeo care for more than just power and money, so she prayed to God that he'd help him find his way.

CHAPTER SEVENTEEN

Romero was sitting in the bleachers watching a baseball game. Although it wasn't the

Cubs vs. the Dodgers in the Stadium, but more like the South Siders vs. the Wood Pile at Salinas Valley Maximum Security Prison, it was still enjoyable to Romero. He and a few more of his homies sat, enjoying the game and some of that "BOMBAY".

"Ay Flaco," said Romero.

Flaco was sitting there high as a kite. He's one of Romero's older homey, from Venice. However since Romero had the biggest dope sack, the deepest pockets that bought the clout that said, "age don't mean shit" . . . Age didn't mean a damn thang . . . at least not for Romero. Still, Flaco was respected for his knowledge of the game, and he still possessed enough clout of his own to survive and have some say-so in some-things.

"Ay Flaco," Romero repeated.

"Whass' up ay," he managed to slur out.

"Ay holmes . . . how many joints left ay."

"Ay fool it's a lot left ay."

The pack of thug's that were seated in the bleachers with these two all laughed at the way Flaco was talking. He looked like a drunk-ass chinaman smoking on the chronic.

"Damn fool . . . that fool high as a kite ay," stated Speedy.

"Ay holmes . . . light another one esse'," requested Romero.

"Damn homey . . . you gon' have a muthafucker around here floatin' ay," Flaco said.

"What esse' . . . I'm already floatin' ay," said Rock.

Big Rock was from the valley. Another one of Big Joes' people. Romero loved and respected him a little bit more than the others just based on Joe's word. It was almost the same as he did Romeo. But Romeo was different altogether, for the simple fact that, being black and vouched for by someone of Big Joe's status, you had to be connected in some kind of way. Everybody laughed at Rock's punch-line as Big Flaco was retrieving the other joints from down in his socks. Romero's mind briefly slid to the streets. His first thoughts were of his little one, little Romero. He envisioned his little smile and the excitement he use to display when he saw his dad walk through the door. Romero had to take a quick deep breath to hold back his emotions. This was a reoccurring effect that smoking weed had on him. Romero justified his reason for not stopping his weed smoking, which was simply fear of him not being able to remember the good in himself . . . which in-fact was truly his little one. He looked down and caught a glimpse of his tattoo. It read; "In Memory Of Big Monster". It didn't say in loving memory because the memory he had of Monster wasn't loving, however, he stilled honored him just as much. Now he did wish that it were Pelon instead of Monster who caught those slugs from the cops. He shook his head vigorously, bringing himself back to reality. Rock handed him a joint.

"Here esse' . . . take this shit ay."

Romero took the joint and sucked the life back into himself. His chest swelled with smoke, and he held it in as long as he could before releasing it. It was like a soothing breeze that flowed throughout his soul, he thought.

"Puff puff pass esse' . . . whass up with that shit ay," uttered Speedy.

"Awe my bad carnal . . . I got lost in the smoke ay."

Again laughter filled the air. Even amongst killa's, some moments were pleasant.

"Ay esse' . . . heads up ay," stated Crow

"Whass' up holmes," asked Flaco.

"Some new fools coming in ay . . . . thass a fish line ay." Crow pointed out.

Romero continued to toke on the weed while Crow and Flaco worried about the fish-line.

"Ay esse' . . . somebody go see if we got any new homies ay," requested Romero.

"Let me hit that again before I push over there ay," said Speedy.

Handing him the joint, Romero had a look in his eyes like, you sucka' ass muthafucka'. He knew why half these muthafucka's hung around him. To them he was a free high, a good meal, and a lot of protection.

Speedy took the weed, hit it a few more times, and tried to pass it back to Romero. He turned it down.

"Naw holmes . . . I'm cool ay . . . walk wit' it ay," he said.

Speedy responded like a fiend. He quickly got up from the bleachers and took off towards the fish-line without thinking twice. He didn't notice that all the fish,(new inmates), were black until he got all the way on them. Yet he continued to look while the C/O's were issuing I.D's and bed-rolls to the fish. Finally, he got one of their attention.

"Ay homey . . . where ya'll comin' from black," he asked.

"The reception loc," responded C.J.

C.J. spoke with an obvious attitude when he answered Speedy's question. Speedy then noticed that all the new inmates were suddenly maddoggin him. He said nothing, just turned and walked away, headed back over to the bleachers.

"What that fool say to you cuz," asked Romeo

"He was just being nosey big homey thass all."

Speedy had made it back across the yard. Everyone was sitting quietly in the bleachers waiting for Speedy's report.

"Damn whass up esse' . . . you look like you just seen yo' worst enemy ay," stated Flaco.

"Where they comin' from," asked Romero.

"Reception holmes . . . them fools act like they got a chip on they shoulders or somptin' ay," Speedy said.

"It might be them black fools from Delano Reception ay . . . I heard it was big melee with the homies and the blacks over there ay," Crow stated.

Romero took a long pull on his joint and let the smoke glide out of his lungs slowly. It was quiet for a second or two before he responded to anything.

"Ay esse' . . . we need to find out where these vatos came from for sho ay . . . so we'll know exactly whass up ay . . . was it any homies in the line ay?" he asked.

"Naw esse' . . . the whole line is all blacks ay."

"Don't trip ay . . . I got this ay," said Flaco.

He walked off quickly from the bleachers headed towards building five where he see's a couple of new blacks enter the building. He followed them inside. As the two black inmates clear the rotunda, Flaco was hot on their trail. The two stopped at the officer's podium, where the officer told them their designated cell-numbers.

"Who is Smith?" asked C/O Tulley.

"I am," answered Pookie Dog.

"You're in cell one-nineteen-low . . . and you Mr. Landrum . . . you're in one-twenty-two up," Tulley continued.

Pookie Dog and K-Ru,(Kevin Landrum), headed to their assigned cells. They felt stares from all the other inmates that were programming in there dayroom. Just as K-Ru reached for his door handle, it slid open. His cell-mate stepped out to greet him.

"Whass up gee . . . where from homie?" asked Bouncer.

"I'm from the West Side Compton Piru."

"Right . . . right . . . they call me Big Bouncer my nig . . . I'm from Dell

Park Piru in Lancaster Ru . . . welcome to hell my knott."

"Thass right love one . . . I'm K-Ru."

"Ay holmes . . . you comin' from Delano?" asked Flaco.

Flaco walked up behind K-Ru, un-noticed. He stood at a nearby table still floating high on a cloud. He took a deep breath before asking his question again.

"Ay black . . ." Flaco called out.

"What up homey", K-Ru asked.

Flaco was too high to notice that K-Ru had an attitude.

"Ay holmes you comin' from Delano reception ay?" he asked.

"Why? Whass up Blood!"

"Ay ya'll had a riot with the homies ay?"

"What fool . . . . you need to kick rocks boy!" Bouncer exclaimed.

The officers at the podium alerted the tower guard of the aggressive language. He then posted on that side of the tower with his mini-14 rifle sticking out the window. When Bouncer made an aggressive move toward Flaco, C/O Tulley pushed his panic button and began yelling, "GET DOWN . . . GET DOWN"! The alarm sounded thoughout the yard. Every inmate inside, and outside of every building, was made to lay out in a prone position on the ground or floor.

Romeo was inside of building three on his stomach, proned out.

"Damn . . . cuz here we go with this shit again," Romeo said.

He was laying next to young crip from the West Side Gangsta's . . . Tiny Scooby.

"Whass' goin' down big homey?"

"Probably just a false alarm cuz . . . don't trip."

The rotunda gate slide open. Two Sergeants, a Lieutenant, and four C/O's came through it and headed straight for Romeo. He noticed them coming his way and tucked his head down in his crossed arms like a scared kid in the dark. All of the officers stopped at the podium first. The officers there had a picture waiting for the Lieutenant. As he made his way over where Romeo was, the two sergeants were ordering some of the other inmates to move out of the path of an escort.

"Mr. Jackson . . . stand up and turn around," ordered the Lieutenant.

Romeo stood up and slowly turned around as one of the C/O's put handcuffs on him. Once the cuffs was on and Romeo was deemed secure, all the officers then surrounded him as if he were a serial killer out of some Hollywood horror flick.

Escorting him out of the three block to the Lieutenants office, they passed by the bleachers where Romero and his homies were still proned out on the grass.

"Ay fool . . . that's one of them black fools ay," stated Crow.

Romero looked up at the escort, focused his sight in between the officers, and immediately recognized who it was. Just as his disbelief was coming to reality, another escort was coming out of the five-block.

"Damn holmes look! . . . What tha' fuck they got Flaco for ay . . . and another one of them black fools ay," stated Crow.

From the looks of things, it was all bad. Every black and Mexican inmate on the yard was now on pins and needles, wondering what was going on.

Romero was still locked in his trance from who he just saw. He was lost in his thoughts. How could he tell his people that one of his favorite people in his world was black, when in this world of ethics that ain't to be tolerated. He went completely blank and just stared at the program office and watched as Romeo and the officers disappeared into the building.

The lieutenant took a seat behind his desk when they got inside his office. Romeo stood right at the inside of the door with his hands secured behind his back.

"Have a seat Mr. Jackson," stated Lt. Shields.

"Whass' all this about lieu . . . I just got to this yard today."

"You're coming from reception, right?" asked Lt. Shields.

Romeo sarcastically ignored the lieutenants' question, as he did his. A few seconds passed in silence before Lt. Shields added a touch of anger and aggression to his tone.

"Right Mr. Jackson!" he exclaimed.

"Man you got my file right there in front'cha," Romeo sad, showing no fear.

Lieutenant Shields dismissed the two C/O's that were posted in his office to ease the tension between he, and Romeo.

"You two can leave . . . I got this," he said.

They stepped right outside the door just in case back-up was needed.

"Man what ya'll gaffle me up fo' . . . I ain't did shit . . . like I said . . . I just got off the damn bus cuz!"

"First of all . . . calm that shit down Mr. Jackson . . . I called you in here because of a situation with one of your comrades and a Hispanic inmate in building five that almost went too far, and I want it nipped in the bud immediately . . . now I know that your're a crip and even though your comrade is blood-affiliated, you still have a lot of influence so there's no need to bullshit me there."

"Whats this situation got to do wit' me . . . I got a T-number not a we-number," Romeo interjected.

"Listen . . . I got the paperwork here . . . . you all were just transferred here from the lock-up facility at Delano for being involved in a race-riot there at reception . . . I . . . let me cut through the chase . . . your homey Kevin Ladrum, A.K.A., K-Ru . . ."

"K-Ru ain't none of my homey . . . . you got the game twisted lieu . . . I'm a crip."

Romeo stood straight up out of his seat to bash the lieutenant with his words.

"SIT THE FUCK DOWN!!!" exclaimed the lieutenant.

"Man I'm just sayin . . . I ain't nobody's muthafuckin' babysitter."

"Mr. Jackson . . . I'm not here to argue with you . . . this is what's going to happen. I'm going to re-call the yard . . . and you, your homey K-Ru and his cell-mate are going to do a little chit-chatting with this Hispanic and couple of his homies. And you're going to get this shit straightened out or I can assure you that your stay here at my prison won't be pleasant at all." said Shields.

◄O►

Meanwhile . . . three C/O's were approaching the bleachers. They got there and gaff led up Romero and Big Flaco, Flaco's dad, and escorted them to the library.

Bouncer and K-Ru was already inside when the officers brought Romeo into the library.

"Whass' up Romeo," said K-Ru.

"What up my-nig . . . what goes on?"

"Awe you know . . . me and the homey almost go into it with one of them punk-ass Mexicans big homey."

"Damn boy you in some shit already."

"Naw big homey . . . but you know a nigga ain't accptin' none from them tho . . . ay . . . this the homey Big Bouncer From Compton." "Whass' up love-one . . . I'm Big Romeo from East Side Mafia."

"Thass right . . . what it do . . . I'm Big Bouncer . . . Compton Piru homey . . . much love . . . I hear you good folks."

"All the time . . . look tho . . . these punk-ass-pickles (C/O's), called me in here on this bullshit . . . they bout to bring these Mexicans in here too so that we can get this shit squashed . . . so is it cool or what," asked Romeo.

"Yeah we straight big homey . . . . a nigga was just marking his tree, feel me," stated Bouncer.

As that was being said, the door of the library flung open. Big Flaco, Lil Flaco, and Romero stepped in. Romero and Romeo immediately locked eyes. He gave Romeo slight-discreet shake of the head and a quick wink to for-warn him not to expose game of them already being acquainted.

"Whass' up holmes . . . I'm Big Flaco ay . . . . ay I know my son was a little stoned when he talked to one of you vato's ay . . ."

"Ay look gee's I offer my apologies for this dumb ass shit ay," Romero cut in and said. "We cool?" he continued.

He stuck out his hand to seal the deal. Romeo took it and shook it.

Officers was right outside the door just in case shit didn't go down like it was suppose to.

"Yeah we cool homey . . . right love-one's," stated Romeo.

"If you say so big homey," said K-Ru.

It was just as it had sounded. Romeo, K-Ru, and Bouncer was cool. But it was a known fact that the Mexicans didn't play fair when it came down to war . . . especially these Southern Mexicans.

When they began to exit the library, K-Ru went first, followed by Bouncer, lil Flaco and his dad. Romeo and Romero dragged out last.

The Lieutenant and his goons were in the hallway posted.

"Ay holmes meet me in the chapel after chow when they let us up ay," whispered Romero.

"Well gentlemen . . . we good?" asked Lt. Shields.

"Yah man we good," stated Romeo.

Romero reached out to grab Romeo's hand to show good-faith to the lieutenant. He had the yard re-called like the threatened to do. Romeo and the others were sent back to their housing units to prepare for count and later chow.

Soon as Romeo got in his cell and made his bunk, count-time was announced. He and Tiny Scooby was accounted for, then Romeo laid down and took a quick nap. Tiny Scooby noticed the frustration on his face and refrained from asking him any questions. He too joined Romeo for a quick nap.

After almost two hours of some much needed sleep, Romeo was awakened by his cellie, Tiny Scoob.

"Ay big homey . . . big homey . . . . It's chow time cuz . . . you goin'?"

Romeo snapped to life, brushed his grill and washed his face real quick. His building was released for chow soon thereafter.

Inside the chow-hall was loud and flooded with conversation. There was also a gunner posted in the gun-tower, strapped with a mini-14 rifle, watching over everything and everybody as they pick up their tray's and sit.

Romeo grabs his tray from the window, bends a corner to go take a seat, and is overwhelmed by the segregation. He made his way to an empty table, followed by Tiny Scooby. White with white, Black with Black, and Mexicans with Mexicans, he thought to himself as he sat down. He took a deep breath and welcomed the bad vibe.

"Ay . . . I'ma go toeh chapel right now loc . . . you want this shit?" Romeo offered to Scooby.

"Hell yeah cuz . . . I'ma growing boy."

Romeo eased his way out of the chow-hall passing a few familiar faces on the way and taking in the head nod's and smiles. What the fuck these nigga's smiling at, he thought.

The chapel was quiet when he got there. He really didn't know what to expect. Romero was waiting for him in the office area. He stopped dead in his tracks three feet from Romero with a cold stare in his eyes. That's when he realized why them other nigga's was smiling. Romero cracked a grin and Romeo returned it, then they embraced as brothers.

"Damn boy . . . . yo' ass always in some shit ay," stated Romero.

"Man . . . it's good to see you cuz . . . you been here long my knott?" Romeo asked.

"Long enough fool . . . whass' up essse' . . . What tha' fuck you doing in jail ay," asked Romeo. "It's a long story loco."

"I know that story already fool . . . here homeboy . . . I know you gon' need some of this."

"What is this boy?" asked Romeo.

"I'm tha man fool . . . what you think it is ay."

"What the fuck!" exclaimed Romeo with excitement.

"It's yo' favorite, you big-head mutherfucka'."

"Oooh wee . . . my boy ain't playing . . . what I owe you fo' this homey?"

"What fool . . . thass' cause I love yo' fat-head ass boy . . . and ay . . . if you need anything else just holla . . . but kind'a keep it on the D-L . . . incognito feel'me."

"Oh all of a sudden . . . what . . . you don't want yo' homies to see the love between us . . ."

"Nw fool . . . but you know how this bullshit goes ay . . . . these muthafucka's wont understand that ay."

"Yeah . . . I kow what'chu up against loco . . . I ain't trippin' tho . . . I hate this shit love one but I feel you tho' . . . ay my nig . . . Big Flaco and Lil Flaco . . . are they???"

"Yah ay . . . . thass the homey's father ay."

"Damn cuz . . . . how a nigga gon do some time with his son cuz," stated Romeo.

"We" . . . . "don't ay . . . . we don't fool," Romero specified. "Ay enjoy that shit ay . . . and when you run out, holla."

"Oh you can't kick it and smoke one wit'cho boy," Romeo said sarcastically.

"Oh you got jokes now huh."

They both laughed then embraced. Romeo then tucked the bag of weed Romero gave him down in his nuts, and headed out the door.

Tiny Scooby was in the cell listening to the radio Romeo had come up on from one of his comrades. When Romeo entered the cell he was smiling from ear to ear.

"What it do lil homey," he asked

"Shiittt . . . . listening to these oldies big homey . . . whass wit' you . . . why you so wired up?"

"Look what I got boy!"

Tiny Scooby sat up in his bunk and looked down. Romeo tossed a the bundle of weed on his cell's table.

"Whoa!" exclaimed Tiny Scooby. "Where you come up on that from Big Homey?"

He jumped off the top bunk and sat besides Romeo on his bunk. The radio was still playing low.

"Ay watch the doe boy and stop asking questions . . . don't trip lil one . . . just enjoy the ride cuz."

This high was different than any other high Romeo had even endured. In his mind right now, he was free. And he owed his new freedom to his homey, Romero. He laid back on his bunk and enjoyed the ride himself.

Tiny Scooby went out to the yard when they called for a yard release. As the day progressed, Romeo cleaned the cell top to bottom, smoke a couple of more joints to the head, then sat down at the table and started composing a letter to Renee'. As he began reading to himself, Tiny Scooby came through the door.

"What it do big homey?" he said.

Romeo turned around from the table and just looked. Tiny Scooby burst into laughter as he hung his jean jacket on one of the homemade coat-hooks.

"Damn cuz you high as a muthafucka' big homey," Scooby said.

"What time is it loc," asked Romeo.

"Its' yard re-call cuz . . . smoke one wit yo' lil homey."

"Look out there and see what tha' po'po' doin' loc."

Tiny Scooby looked out the cell doors' window to check the surroundings. As he was doing so. C/O Motta stepped right in front of the door.

"Oh Shit!" said a spooked Scooby.

C/O Motta was standing there sorting through a few pieces of mail.

"Jackson," he called out.

"Yeah?" Romeo answered from the back of the cell.

"Last two," said C/O Motta.

"Uhh . . . Nine-Fo'."

Motta handed two letters through the side slit in the cell-door. Romeo quickly looked to see who it was that the letters were from. When he saw that both were from Kia, he just threw them atop the desk without opening them.

"Did they take count loc?"

"Yeah big homey . . . . they already did that shit."

"Light this up then lil nigga."

Romeo threw a joint at Tiny Scooby to light up. They smoked and laid back listening to the oldies. Romeo fell asleep thinking about Renee', and his precious little one.

CHAPTER EIGHTEEN

Today was no different, Romeo thought. He woke up this morning feeling like he had a hangover from yesterday's bullshit. Same old shit, day-in and day-out he said to his self. It's been just that for the past year and eight months. If it hadn't been for the relationship between he and Romero, things would've been much worst by now. The Black's and Mexican's on this yard would've been at one another's throats a long time ago.

Romeo didn't mind anyone knowing about the connection between he and Romero. However, Romero on the other hand was up against a whole different set of rules that fortunately Romeo understood. Regardless of these circumstances, he still had a lot of love for Romero and his family.

When Romeo got back from breakfast his head was cluttered with thoughts. He shook his head in attempts to break his thoughts up from being so crowded.

"Ay lil homey . . . twist us a couple of blunts and about ten or fifteen joints for the yard cuz," he requested from Scooby.

"Damn big homey, what'chu' got goin' this mo'nin' a smoke-out?" asked Tiny Scooby.

"Naw cuz I just wanna hit a few of my nigga's wit a little sumptin'."

"Cuz you straight . . . you sounding down big homey."

"I'm straight loco . . . just tired of this same ol' bullshit everyday cuz . . . gimme one of them joints now loc."

Romeo lit up one of his homemade incense, then lit the joint. He sat on the toilet while Tiny Scooby rolled up the rest of the joints, and the blunts he requested. He just sat there quietly smoking and thinking to himself and waited for yard-release. Finally he heard the announcement over the P.A.

"Thass' yard cuz . . . gimme them two blunts."

"Here big homey."

The sun beamed through the front opening of the rotunda as Romeo and Tiny Scooby exited the building. Romeo briefly stopped by the curb-side and scanned the yard. He spotted Romero immediately, as did Romero him. They shared a head-nod as if to silently greet one another with a, "what's up love one", from a long distance. Romeo smiled then he, and Tiny Scooby peeled off to the right headed towards the one-block.

"Whad'up locos," stated C.J.

He approached from behind. Romeo immediately recognized the voice, spun around, and embraced his comrade.

"Hey my nigga' . . . what it do."

"Shit . . . just chillin' big homey . . . bout to buss some laps."

"Wanna smoke one wit' cho boy?"

"Hell yeah cuz!"

Romeo pulled one of the blunts from his jacket pocket, along with his tiny bic lighter.

"Damn loc . . . where you come up from?"

"There you go my nig . . . asking questions like the feds or sompthin' . . . . . ay Tiny Scoob check this nigga' fo' a wire cuz."

Tiny Scooby guestred as if he were going to search C.J. jokingly.

"You bet'not touch me lil nigga."

They all laughed and headed over to the bleachers next to the basketball court. It was a few more fella's already posted at the bleachers when Romeo, C.J. and Tiny Scooby pushed up.

"What up loc's," said Romeo.

"Whass' cracking big homey," Blue Devil responded.

"Same ol shit Dev . . . whass' new wit'chu love one." Romeo said.

"Ay big homey, they say the Mexicans supposed to be disciplining one of they own today."

"Oh yeah," Romeo said.

Devil went into details of what the whole ordeal was going on with the Mexican issue. Romeo and Tiny Scooby sat and listened to all the details. It was never enough information to begin with, with all the different so-called codes of silence.

"Now is that what you know or what your heard cuz?" asked Romeo.

"One of they peeps put me up on that one loc."

"Damn . . . you say he got caught stealin' huh.

"Yah cuz . . . from the Woods."

"And what the Woods talkin' bout, asked Romeo.

"I don't know all that . . . I know them Mexicans supposed to be gettin' off on the boy."

"Which one was it cuz?"

"I think my boy said Lil Flaco."

"Awe shiiitt . . . his daddy one of they heads . . . they ain't bout to do not'n to that one," sated Romeo.

"Yeah thass' the same one thass' been gettin' into all kind of shit since we got here last year big homey," sated C.J.

"Fuck'em all," Romeo said. "It'll come to bite'em in the ass one day . . . ay cuz, here, light this other blunt," he continued.

He pulled the blunt from his pocket and handed it to Blue Devil. As soon as he lit it up, an announcement came over the P.A. system.

"ATTENTION ON THE YARD AND IN THE HOUSING UNITS . . . THE FOLLOWING INMATES HAVE VISITS . . . JACKSON T-94, GARCIA T-33, VALDEZ J-01, BROWN P-33 AND BROWN D-91 . . . GENTLEMEN YOU HAVE VISITS . . . REPORT TO VISITING."

"Whoop . . . that be me my nigga's . . . ay Scoob . . . just blow them with the homies cuz . . . I'll be back wit' a fresh load."

He leaped off the bleachers and made a dash for the building out of excitement. The tower guard yelled to him to him over the P.A.

"NO RUNNING ON THE YARD!"

Romeo stopped in his tracks. He had to take a deep breath and remember where he is . . . and what could've just happened. He turned, looked up the guard, and patted his chest as if to apologize. "My Bad," he said.

Romeo was quickly in-and-out of the block in less than ten minutes. He was freshly dressed and smelling like he had just come from a Muslim convention. As he headed towards the vising room, he passed by the bleachers where Romero and his homies were posted. They gave each other a brief glance and Romeo kept the line moving. By the time he reached the peg-gate an officer was already there to let him through.

"Thank you," Romeo said.

He walked through the gate with a smile. It was as if he were escaping a bundle of racial atrocities. Each group on this yard was packed with racial hatred, rather it be the Black's, Whites's, or the Hispanic's. There was not one area where interracial activities played a part.

Romeo shook it off as he approached the officer's desk inside of the visiting room where he checked in with the visiting officers.

"Jackson T-94," he said, handing the officer at the desk his I.D.

"Mr. Jackson, you're at table twelve.

Romeo turned around shining like brand new money, suited in his spiffy penitentiary blues and P.I.A. tennis-shoes, spotted Kia sitting at the table waiting patiently. When he finally reached the table, she stood up and greeted him with a luscious wet kiss.

"Hey baby," she said.

"Whass' up with you sexy," he responded.

She was wearing a smile on her face that almost outshined the sun. she was very happy to see that her presence put a smile on her Romeo's face.

"Nothing baby, just missing you . . . . whass' been up with you . . . are you okay," she asked.

"I am now," he said with a smile.

Kia smiled even more with that comment.

"You got my thang baby girl?" he continued.

"Dang . . . . you just messed our moment up . . . is that all you care about."

She briefly got upset at Romeo. She thought was really the reason for his happiness. Turned out, she really wasn't. Soon as she snapped, so did he.

"Hold up nigga . . . you get paid fo' what'chu do bitch . . . it ain't no puzzle to this game muthafucka', what'chu' trippin fo!"

Kia dropped her head in sorrow. Romeo's words had viciously stabbed her in the heart. She felt the point of each one of his words pierce her emotions.

"I'm sorry Romeo . . . but you know it ain't about the money with me . . . I want you baby . . . you know I do."

"Knock it off girl . . . you already know the deal. And you don't want me. You just infatuated with this lifestyle girl . . . com'on now."

"Naw baby it's you . . . I know what I want."

"Oh yeah, well wantin' and needin' is two different thangs baby girl . . . I'm trying to keep it real wit' you instead of stringin' you along wit' a bunch of bullshit like the rest of these nigga's be playin' that game, feel' me."

"I mean, you might want me, no doubt . . . but you don't need me or this lifestyle . . . and plus, I need my son, so therefore I need his mama, feel' me."

Kia just smacked her lips as quietly as she could and shook her head in disappointment.

"Look baby girl . . . I appreciate everything you do for me. Right now I do need you, but I'm not gon' make no false promises to you, you do mean mo' to me than that," he concluded.

"Okay . . . okay baby, I got it . . . you hungry," she asked.

Rome grabbed her by the hand, they both stood up and headed for the vending machines. Kia purchased a few items out of the machines quickly. After, they stepped a few feet to the left where the microwave oven's were. Romeo put his back against the wall and tucked himself in-between a wall and one of the vending machines. Kia then handed him three log-like items from down in her pants.

"Whatch out baby girl while I do this real quick," he stated.

As Kia warmed the food in the microwave, and watch the two offers discretely, Romeo gently, but swiftly, tucked all three logs into his ass-hole one-by-one. By the time she was finished warming the food, so was he with stuffing his vault. They then made their way back to their table to eat and enjoy the rest of their visit.

"Ah . . . ooh this shit is hot baby girl." "I am too baby," she flirted.

"Girl you crazy," he laughed and said.

He was happy to see Kia back to enjoying herself. He would've hated if he would've had to cut her off the team.

"Yeah . . . crazy bout yo' ass," she said.

Romeo fed her some of his burger and nachos. Her whole face brightened. This was a relief to Romeo, plus him being surrounded by all this freedom, babies crying, sexy women, and a bunch of colliding conversations about something other than the bullshit ass penitentiary lies he hear almost every day. This really re-set the mood.

He and Kia ended up taking a couple of pictures and enjoying walking in circles around the visiting yard. Kia rested her head on his shoulder as he held her hand and turned the rest of the day into her day.

⋈

Meanwhile on the yard, at the bleachers where Tiny Scooby is hosting a jail-house smoke-out, he and some of the other young crip's were still clowning around. They were all kind of stuck in laugh-land from the effect of the chronic smoke.

"Cuzz . . . I'm high as a muthafucka's loc's" stated Lil R/C.

"Shet up nigga . . . you was high when you was born cuz," Tiny Scooby said.

Everybody burst into laughter except for Blue Devil.

"Ay loc why you getting' at the lil homey like that cuz," grudged Blue Devil.

"What homey . . . I'm bullshittin wit the homey . . . what'chu trippin fo cuz."

"So what I'm trippin cuz . . . whass next nigga . . . you wanna see me bout somp'n nigga."

Blue Devil stood up around over Tiny Scooby. Then R/C, Ric-Roc, and C.J. all stood up around Blue Devil.

"Ay . . . both of ya'll need to chill cuz . . . if the big homey was here ya'll wouldn't be trippin on each other . . . especially out here on this yard loc."

"It ain't me cuz . . . thass' that nigga loc," exclaimed Tiny Scooby.

"Fuck you nigga," shouted Blue Devil.

"Naw nigga . . . . fuck you cuz," T-Scooby shot back.

C.J. looked and saw that it was pure hatred glowing in the eyes of Blue Devil. He now understood why Blue Devil was acting like this. Romeo had left Tiny Scooby here with the sack to smoke with the rest of his homies, but Blue Devil took it as if Romeo left him in charge.

Blue Devil was in-fact wrong because with Romeo there is no in-charge. He loved all his loc's, and everybody had say-so. And the one thing that Romeo didn't tolerate, was hatin' on one another.

"My nig . . . you need to kill that bullshit wit the lil homey loc," said C.J.

"That lil nigga need to stay his young ass in his place then loc."

"Cuz . . . I ain't said a muthafuckin' thang to yo ass nigga," said T-Scooby.

"It'll be wise if you don't say nothing else nigga," threanted Blue Devil.

"That nigga actin' like he somebody's Gee or something' cuz."

"What . . . knock it off loc . . . that don't even sound right . . . light somp'n up T.S. cuz," C.J. said.

Tiny Scooby pulled a few of more joints out of his stash and laid them and the lighter on the bleachers. C.J., Ric-Roc, and Blue Devil lit' em up and they all smoked in silence.

Romero and his homies were still posted in their bleachers, on the other side of the yard, also enjoying some chronito. Big Flaco was just walking up.

"Ay holmes whass' up ay," he said.

"Whass'up esse'," said Romero.

"Ay Youngster, you seen my son ay?"

"Not lately ay . . . the last time I saw him was at breakfast esse'," said Youngster.

"Whass' up esse' . . . nobody's seen the little homey ay," Romero asked.

"Nope esse'," followed Payaso.

Even Sleepy was shaking his head no.

Romero stood up in the bleachers and scanned the yard to see if could notice lil Flaco out roaming around. Then he quickly glanced at his watch.

"It's almost count time ay . . . . he'll show up somewhere ay," stated Romeo.

"Yeah . . . his little ass probably fuckin' off in a cell wit one of the homey's ay . . . if one of you vato's run into his ass esse' tell'em I'm lookin' fo' em ay," Big Flaco said.

Everybody sat quietly as Big Flaco pushed off. Romero thought it to be rather strange for little Flaco to be missing, especially with all this weed that's being smoked out here with the homies. Romero figured that it was just as Big Flaco suggested, that he was probably somewhere fucking off.

◄◦►

Visiting was over. The officer's was strip-searching all the inmates before they were allowed to go back to the yard. When Romeo was finished being searched, he and a few other inmates were released back to the yard.

Romeo was walking with Big Vamp from Compton N-hood.

"Ay that was yo' girl cuz," asked Big Vamp.

"Naw . . . thass' my lil hood snow-bunny cuz . . . ever since a nigga laid this pipe and exposed her to this platinum tongue, she been sprung loc . . . that bitch be irritatin' me sometime cuz, but she do the damn-thang fo' yo' boy tho." stated Romeo.

"I feel you loc . . . but a nigga can't complain. You need all you can get in this mothafucka'," Big Vamp said.

"Yeah . . . I feel that one my nig."

"Hold up homey . . . my son should be catching up wit' us."

"Yo' who cuz," asked a surprising Romeo.

"Yah . . . love one, that was his young ass at the table wit' me and mom's cuz . . . his dumb ass caught a punk-ass car-jack with his so-called homeboys, and they rolled over on my lil nigga cuz . . . here he come now."

"Whass' his name love one," asked Romeo.

"Oh he lil Vamp, from da'hood . . . the homies call'em Lil Vee tho'.

"Damn cuz, how much time he got loc?"

"They broke'em off eleven wit' eighty-five."

Romeo shook his head in disgust. He couldn't fathom how Big Vamp could sound so proud of his son being Lil Vamp. Then he thought to himself about his own little one.

"Damn cuz . . . that'll hold'em. Man I don' ran into a couple of homies thass' locked up wit' they son's . . . I don't think I'll be able to do it," Romeo said.

"Yeah well . . . I'm glad he here wit' me, than in a pine box loc. Anyway my nig you must ain't met Mr. green yet . . . he here wit two of his son's."

"Damn cuz . . . two?"

"Two my nig . . . they all in one-block. Mr. Green be on they ass too, with his old grouchy ass."

"Dammit', how much time they got?" asked Romeo.

"He got life-without . . . . one of his boy's got twenty-to-life, and the other one just got a gang of time . . . I think thirty years or something' like that.

"Ya'll must be talking bout Mr. Green an'nem," said Lil Vamp.

Romeo turned around to where the voice was coming from and was surprised to see a little miniature Vamp standing there. He looked and sounded just like his daddy. Fear charged through Romeo's thoughts like a raging tornado, twisting his mind in all sorts of directions, all ending in disaster.

"What it do lil homey," Romeo spoke

He looked up a Romeo and stared straight into his eyes like he was looking for a challenge or something.

"I'm straight homey . . . where you from cuz," he asked Romeo.

"I'm Romeo loc, from East Side Mafia Crip's." Romeo said.

"Right, right . . . I know a gang of yo' lil homies cuz."

Big Vamp got a little irritated with his sons' arrogance.

"Boy what I tell you bout that kinda'a shit," he yelled. "Don't trip Romeo, he just puttin' a little extras on it loc," he added.

Romeo just laughed. He got kind of confused with Big Vamp's sudden change from big homey to father in just seconds. At least it was change for the better, Romeo thought.

"It's cool cuz . . . I remember when I used to be on nigga's like that," Romeo said.

"YARD RE-CALL . . . GENTLEMEN REPORT BACK TO YOUR ASSIGNED HOUSING FOR COUNT . . . YAAAAARRRRDDDDD RE-CAALLLLL."

They stepped onto the track to listen to that announcement. Romeo and Big Vamp gave one another a pound-pound of the fist.

"Well it's bout that time love one . . . ay cuz when we come out for the night yard loc, holla' at me, I'ma have a little somptin' fo' ya'," stated Romeo.

"You doin' it like that my nig," Big Vamp asked.

"Don't trip cuz, I got'chu . . . Ay lil homey, you keep yo' head to the sky loc."

Little Vamp just gave Romeo a head-nod and started pushing towards hi building.

"Don't tell that lil nigga that cuz . . . . his head already too big as it is." Stated Big Vamp.

Romeo recognized the embarrassment that was being imposed on Vamp's little one, and sympathized wit him. Romeo also understood the hurt Big Vamp was imposing on himself, by blaming himself for the self destructive path that his son was choosing. Romeo felt it in his heart to say something, but he thought, who was he to say anything, when he's living the same way.

CHAPTER NINETEEN

Renee' sat up in her bed sorting through her thoughts. Tonight, she was having a strange feeling sitting here alone after midnight, heavily thinking about her Romeo. She and her little Romeo constantly prayed, together, for God to watch over Romeo and bring him home safely. Every since that little chit-chat Renee' had with Ma'Ma', worry has conquered her thoughts. Renee' got out of bed, went into the kitchen, warmed her up a glass of milk, and then took a seat on her living-room couch to finish her thinking. The darkness of the house enhanced her thoughts. She sat and just stared at the Glade scent dispenser that was plugged into the outlet next to the lamp stand, which was her only source of light at the moment. Ma'Ma' had shared some real shit with her, she thought. Maybe she should go see her Romeo and stop being so damned stubborn. She found herself literally beginning to speak out loud to herself. She set her glass of milk down on the table in front of her and tried to gather her thoughts. This shit is crazy, she thought. I'm sitting here, can't sleep . . . do he realize or even understand the heartache and pain this shit is causing for me and his son, she wondered. Then the thought crossed her mind that he probably didn't give a fuck. "Oooh . . . he make sick," her heart screamed inside.

"Not long after her Romeo-bashing in her thoughts, she returned to her seat on the couch and calmed it down a little. Who was she trying to fool anyway? She knew for a fact that Romeo truly loved her and his son dearly . . . more than his own life. Suddenly she realized what was actually going on in her head. She was persistently trying to harvest an excuse not to go visit Romeo. She knew her little Romeo was alright. He understood the situation. Of course he was hurting because his dad had to be away, but she knew even the little one knew his dad loved him dearly. "You need to stop playing with the game," she said to herself. Finally she was able to smile when she thought of how proud her Romeo would be of his baby girl being this strong black woman instead of a little cry-baby.

"Renee' took a deep breath. Her mind was made up. Tomorrow is Saturday, she's already approved for visitng, lil Romeo is spending the day with Ma'Ma' and little Romero, so her day is free . . . she's going to see her Romeo.

"It was good, she thought, that little Romeo had plans because she was adamant on not taking her baby to nobody's jail . . . at least not at the moment. She got up from the couch, quickly finished her now, cold milk, then made a b-line for her bedroom. She decided to sleep on her decision, even though her mind seemed to be made up. As she lay down in her bed, excitement raced though her entire body. Wow, she thought. She just couldn't get Romeo out of her head.

"It must be true love," she whispered to herself.

She leaned over to her night stand and grabbed hold of a picture frame that possessed a recent a photo of her two Romeo's. Smiling she allowed her heart to marinate on how sexy he look as a father, and how much the little one looked just like him.

"I'll be a fool to lose you again," she whispered to the picture.

Renee' closed her eyes, hoping for Romeo's voice to respond . . . . "You won't baby girl . . . I love you and I always will . . . I am you life," she imagined him saying. She fell asleep with a smile on her face and the picture locked in her embrace, close to her heart.

It was six A.M. when Renee' sprung back to life. She got out of bed and noticed that she had slept holding the picture of her two favorite men.

She smiled, then stretched, got out of bed, and enjoyed a hot shower. Afterwards she woke her little Romeo.

"Hey . . . wake up little man," she said softly.

"I'm up already mommy."

He was indeed already awake. He was just lying in his bed thinking about his hero, and hoping he was here with him.

"Then why was your eyes closed," Renee' asked.

"I was just thinking bout my daddy . . . if he was here was probably be going fishing or something'."

"Awe baby . . . he wish he were here with you too, I'm sure . . . are you gonna' be alright today at Ma'Ma's?"

"Yeah!" little Romeo exclaimed. "I'ma big boy now and plus I know my dad would want me to be having fun until he got home."

"He sure would baby."

Renee' almost burst into tears. She was a proud of how her little Romeo was handing his daddy's absence.

"Okay . . . what you want for breakfast baby?"

"Ummm . . . cereal."

"Yep."

"Okay then . . . . cereal it is . . . I guess I'll call Ma'Ma' and little Romero and let them know that we'll be on our way in a little bit."

Renee' was all smiles this morning. Last night she indulged in very long conclusive talk with herself. She realized that Romeo would've wanted her to keep on living as if he were still there. As little Romeo had just said.

She and the little one went about their business for the morning. She picked up the phone and called Ma'Ma about six-forty-five.

"Hello . . . Ma'Ma' . . . are you awake?"

"Yes sweetie . . . who's this?"

"Ma'Ma' it's me . . . I'm just calling to tell that I'll be there shortly to drop lil Romeo off."

"Oh, okay . . . I didn't recognize you voice sweetie . . . you sound a little excited, what's up?"

"Well I decided to take your advice Ma'Ma . . . I'm going today."

"What traffic, it's Saturday."

"I know, but it's a lot of people that's going to be visiting today."

"Oh, okay . . . I see what you're saying."

"Yeah, you hurry now."

Little Romeo was finishing up his cereal as Renee' hung up the telephone. He had cleaned and already dried his dishes as she was entering the kitchen.

"You ready mom?" he asked.

"Sure am . . . are you done eating?"

"Yep."

"Okay . . . go get your stuff and let head out."

Little Romeo took-off to his room and grabbed his duffle bag. Renee' made sure that the house was locked up and they were soon on their way up the boulevard. She got to Ma'Ma's house quick. It was a little past seven when she got there. Little Romero was still in his pajamas when he ran out the house and darted to the car to help to help little Romeo with his bags. Ma'Ma' with a pair of crossed fingers as if needed some luck along for her trip. And then off she was, to see her Romeo. By the time Renee' hit the highway, her stomach was flooded with butterflies. What if some other bitch was already up there visiting him, she thought. She slowly took a deep breath then answered her own curiosity . . . . oh well, she said . . . she was definitely on her way to re-claim once again what was truly hers.

CHAPTER TWENTY

I t was count time in hell. Tiny Scooby was standing at the cell-door and Romeo was at the desk in the rear of the cell. Soon as the C/O made his rounds and counted them, it was on once again.

"He gone big homey."

"Keep yo' eyes on that fool love one . . . I'm just gon' twist us up something' for right now real quick," Romeo said.

He pulled out enough weed to roll up two joints. He then put the rest of it back in his human vault, real easy. Being a vet at this game, it didn't take much effort. By the time Romeo had gotten the two joints rolled, Tiny Scooby noticed that something wasn't right with the C/O's.

"Hold on big homey . . . don't light that shit yet."

"Why . . . . whass' up dog," asked Romeo.

"I don't know . . . but it look like they finna' walk again cuz."

"Watch out my nig . . . let me see."

Romeo stepped up to the door to make his own assessment of what was going on. When he saw that the officers brought the population board out to the podium, he concluded that they maybe fucking up the count.

"These dumb ass muthafucka's cain't count cuz . . . thass' all it is."

The building tower guard announced a recount and ordered everyone to stand with their I.D.'s in-hand. Romeo and Tiny Scooby stood at the front of their cell in compliance. It was a tight fit with two people standing by the door, but they managed. In building one, officer Ochoa was recounting, which confirmed that she was one head short. She approached her partner, c/o Samuels of the podium.

"Hey Sammy . . . how many empties we got?" she asked.

"None," C/O Samuels replied.

"No shit . . . well I got one empty in cell 224."

"Check the Medical sheet," said Samuels.

"We had no bodies on the D.M.S. (Daily Movement Sheet), today."

"Well shit if we got an empty, he has to be somewhere . . . . look on the pop board and see what's the name."

"I got the name . . . it's Jiminez . . . I'm calling the sarge."

Ochoa called the sergeants office immediately. She was nervous, being a fairly new employee of C.D.C, she didn't know what to expect.

"Sergeant Cohan office," he said when he answered the call.

"Yeah sarge, this is Ochoa in A-1 . . . I have an empty, when in-fact we have no empties listed in this building."

"What's the cell number, name, and C.D.C. number, Ochoa?" asked Sgt. Cohan.

"Uhhh, the name is Jiminez, A. his number is F-33619, and he was housed in A-1, cell 224 low sir."

"Okay let me run this by central control and I'll get back to you," said Cohan.

"Okay," Ochoa replied.

She hung up with the sarge and took a second look at the D.M.S. Romeo was still at the door watching what was going on with his building C/O's. When he saw that one of the officers was leaving the building, he got frustrated.

"Cuz . . . . look like sump thin' up in another building . . . fuck'em I need to smoke sump'n right now."

Tiny Scooby laughed, reached up on one of their shelves and grabbed one of the homemade incense they kept handy. They were made from new mop strings and Muslim oils. He lit the end of the string and blew out the flame, which left a small cherry like tip burning at a slow pace. It let out a thin smoke and musky/sweet scent that lit the cell up quickly with its smell.

Romeo took a long whiff then lit the joints. He pulled on it hard, filling his lungs with its smoke. Now closing his eyes and holding his breath, he held the joint out towards Tiny Scooby so he can hit it. Romeo then sat quietly and let the chronic smoke marinate his system and serenade his mentals. When Romeo released the smoke from his lungs, he also let out a long aaaahhh, for proof of satisfaction, and then a short flurry of coughs. Tiny Scooby took the joint and took it easy as well, after seeing how it treated Romeo at the end.

"Damn big homey . . . you take this shit to the extreme."

"Nigga', puff puff pass cuz."

"Here."

Tiny Scooby rushed into a quick pull of the joint before passing it to Romeo and couldn't handle it. He burst into a frenzy of couching.

Now Romeo burst into cloud of laughing with smoke everywhere. Romeo just so happen to glance out the cell-door's window as he was laughing at his little homey. He noticed the C/O's taking count on the other side of the building.

"Awe shit loc!!! Put that shit out cuz!" exclaimed Romeo.

"Whass' big homey?'

"Put that shit up loc . . . they countin' again cuz . . . oohh, dammit . . . they opening' all the doe's too cuz . . . damn!"

Romeo and Tiny Scooby scrambled in a panic. Romeo reached down into his locker and retrieved a bottle of baby powder. He shook it up frantically, then twisted the top, and commenced to squeezing it so that it would send powdery poofs into the air. They both sat quietly, and nervous awaiting their fate.

When Sergeant Cohan finally made it over to building one, he was furious. He, Lieutenant Diaz, and Captain Jones all entered the building together. They didn't bother stopping at the officer's office or the podium. They all looked like warriors on a serious mission as they strolled over to cell 224. C/O's Samuels and Ochoa fell right in line and followed. Ochoa waved her hand up towards the tower guard, gesturing for him to pop the door. The door flew open with the help of the sergeant snatching it. Popper was standing there glassy eyed, and the Sergeant began drilling him. "Where the hell is your cell-mate!"

"Huh," Popper replied.

"Where the fuck is inmate Jiminez!" shouted Cohan.

"Huh," said Popper, again.

"Your fucking cellie . . . where is he," Cohan demanded. "Oh . . . I don't know ay . . . he ain't came in here all day ay."

"Lock it down!" commanded Captain Jones.

The Lieutenant got on his radio. Seconds later, four more C/O's came to the building to assist the officers.

"Cuff this one and take him to medical and test him. Radio this in to control . . . emergency head count . . . have all inmates step outside their door's with an I.D. in-hand immediately. Get on it pronto," ordered Lt. Diaz.

All of the officers began to scramble to carry out the orders that were just dished out by the lieutenant. He and the Captain were furious . . . an escape on their watch. They knew if this was so, then it would be hell to pay for the man who'd have to deliver the news to the warden.

Romeo and Tiny Scooby were still waiting to be counted. They were sitting quietly and staring straight ahead listening for keys, until Tiny Scooby broke silence.

"Damn big homey . . . that shit still stank," he whispered.

"Thass that fire boy, I told you . . . now shet up and stop watching me nigga'."

When the door slid open to Romeo's cell, his entire body tensed up like he was preparing to be hit by Mike Tyson, that's when they heard it.

"EVERYBODY STEP OUTSIDE YOUR DOORS WITH YOUR I.D.'S . . . . SHOW IT TO ONE OF MY OFFICERS AS THEY

PASS . . . . DO IT NOW!!!" Captain Jones ordered.

That announcement set about twenty pounds of relief in Romeo's thought's. With all the cell-doors open it would be harder for officers to tell where the actual smell was originating from, when it-fact the smell wasn't in the air but on their clothing. Romeo immediately realized this and quickly stepped back into his cell and grabbed a small bottle of some Muslim oil. He squeezed a few a drops in the palms of his hand and quickly stepped back outside his door. Romeo was rubbing his hands together then he hit his shirt with the scent off his palms, afterwards he shook both of Tiny Scooby's hands also.

"Here cuz . . . rub some of this shit all over you loc," whispered Romeo.

"Whass up big homey?"

"You stank nigga' . . . rub some of this on."

"OH."

They both began applying the oil to their clothing. Tiny Scooby was feeling on his chest like he'd just swallowed a bottle of Spanish-fly and popped an X-pill. By the time the officers had gotten around to Romeo's cell, the chronic smoke, baby powder, and Muslim oil scents had bonded with the penitentiary's cement, crusty feet, and musty ass scent that was proturuding from the cells.

The tower guard followed every move the floor-officers made. He was their god. Only his power wasn't of a spiritual nature, it was the nature of knowing the power of his mini-14 when it knocked a plug out of a muthafucka's ass.

Romeo and Tiny Scooby was accounted for then allowed to go back inside their cell. Romeo quickly turned on the oldies on the radio to calm his nerves. Tiny Scooby remained at the door and continued to watch the officer's movements nervously.

"Sit'cho ass down somewhere cuz . . . it's over my nig," Romeo stated.

"I'm trying to see what they doing big homey."

"Nigga' squat!!! We finna' blow another one in a minute loco . . . they aint trippin on us cuz."

"Ooh C/O Nunez and' nem' just left cuz, and the bitch is up in the office."

"Good . . . blaze that other joint up then loc."

Once again it was on . . .

Romeo was back in the norm. He and Tiny Scooby was smoking life again. Romeo still wondered in his thoughts what the hell was actually going in out there. He had a gut feeling that something wasn't right, and it had to be more than just a head-count.

The C/O's had completed their count in building one also. However, the sergeant and lieutenant, was still in the building. Captain Jones had returned to his office, he was designated to be the bearer of the embarrassing news to the Warden.

As C/O Ochoa and her partner, Samuels was searching Popper and Lil Flaco's cell, a call came over the radio from one the S&E's (security and escort officers).

"S&E one to control"

"Go ahead S&E one . . . this is control."

"Control, we have located inmate Jiminez, C.D.C. number-frank-33619."

"Control copy . . . what is that inmate's current status and location S&E one requesting medical staff to 10-20 the chapel."

When the sergeant heard this over the radio, he turned beet-red in the face.

"All available officers' report to the chapel immediately!!!" shouted Sgt. Cohan over his radio.

Lieutenant Diaz was pissed. He walked out of the building by himself and headed to the chapel. Everybody knew that the Warden was going to roll some heads on this one, so Cohan, Diaz, and Jones started their every-man-for-himself game.

When Cohan finally made it over to the chapel, Diaz and Jones were already there. Little Flaco's body was sprawled out behind one of the office's desk with yellow foam around his mouth and his eyes were bucked wide open, like he enjoyed too many banana pop-rocks, got scared as hell, and just croaked.

The M.T.A. (medical training assistant), in other words, the nurse was looking over the body.

"What's the cause," asked Cohan.

Diaz and Jones were standing there awaiting that same information.

"From what I see before me . . . . overdose . . . . here you can see the fresh needle marks on his arm." The nurse replied.

The nurse pointed out the four little red dots on lil Flaco's arm. They sort of looked like tiny little flea bites that tracked along what used to be a vein. Sgt. Cohan turned and started screaming at his officers.

"Keep this out of the air . . . . after chow, I want building one torn apart top to bottom . . . strip'em down to state issue!"

"Ay sarge," said C/O Gaines.

He pointed at the body as he addressed the sergeant.

"Yeah," said Cohan.

"Uhhh, I believe that's Javier Jiminez's son sir . . . he's one of the lifer's in five block . . . . goes by the name of Big Flaco, and that's little Flaco sir if I'm not mistaken," Gaines said pointing at little Flaco's body.

"Shit . . . okay, bring him to my office."

"No . . . bring him to my office," Diaz interrupted.

"Radio in control-feeding, one building at a time . . . I don't want no info passed between buildings . . . and get that damned body out of here!" screamed Cohan.

He jumped furious when Lieutenant Diaz stomped on his authority. However, he refused to be used as a scapegoat. He and Diaz went to the program office and waited for the C/O's to escort Big Flaco to Diaz's office. As they waited . . . they argued.

"I'm not going to be your fucking fall guy on this one," Cohan said.

"You're the Supervising Sergeant ass-hole . . . don't . . ."

"No!!! You don't, you fucker!!! Don't try and pin this bullshit all on me!" Cohan shouted, sounding like he'd just shattered his vocals.

"Like I said . . . You're the Supervising Sergeant . . . you're the one with direct supervision over security and all other activities on this facility . . . FUCKER!" replied Diaz.

It looked as if Cohan wanted to snatch Diaz by the neck and add one more to the body-count. Sgt. Cohan was one of them big ass corn-fed-ass-red-neck white boy's from the south, whereas, Diaz was just a frail-ass Mexican with more authority. But neither one of them was afraid of the other.

Two C/O's had finally brought Big Flaco to the office where Diaz and Cohan were. They made Flaco stand by the door of the Lt.'s office, then turned and left immediately.

Big Flaco stood by the door's entrance quietly. Both Cohan and Diaz waited to see which one of themselves would take the lead. Diaz ordered Flaco to enter and have a seat.

"What's this all about sir?" asked Flaco.

Cohan and Diaz looked at one another. Cohan was thinking to himself, this one of their O'Gee's, if this go wrong . . . shit can and will get hectic. As far as Diaz was concerned, he just didn't know how this lifer was going to respond to his son being dead.

Cohan decided to take the lead and make a power move.

"It's about your son Mr. Jiminez . . . did you know that he was doing drugs in my facility?!" stated Cohan in an aggressive tone.

"What! What the fuck is this ay," shouted Big Flaco.

He jumped to his feet furious. His first thought was they had caught his son with some "TAR" (heroin), and now they trying to play him out to be some kind of fatherly snithch.

"Now hold Mr. Jiminez," said Diaz. "It seems your son had overdosed himself with some heroin . . . my officers found his body in the rear office of the chapel during the seventeen-hundred-hour count," he continued.

Cohan looked at Diaz with another evil-ass look. Furious once again at the way Diaz played his way into the good-guy position with this convict. Big Flaco just dropped his head to this disastrous news in digust.

"Naw man . . . NO!!! Naw holmes . . . thass my little homey ay," cried Flaco.

"Little homey . . . I thought that was your son," Cohan replied sarcastically.

"Hey!!! Fuck you ay."

"Hey!!! Hey!!! Mr. Cohan step out my office," ordered Diaz. "I was . . ."

"Step out now!" Diaz shouted.

Cohan walked out swiftly and slammed the office door almost shattering it's glass. He was steamed. He thought to himself, this punk-ass motherfucker was not going to get away with this continuous undermining of his authority.

Diaz remained inside the office with Big Flaco.

"Look Mr. Jiminez, I really am sorry about your son . . . but we need to get down to the bottom of this."

"The bottom of what ay . . . you vato's don't give a fuck about us ay . . . you just want to fuck over somebody fo' this ay . . . well not with my help . . . I don't know shit ay . . . his blood is on you motherfuckers hands ay! exclaimed Big Flaco.

He stormed out of Diaz's office and asked Sgt. Cohan can he be escorted back to his block. Cohan head-nodded to one of the S&E's standing nearby. The S&E officer then gestured to Big Flaco to follow, and they both left the program office. Cohan was almost amused at the Diaz's tactics backfired on him. He looked through Diaz's office window and caught his eye. He gave him a little devilish smile, like ha-ha' motherfucker. Cohan then walked into his own office which was next door to Diaz's, and answered his ringing phone. The Captain was calling to inform him of an immediate meeting in his office. When Cohan was leaving his office so was Diaz. They exchange looks again but no words.

Captain Jones was sitting at his desk when they arrived. They entered his office silently and waited for Jones to start this so-called meeting.

"This is what's what," Jones said. "I've assessed the situation and come to the conclusion of this being an isolated incident . . . Aaaahhh . . . . the deceased, cell-mate has confessed to using the drugs with the deceased. He also tested positive and informed me that the drugs came form Jiminez, the deceased inmate . . . Now this is what I want, lock it down for the rest of the evening and we'll resume normal program tomorrow at second watch. That'll be all gentlemen," he concluded.

Cohan and Diaz exchanged another look, then exited the lieutenants office. They proceeded down the corridor of the program office toward their own separate offices, silently. Worry was painted on the both of their faces. Cohan entered his office first, closing the door behind him. Lt. Diaz walked past his door, which was directly across from Cohan's, further down the to the vending machines, where he purchased himself a coke. It was already implanted in his plan to make Cohan the fall-guy for this incident, regardless of what the captain assessed. He wasn't going to be the one who loses his job or rank, if it came down to that.

CHAPTER TWENTY ONE

Romeo woke up the next morning to the awful sound of a guards jingling keys. As he took a deep breath, the smell of the cement made him sick to his stomach when he compared it to the dream he was indulged in last night. He dreamt he was on a yacht with his junior Romeo and his beautiful wife Renee' chillin' with no worries, and enjoying the freshness of the ocean's freedom. He shook that off, brushed his grill, and washed his face.

"Hey wake up lil nigga, it's time fo' breakfast loc," Romeo said.

Tiny Scooby squirmed his way from under the cover and yawned like a baby tiger.

"What time is it big homey?" he asked.

"Time to get'cho' young ass out the bed," replied Romeo.

Romeo turned on some music and sat at the desk. He then pulled out his stash and began rolling up several fat joints to begin the day. When he finished rolling a few, he immediately lit one up and started his smoking ritual. By the time the doors were racked for breakfast Romeo was ready for whatever the day had in store.

At the chow-hall, they entered in the A-side dinning. They grabbed their tray's, got some juice, and took their seat near at the front, close to the scullery. Soon after they were seated, Big Vamp and C.J. joined them for their Sunday breakfast.

"Top of the morning loc's," stated Big Vamp.

C.J. was sippin' on some of the states finest gunpowder mixed with water, that some refer to as coffee. Tiny Scooby nodded his head, greeting them as they sat with them.

"Ugh . . . this some scandalous shit cuz," stated C.J. as he frowned at the coffee's retched taste.

"Whass' that loc," asked Romeo.

"This coffee cuz . . . this shit super strong and nasty as fuck."

"Don't drink it then," Tiny Scooby said laughing.

"Shet up lil nigga," he replied. "Oh yeah big homey . . . they found that mexican's son dead yesterday loc." C.J. added.

Whaaaaa' . . . what Mexican." Asked Romeo.

"That O/G one . . . umm . . ."

C.J. was snapping his fingers like he was jamming to some popular music, when actually he was trying to remember a name.

". . . . Damn cuz . . . . I cain't remember that fools name . . . . but you remember cuz . . . his son was the one who came over being nosey when we first got here," C.J. continued.

"Big Vamp took a sip of his coffee as he listened to C.J.

"Big Flaco," Vamp said

"Damn O/G, how you drink that shit like that cuz."

"Years of nothing else love . . . behind these walls you learn to survive the best way you can loc," answered Vamp.

"You ain't never lied," interjected. "Ay . . . who kilt'em . . . one of them?"

"Naw cuz, I heard he o-deed off that black shit . . . . word is he got some bad shit from the wood's . . . it was fucked up batch," Vamp said.

"Damn thass' fucked up," Romeo sympathized. "I don't understand how he was doing time on the same yard with his son, let alone . . . but to let him put that bullshit in his veins . . . thass' some crazy shit cuz."

"Like I said . . . . years of being behind these walls loc, prepare you to accept a whole lot of shit thass' not understandable."

"Ain't that Big Flaco at the table over there big homey," asked Tiny Scooby.

They all looked in Tiny Scooby's line of sight over at the table where indeed Big Flaco was having breakfast with a few of his comrades. They were glued on him as if they were scientist observing a test rabbit.

Big Flaco's eyes were locked on two white boy's coming through the line with their trays and heading for the coffee dispenser. He got up from the table, followed by one of his little homies that was sitting with him. They met up with the two wood's by the coffee dispenser.

"Ay esse' . . . we need to talk after chow ay . . . when the yard opens ay meet me at the hardball courts," Big Flaco aggressively demanded.

Spanky and Kaos stopped dead in their tracks when Flaco and his little homey approached and made this demand. Spanky just shook his head in aggreeance and kept the line moving, leaving Big Flaco and his homey there staring at the back of he and Kaos' heads. The two of them made it over to the table where two more white boy's were sitting. Tommy-Boy and youngster.

"Ay homeboy . . . what was that all about," Kaos asked Spanky.

"Don't know wood . . . he say we need to talk after chow . . . so we're going to talk after chow."

"I heard his son fucking o-deed yesterday bro," said Youngster.

"Yeah . . . he o-deed off a bad batch of tar bro . . . what a way to," said

Tommy-Boy.

"What the hell that got to do with us," Kaos asked angrily.

Kaos was one of them shit startin' white boys. It wasn't that he was all that tough, it was that he knew he had an entire race to back him up if anything was to go haywire. Especially with another race.

Spanky raised an eyebrow and looked deep off into Kaos' eyes as if he were trying to see his soul.

"If that's what he wants to talk about . . . then we'll find out after chow wont we . . . now enjoy yo meal killa'," Spanky said directly at Kaos.

Romeo and Big Vamp headed out the chow-hall followed by Tiny Scooby and C.J. They all grabbed their lunches and kept it moving around the track, back to their buildings.

"Here loc." Romeo said, handing Big Vamp a small ball of some weed wrapped in plastic.

"Good lookin' out cuz," Vamp replied.

"Fo'sho loc . . . I know you blow and it's a little somp'n in there to check you a few groceries to put in yo' locker cuz."

"Damn love one . . . again I say good on the lookin' out . . . a nigga like needed that."

Romeo chuckled a little bit at Big Vamp's happiness of him handing him a dope sack. Vamp tucked it down in his pants under his nut-sack to secure it. Tiny Scooby and C.J. followed right behind Vamp and Romeo while they talked, then Romeo turned and handed them two joints and a lighter.

"Here cuz . . . light them up."

"Both of em big homey?" Tiny Scooby asked.

"Ya'll can share if you want to . . . me and Vamp smoking one to tha' head. Here C . . . thass' for you."

Romeo tossed C.J. a small ball of get high and come-up also.

"Good lookin' big homey . . . gimme my joint slick-ass lil nigga."

Everybody lit up and enjoyed the walk back to their cells. When Romeo and Tiny Scooby got back to their cell they immediately blazed another joint along with an incense. Romeo wanted to be good and high by the time the yard opened.

It was ten-fifteen when the yard-release was announced. Romeo was up and out before Tiny Scooby even jumped off his bunk. He caught up to Romeo at their normal kicking it spot, on the bleachers over by the basketball court.

"What up big homey."

"Heyyy cuz . . . whass' hattnin'." Replied Romeo

"You see the Mexicans over there pow-wowin' now . . . and there go the wood, Spanky, on his way over there too."

Tiny Scooby's informative description of the situation was accurate. Only he left out the fact that Spanky was accompanied by three of his compadres, Youngster, Kaos, and Tommy-Boy. They all approached the bleachers where Romero, Big Flaco, and a couple of more younger Hispanic thugs were posted. Spanky led the pack. Walking with his had tucked down in the front of his pants. He and his boy's came to a stop in front of the bleachers to where they were staring directly into the eyes of Romeo and Big Flaco.

"What's on you fella's mind," asked Spanky.

"Word is ay . . . you vatos sold one of our people some bunk shit ay," Romero stated.

"Hold it bro . . . are you asking or is this what you know," a tempered Youngster said.

"Ay fool," Flaco exclaimed. "Watch your fucking tone ay."

Spanky snatched his hand out down in his pants as if to pull a weapon. Instead he held it up at Youngster and Big Flaco in a hold-it motion.

"Whoa, fella's fella's . . . let's not let this become a misunderstanding that's get's out of hand here . . . I thought you asked us here to talk bro."

"My son is dead fool . . . it's already outta' hand ay!"

"Look bro," Spanky broke in. "I'll check with my people . . . but I doubt seriously that it was one of us bro."

"Ay bro . . . yo' son was mainlining that shit with his homeybody bro!" exclaimed Youngster.

"What holmes!" shouted Romero.

"His cellie, homeboy," Youngster added.

All of the Mexicans that were there posted in the bleachers go quiet and had a dumbfounded look on their faces. They all looked at one another and noticed that their looks was all the same.

"Ay fool . . . is this something you heard or something you know ay," Romero said, returning Youngster's words.

"Ay esse'," Big Flaco gritted through his teeth. "Trae me Popper esse' . . . rapido!"

Popper was Little Flaco's cellie. Big Flaco had just requested his presence pronto. But just as he finished his request, their little pow-wow was interrupted.

"Ay holmes . . . ain't that Popper right there ay." said Cornejo.

He pointed over towards building five. Popper was being escorted over to the program office with bags of what looked like his personal property. Yeah . . . looks like some underhanded game is being played bro . . . but it ain't with us, said Kaos.

Big Flaco said something In Spanish to his little homies. Two of them started moving quickly and aggressively towards the escort.

"What the fuck you say esse'," Flaco flared.

He was trying to watch both, his two little homies that just peeled off from the bleachers, and the woods that was standing right in front of them. Just as the two young Hispanics was making their approach closer to the escort, Big Flaco engaged himself in a pushing and screaming match with Kaos.

"Fuck you puto' . . . this is my son motherfucker!"

"Ay bro . . . what the fuck . . . don't you ever put your fucking hands on me dude!" Kaos yelled back.

"Or what esse' . . . what the fuck you gonna do ay!"

The two squared off in front of the bleachers. The tower guard that was posted in the tower located above the dining hall noticed the ruckus and leaned out the tower's window with his mini-14 rifle and yelled out, "break it up at the bleachers. This drew the immediate attention of all the officers on the yard, including the S&E's that were escorting Popper. One of the S&E officers' posted Popper up against the wall next to the entrance of the chapel. He then took two steps forward and stood next to the other S&E's. Big Flaco began yelling again at the top of his vocals.

"Fuck you motherfuckers ay . . . . somebody killed my boy ay . . . and somebody got to pay holmes!" he screamed.

Obscenities were being yelled from both men. All of the officers began to make their way towards the ruckus swiftly. That's when Big Flaco's two little homies made their move. One grabbed Popper by the neck, from behind, bending him backwards while the other filled his chest with holes like he were shooting him with an automatic machine-gun, only he was using a homemade shank. By the time Popper's body went limp and hit the ground, his two assailants vanished through the chapel doors unseen by anyone that would've mattered. When Big Flaco saw that the mission was complete, he calmed his situation between he and Kaos by raising his hands into the air. The tower guard then scanned the yard. As he was doing so he noticed the body laying on the ground over by the chapel and laid the yard down.

"GET DOWN!!!! EVERYBODY DOWN WHERE YOU STAND

NOW! He yelled via the P.A. system.

The S&E's responded to the area, at the bleachers, where Big Flaco made a big scene. The tower guard started yelling, "NO!!! NO!!!" and was pointing towards the chapel. One of the C/O's, which was C/O Hernandez, noticed where the tower guard was pointing.

"Awe shit . . . what the fuck!!!" he yelled.

Hernandez immediately ran back over to the chapel where he had left Popper standing, to find how now sprawled out across the pavement in a pool of his blood. Popper's eyes were beamed straight into the sky, with a surprised look on his face. The same look that appeared when he was first grabbed and bent backward. It was as if he froze from the look on his face, however, his body was shaking vigorously and his blood was everywhere, like spilt milk. C/O Hernandez called it in and within seconds, C/O's swarmed the area.

Romero and Big Flaco exchanged looks with one another as they laid out in prone-position on the ground. That's when Romero realized that Flaco had spontaneously planned the whole thing.

Big Flaco had sent his little homies on a kill mission. He had caused a diversion by picking a staged fight with the woods without them knowing. Spanky looked up from where he was laying. So did Kaos and Youngster. Redness filled in Youngsters head like a thermometer about to burst.

"Ay bro!!!" exclaimed Youngster. "What the fuck you trying to do . . . get us caught up in ya'll bullshit or what!"

Even Romero was pissed at how Big Flaco went about this little kill-scheme. However, he had no choice but to ride with it.

All the C/O's fanned out around the yard while the medical staff tended to Popper. The Central Control Watch commander called for an immediate yard-recall, by races. The Hispanics were recalled first, then the Whites, then the Others and Blacks were recalled last.

When Romeo and Tiny Scooby got inside their cell, Romeo slammed the door and immediately lit up a joint. About thirty minutes later he thought that he was trippin' out. The Administration re-opened the yard. When Romeo heard the announcement, he jumped up and started scrambling to get ready. He quickly took out some weed and started rolling up some joints.

"Ay cuz . . . watch that doe loc while I do this."

"You cool big homey . . . they say in ten minutes and the pickles is in the office," replied Tiny Scooby.

"Yeah . . . still watch'em tho nigga' . . . . these muthafucka's is up to something', why tha' fuck they letting' us back out so quick."

When they were finally released to the yard, Romeo went straight over to the Black's set of bleachers and had a seat. He waited until a few more of his homies showed up before he started lighting up the joints.

"There go the homey Pugz cuz . . . I'ma go holla' real quick," said Scooby.

"Nigga' wave him over here . . . . cuz might wanna' hit somp'n to get his head together."

"Tiny Scooby didn't have to wave or leave. Pugz was already on his way over. Every Black on the yard knew that when Romeo hit the yard it was major smoke sessions jumping off.

"Whad'up big homey," C.J. said from behind.

Romeo turned and greeted C.J. Other than Tiny Scooby, C.J. was one of Romeo's most trustworthy comrades, although Romeo didn't really trust none of these nigga's.

"What up cuz . . . what it do my nigga'."

"Ay big homey . . . I need to holla' at'chu' cuz."

"Whass' crackin' love one?"

Romeo jumped down off the back of the bleachers, and he and C.J. stepped off to the side where they could talk incognito.

"Cuz I heard it through the grapevine that Blue Devil was the one that sold that Mexican that bullshit ass dope big homey."

"And?" Romeo asked

"Cuz you know we ain't supposed to do business with them fools."

"What!" Romeo exclaimed. "Cuz that ain't our problem . . . thass' they rule loc . . . they ain't supposed to deal with Blacks love one."

"Yeah I feel you big homey . . . but you and I both know them punk-ass mexicans gone try and start some shit iff'in it's true . . . feel me."

"So what cuz!!! I don't give a flying fuck bout what no Mexicans gon' do my nig . . . this Crip!" expressed Romeo.

"Right . . . right . . . ay what it do tho . . . what ya'll bout to get into?"

C.J. quickly changed the subject. He felt the heat building up inside Romeo. Just then an announcement came over the P.A.

"THE FOLLOWING INMATES HAVE VISITS."

It was loud and in super-stero. Romeo heard his name and his heat turned to a cool breeze.

"Damn loc . . . thass' me they just called, huh?" Romeo said surpisingly.

He handed Tiny Scooby and C.J. the rest of the joints he had on him then headed back to his building. When he got to his cell, he left the door open while he quickly brushed his teeth and got dressed. He pulled his shirt over his head and put a few drops of Burberry Weekend in his palm and rubbed it on his shirt and dabbed a little behind his ears. As he was about to leave his cell, C/O Potts popped his head in.

"What's that I smell?" asked Potts.

"What?" replied a nervous Romeo.

"That cologne . . . what kind is it?" he asked

"Oh thass' that Burberry Weekend . . . you don't know nuttin' bout that tho," Romeo said, relieved.

"Here you go Jackson . . . have a good one."

Potts handed Romeo his visiting pass and returned to the podium. Romeo took it, relieved, and headed out the building on to the visiting area.

Romero was in the bleachers on the Mexicans side of the yard. He was watching the soccer game that was being played on the grass by the Piasas. He noticed Romeo walking around the track in his Sunday's best. Romero smiled to himself. He recognized the shine on his boys face and the bounce in his step from the distance. He knew Romeo had to be on his way to a visit, and he was happy for him. As Romeo passed the bleachers where Romero was posted, they made eye-contacted and gave each other a head-nod. Romero gave a second one attached with a smile, as to say, "have a good one love one." Romeo winked and kept it pushing.

When he finally got inside of visiting, his shine was at a full glow. He stepped up to the officers desk and handed his I.D. and pass to the C/O.

"Table twenty-two, Jackson," the C/O said.

Romeo turned and was surprised to see that it was Renee' sitting at table twenty-two. He stood there and looked for a brief second then shook it off. When he realized that she was still there and that it wasn't a dream, he took a deep breath and made his way to his table.

"Hey baby girl, this is a pleasant surprise," he said.

She stood up and hugged him tightly, and returned the "hey babe", in a very sweet and soft tone. Then they both had a seat at the table.

"So what brings you here," Romeo asked.

"Does it matter . . . I'm here," Renee' replied.

"Look baby girl . . ."

Renee' cut off into Romeo's words like a hot knife through butter.

"NO, you look," she said. "We love you Romeo, and I'm here to support you . . . but Mr. Jackson you need to think about where your loyalty lies . . . it's either with me and your son, or the streets and them so-called homeboy's of yours."

Romeo was speechless for a second or two. Renee' also remained silent to let words marinate on his heart.

"So it's like that," he finally said.

"That's how it got to be babe . . . . because me and my baby comes first or nothing' . . . we're second to none."

"So what exactly is it that I need to do," asked Romeo.

"It's very simple . . . you got some mail coming from us for Father's Day . . . read it and make your decisions babe."

Renee' got quiet and grabbed Romeo's hand and held it for a minute. She looked deep off into his eyes and saw the decision that he would make.

"We really do love you Romeo and we truly need you." Renee' stood up to leave, but held on to her hand tightly.

"Don't go." He whispered.

"I have to go baby," she replied. "Remember that we love you babe," she concluded.

She slipped her hand out of his grip, turned to leave, and then paused. Renee' turned back and reached up and wrapped her chocolateness around his neck, and plated a heavy-wet kiss on his lips, then left. Romeo just stared at his sexy Renee' as she vanished through the double doors to freedom. It was like losing her all over again. In that moment Romeo thought, no . . . I wont lose her again . . . I can't lose her or my son.

CHAPTER TWENTY TWO

Romero was still posted in the bleachers when Big Flaco and a couple of his younger homies pushed up and joined him. Romero didn't say a word to any them as a few more Mexicans filled the bleachers. Before you knew it, there were groups of Mexicans here, and groups of blacks there, spread all across the yard . . . something wasn't right . . . tension was thick.

"Ay esse'," Big Flaco said, pretty much talking directly to Romero, since he was the one who held the keys to the yard. "This is Pelon, from El Monte ay . . . he just told me who sold my son that trash ay."

"Oh yeah . . . who ay?" asked Romero staring straight ahead.

"Lil Flaco was getting it from a black ay," said Pelon.

Romero pushed to the edge of his seat. He understood, but was yet irritated by Big Flaco's persistence of making this incident of his son's stupidity a big issue.

"What!" he shouted furiously. "That all you got homey . . . was you buying the dope from the black too esse' and why didn't you say anything sooner ay . . . what fucking black ay . . . !"

Not only was Romero at the edge of his seat, but his patience was also riding very close to it's edge.

". . . You got the fucking homies all riled up on some he-say she-say bitch shit ay . . . first it's the woods now it's the blacks huh . . . what'chu' want a war or what ay!" continued Romero.

"Ay esse'," Big Flaco said. "Why the fuck you getting' all crazy for esse' . . . I called this meeting to discuss the issue ay, and the homey right here just trying to help us with a little information esse'."

Romero wasn't paying any attention to what Big Flaco was saying. He had his eyes glued on his boy returning from his visit, and was wishing he could've been out there with him. Thoughts quickly began to fill in his head. He couldn't let what Big Flaco was brewing go down. Romeo was like his own blood brother.

◆◇◆

Big Vamp and Tiny Scooby saw Romeo returning from his visit. They both met up with him at the A-gate he was coming through.

"Whass' up homies," he said.

"They bout to lock us down cuz," Tiny Scooby said.

Romeo looked at Vamp. "What happened homey," he asked.

"C.J. confirmed that info on Blue Dev cuz . . . . now I don't think the Mexicans know fo'sho', but I'm sho' they suspect somethin's up."

"Well we cain't do nuttin' now . . . we'ah holla when these pickles sort they hang out."

Just then the announcement came over the P.A. system; "YARD RE-CALL . . . ALL INMATES REPORT BACK TO YOUR ASSIGNED HOUSING UNITS IMMEDIATELY . . . YARD RE-CALL."

"Ain't no tellin' how long this one gon be cuz." said Tiny Scooby.

"Right . . . you know how these muthafucka's like to drag shit out when it's with the Blacks and Mexicans cuz," Vamp added.

"Yeah I know loc . . . . this shit get dumber and dumber by the day cuz . . . and I'm bout tired of it." expressed Romeo.

"I been tired of this shit cuz," said Vamp.

"Ay Scoob . . . how much weed you got left on you?"

"Umm, bou eight sticks."

Give'dat to the homey loc . . . them should hold you fo' a minute cuz . . . I cant get to the vault right now."

"Aw, don't trip cuz . . . this cool . . . I appreciate that."

Romeo and Big Vamp exchanged hugs and departed, their separate ways.

<hr>

Romero and Big Flaco was in their cells laid back in silence on their bunks, awaiting count. With his eyes shut, Romero's thoughts overwhelmed his mind, causing him to raise quickly in his bed as if he were having a nightmare. He sat up and paused in that brief moment then reached up in his locker and pulled out his letter box. He then began scanning over a few old letters. Big Flaco sat up in his bunk, and stood to his feet as he heard Romero ruffling through some papers.

"Ay holmes," Big Flaco said with suspicion. "What's with you and this black vato, Romeo, ay . . . I see how you and this fool communicate sometime through looks ay . . . what up with that ay . . . is it because your name is the same or what esse'."

Romeo remained silent. Big Flaco's sudden curiosity caught him off guard and because of his clouded thoughts he wasn't able to react as quickly as usual.

"Oh . . . what esse . . . . that cat got'cho' lengua, (tongue), holmes," Flaco said. "You holdin' somethin' back homey . . . what is it esse'." Romero leaped off of his bunk and landed towards the door, angry and very much on the defensive.

"You know what ay . . . you dunno shit fool!" he exclaimed.

"Yeah esse' . . . thass what I'm trying to find out now . . . what is it that I don't know ay?"

They both stood in front of one another and faced off in a furious manner. Romero stared, then walked past Flaco to the back of the cell and sat atop the desk. He paused and propped his chin on his bawled fist, and sighed.

"I know Romeo ay," he said.

"What you mean, you know'em esse'?"

"I know'em from the streets ay . . . and I can vouch for'em holmes . . . he works for me out there ay."

"Not in here he don't fool . . . we under a whole new set of rules up in this motherfucker ay."

"Ay, believe me esse' I know that . . . but I also know that he's a firme, (good), vato ay . . . and that's way more than I can say for some homies."

"What!!!" Big Flaco exclaimed. "You sound like you on his side ay . . . where yo' loyalty at esse'."

"Don't get crazy fool I still run this yard ay! Now we gon' get down to the bottom of this bullshit ay but it's gon' get my way esse' . . . comprende holmes." Stated Romero.

"Ora le' carnal," stated Flaco. "We pushing a line on me now esse'."

"Like I said holmes . . . my way ay . . . and don't you ever question my loyalty again fool . . . . sedio ay."

Romero had made himself as clear as he could to Big Flaco then he calmly grabbed a Twix candy bar from his locker and jumped back on his bunk.

Flaco snarled to himself and just stared at a wall. He knew that Romero was here pushing a line under Big Joe's authority, and Big Joe wasn't a muthafucka' you wanted to cross, it just wasn't good for the living. After that thought, Big Flaco too grabbed a snack out the locker and laid back on his bunk while silence took over, after the ruffling of candy wrappers.

This silence was contagious throughout most of the cell-blocks. However, in Romeo's building, C/O Flores was making her rounds with the mail.

"Jackson," she said as she stopped at Romeo's door.

He jumped off of his rack in excitement and floated up to the door.

"Yeah," he said.

"Last two Jackson," she asked

"Oh, my bad . . . it's T-94."

Flores looked though the stack of mail she was toting and located several letters addressed to Romeo. She dropped them on the floor then gently kicked them under the door.

"Oooh somebody really loves you huh Jackson," she stated. "how many kids you got Jackson?"

Romeo gave her a little devilish smirk through the window.

"Not enough," he said. "And I only got one little one, Romeo Jr." he continued.

Flores smiled and moved on. Romeo pinned his face against the window of his cell-door and watched as she swayed her ass side to side in that tight ass jump-suit she had on.

"Mmm . . . Mm . . . mm," he said.

"Oooh she on you big homey," Tiny Scooby voiced from the background.

Romeo paid no attention to Scooby's comment. All of his attention was on the stack of mail he held in his grasp. He began shuffling through the letters until he came upon the one he'd been waiting for . . . the one from Renee' and Romeo Jr.

"This the one I been waitin' fo' cuz . . . my lil nigga' and my sexy chocolate," he said.

He anxiously ripped open the letter. It was in an oversized manila envelope. As he tore intro it, he sat on his bunk.

"Damn big homey . . . you hit big today . . . who wrote?" asked Tiny Scooby.

He looked down off the top bunk and saw that Romeo was glued to his letter and wasn't paying anything else any attention, including him. Tiny Scooby stared for brief second or two then he felt a little touch of hurt and loneliness, from him not receiving any mail. He then just laid back and allowed Romeo to soak up the love ones had sent him.

The first letter Romeo read was from his mini-me, Little Romeo. It read;

> "Hi Daddy,
>
> I miss you a lot. When are you coming home?
>
> Mommy miss you too daddy. Daddy we love you and we need you to come home soon. I love you very much daddy, and we wish a Happy Fathers' Day.

LOVE,

Romeo Jr."

Romeo sat in silence staring at the paper he was holding in his hand that was filled with so much genuine love, he almost cried aloud. He just smiled as he reminisced on that bright smile that Little Romeo brightened his life with. He took in a deep breath of air, then laid little Romeo's letter on his pillow. Romeo then pulled Renee's letter out the envelope. It read;

"Hey Handsome,

I'm writing you to wish you a Happy Father's day. Your mom and Ma'Ma' send their hellos' and love to you. Well I hope you're being good and taking good care of yourself in there. Romeo we really miss you and need you home. Hopefully you'll find it somewhere in your heart to come on home and be a loving father and husband. Oh yeah babe if you run into Romero, tell him that we're all praying for him and the boy's send their Love and Happy Father's Day.

Like I was saying sweetie, a loving father and husband. I hope you enjoy the pictures we sent and Little Romeo made you some things at school. He really loves and miss you Romeo . . . please try and change for us . . . ."

Romeo closed his eyes and squeezed his emotions, only this time a tear escaped. When he re-opened his eyes he had to push himself to re-focus on the letter. It had a dedication after the sentence he had read, "please try and change for us." The dedication was, "Lost Without You" by Robin Thicke. Then the letter ended with a heartfelt, *Love always . . . Renee'*. Romeo glanced down the page further and saw a P.S. under the P.S. it had the words, WILL YOU MARRY ME? This sent a shock through Romeo's entire body. He felt like the bitch now, like when her man proposed to her. This was somewhat confusing to this gangster ass nigga. How could he be feeling this . . . what the fuck was goin on in his head, he thought.

Romeo knew that he loved Renee', but never imagined this love shit to be for him until now. It was like he was feeling sick for her to be in his life in that instance. He stared out the back window thinking and by a mere coincidence, Robin Thick's song came over the radio and sent Romeo into a deep trance.

He snapped out of the trance when the song ended and a commercial came on. He cut the radio down and then reached to retrieved the pictures out of the envelope. He noticed that it was another letter down inside the envelope. He pulled it out to see that it was actually a poem sent by his little man. On the paper it had Little Romeo's actual foot-print. He then read the poem to himself. It read;

Walk a little slower daddy, said a child so small

I am following in your footsteps and I don't want to fall. Sometimes your steps are very fast, sometimes they're hard to see; So walk a little slower-daddy, for you are leading me. Somebody when I'm all grown up you're what I want to be, Then I would have a little child who'll want to follow me.

And I would a want to lead just right and know that I was true: So walk a little slower daddy, I'm right behind you.

Romeo just stared at his son's footprint on the paper. He then closed his eyes and tried squeezing again, attempting yet again to hold back his tears. Yet again unsuccessful, his eyes overflowed. Flooding his cheeks with emotions. He continued to just stare at the paper. It read, FOOTPRINTS, at the top of the page, and Romeo figured that was either the title or the creator of the poem. Then he smiled to himself because he knew that Renee' was the real reason this poem was sitting in his heads. Damn, Romeo thought, Renee' is pulling out all the stops to get him to change. He laid back on his bed resting his head on his pillow. He drifted off into a deep sleep, tired and worn out from being away from his true love ones.

It seemed darker in the hallway as Romeo was slooped down in a corner. Back to that horrific nightmare was where Romeo drifted. That urge to pee, the darkness, the flames from the gunfire, his uncle K-D and Wack leaving, and the thud form his dad's body hitting the kitchen floor all came back to haunt him while he was sleeping in this hell hole.

He was awakened by C/O Motta banging on the door the next morning.

"Jackson . . . Hey Jackson," yelled Motta.

Romeo rose in his bunk squinting his eyes trying to focus quickly on who was calling out his name.

"Yeah, whass' up man," he replied.

"You need to report to the lieutenants office after chow this morning," stated Motta.

"Fo' what," Romeo grunted.

"Hey, I'm just the messenger," Motta replied

C/O Motta then turned and left the door. Romeo sat up on the edge of his bunk and gathered his thoughts. He had an urge to release come tears, remembering that he'd just witnessed his father die again.

"Whass' up stupid . . . whass' wrong wit'chu'?" he heard in his head.

Romeo closed his eyes tight. The voice he was hearing in his head continued.

"You must be stupid for real ass-hole . . . if it happened to you, what makes you think that it wont happen to little Romeo . . history is known to repeat itself."

He stood up and opened his eyes.

"Whass' up homey?" asked Tiny Scooby.

Romeo shook off the nightmare. He brushed his teeth and washed his face, then quickly rolled a joint and lit it. He hit it a few times then offered it to Tiny Scooby.

"Get'cho'ass up cuz . . . wanna hit this shit?"

Damn big homey . . . what time is it?"

"Time fo' you to get'cho' ass up lil nigga . . . and twist up some mo' of

these loc . . . I gotta' go to the lieutenants office cuz."

"Fo' what cuz?"

"I don't know loco . . . yo' guess is betta' than mines."

Romeo continued to smoke on the joint while Tiny Scooby got his life together for the day. When the doors popped for breakfast, they both head out together.

"Ay loc . . . my eyes red?" Romeo asked.

"Naw cuz, you cool,"

It was almost eight-o-clock when Romeo finally got to the lieutenants office. Big Vamp, Romero, Big Flaco, and Shotgun was already inside. When Romeo entered everyone gave one another head-nods and they all waited until the lieutenant arrived.

Ten Minutes had passed before Lieutenant Booker walked in and took his seat behind his desk.

"Gentlemen," he said. "I've been informed about a situation on my yard . . . now . . . I can bring my security squad in here to tear your houses apart, or we can solve this issue now . . . so what's it going to be?"

"Say Lieu'," Romeo spoke up. "It's just one big misunderstanding."

"Yeah sir," Flaco butted in. "We were trippin off of my son's death

ay . . . and I do apologize for the misunderstanding."

"So what was the so-called misunderstanding?" asked Booker.

"We found out that they was planning a spread for his son's death," Romeo said, "But when we first saw the groupin' . . . well you know how that go Lieu."

"Yeah . . . I got a kite to them late ay . . . which was my bad ay," said Romero.

"Well now . . . let me first say I'm glad to hear that," Booker said. "So this is what's going to happen fella's. I'll report this to my Captain and I'll recommend to resume normal programming by noon . . . . now . . . it's not a promise he'll agree. But I can promise you this . . . if the Captain does lift this lockdown and this shit isn't kept in-tact, there will be hell to pay . . . do I make myself clear."

Everyone remained quiet and allowed the lieutenant to talk. He drifted his eyes into the eyes of each individual in his office listening, including his officer.

"I'll take the silence as a yes," he added.

He then waved his hand in a, ya'll go, motion. Big Vamp walked out first followed by Shotgun and Big Flaco, then Romero. Romeo was the last to leave.

"We cool lieu," he added before he left.

"I hope so," the lieutenant replied.

When Romeo excited the lieutenants office into the hallway, Romero was slow-dragging his way out with Big Flaco. Big Flaco turned and faced Romeo as he made his way in their direction.

"Ay holmes . . . you people the one who sold that bullshit to my boy ay," Flaco said with anger.

Romeo held his hand up, as in halt.

"Hold it homey . . . first of all, you don't know me cuz . . . and second, we ain't gon' discuss nothin' in this muthafuckin' hallway loc." Romeo replied.

"We don't have to disucss it at all fool!"

"Why you still talkin' then cuz!"

"Ay esse' . . . I told you I'd handle it ay," Romero butted in.

"Big Flaco gave Romero a hard look then proceeded out the door.

"Handle what cuz," Romeo said.

"Ay fool meet me when they crack the yard back open ay . . . I need to holla at you homey."

Romero had some concern in his tone. After he had made his last statement he left in a hurry. Romeo also shook that spot and headed back to his building.

When he finally made it back to his building, the floor officer allowed him to detour over to C.J.'s cell.

"What up dog," he said through C.J.'s window.

C.J. jumped off his bunk and went to the door.

"Ay what it do big homey?"

"The lieu said he was gon' recommend that we be let up off this dumb ass shit in a little bit cuz. When and If we do I need you to tell Blue Devil I need to holla loc."

"Fo'sho cuz . . . and good lookin' on that fire my nig . . . that shit was A1 loc."

"Yaee, yaee . . . I told you boy . . . oh yeah cuz, that bullshit posed to be squashed with them mahendas too loc, but let all the homies know to stay on they P's and Q's cuz . . . and do me a favor and get that message to the Damu's too loc."

"Fo'sho big homey."

Romeo went on to his cell where Tiny Scooby was waiting to hear the Foe-one-one. As he approached his door, he could smell the sweet aroma of incense. He smiled to himself knowing that his little homey knew what he would want to do as soon as he go in the cell.

"What up my knott," he said when he entered. "Nigga' what'chu waiting on . . . I smelt the incense cuz . . . blaze that shit up loc."

Tiny Scooby jumped off the bunk and lit up a fat chronic stick. They didn't even discuss the yard issue that was brewing until it was time for yard-release.

The announcement came over the P.A. about twenty minutes after shift-change, which was a two-o-clock. Romeo was already good and high. So when the doors racked, he was on a mission to the chapel. He shot out of the building like he had somewhere to be in a hurry. His hurry was to get across the yard un-notice as fast as he could, which he did. He got inside the chapel and took a seat in a chair far away from the front doors of the chapel. While he waited on Romero's arrival, he pulled a manila envelope from under his shirt and began reading over the letters and the poem from Little Romeo and his lovely Renee'.

CHAPTER TWENTY THREE

Renee' was in her kitchen when the phone rang. It was Ma'Ma' calling from her cell phone.

"Hello Renee' . . . sweetie."

"Yes this is me Ma'Ma' . . . what is it," Renee' asked.

"Well I'm at the boy's school, it seems they were involved in some kind of fighting."

"What! . . . where are they at now . . . are they okay?"

"Now calm down sweetie . . . I'm here with them now, but the Principle needs for you to confirm permission for little Romeo to be released into my custody."

"Huh . . . I'm on my way!"

"Sweetie listen . . . it was gotten way outta' hand here at the school today and I want to get the boy's away form here as soon as possible."

"Ma'Ma' what's going on, they never needed any confirmation for you before . . . you've always been able to pick him up."

"I know sweetie . . . look I'm going to put the Principle on the phone and he wants to verify that it's you so he's going to ask you a few questions . . . just calm down Renee' and I'll explain everything to you when we get there."

Renee' took a deep breath as the Principle was getting on the phone. He just asked her for her drivers lecense number, home address and number, Little Romeo's birthdate, and her maiden name to verify that it was in-fact her that he was talking to. When the questions was answered, Renee' slipped in a question of her own.

"What happened sir?"

"Well Mrs. Jackson, there was a disturbance in our lunch area this afternoon and the authorities urged that we suspend the children that were directly involved until we sort this matter out."

"A disturbance!" she shouted. "What kind of disturbance are you accusing my son of being involved in?"

"Look, I'm very sorry Mrs. Jackson. I could imagine how upset you must be . . . but there were a few fights between some of our Black and Hispanic students . . . a few of the students were arrested while a few of them are just being suspend. Mrs. Jackson I'm sure Mrs. Ramirez will fill you in on all the details that has been explained to her . . . . and again I'm very sorry this has happened."

The Principle handed the phone back to Ma'Ma'. She quickly got back on the phone with Renee and told her that they were on their way, and hung up the line.

Renee' sat at her kitchen table thinking about what coul've possibly happened, and how was her little man involved with this kind of madness.

When Ma'Ma' pulled her Lexus into Renee' driveway and parked, Renee' stepped out onto the porch. She and Ma'Ma made eye-contact and shook their heads as Little Romero and Little Romeo exited the car with their heads hanging low.

"Little Romeo, you go to your room, and you mijo, you have seat in the living-room,"

Ma'Ma' ordered the boy's.

"Ma'Ma' what happened," asked Renee'

Renee' was trying her best not to let her anger show. But the suspense of not knowing was weighing heavy.

"Sweetie sit," Ma'Ma' said. "Listen sweetie . . . the boy's got themselves into a little scuffle that they really don' t understand."

"What! . . . a scuffle with who?"

"With each other dear," Ma'Ma' said, dropping her head as if she were embarrassed.

"What! . . . what the heck they fighting each other for?"

"Some of the other kids at their school decided they were going to riot with one another."

"Riot!!! Over what!"

"Only God knows sweetie."

"So what did it have to with our little ones Ma'Ma' . . . . som . . ."

"Wait now let me explain the whole thing sweetie . . . now it wasn't Little Romeo's fault at all. Little Romero was being influenced by some of the older Mexcian children and he picked the fight with Little Romeo because the other children were telling him how Mexicans supposed to hate the Blacks, because Blacks hate Mexicans . . . now what's done is done Renee' . . . what matters now is what they're taught from this point on . . . they're confused little boy's without their fathers and we're all they got right now . . . hell mija, we're all we've got."

"Ma'Ma' . . . oh my God . . . I knew something like this would happen."

"Now keep your head sweetie . . . I'm gonna go . . . I'm goin to leave the both of them with you so you can give what you know . . . they'll be out of school for a couple of days so I'll pick them up tomorrow." Renee' had her head hanging low as she was listening to Ma'Ma'. What was she to say to two little boys, she thought.

"Sweetie listen," Ma'Ma' added before she left. Renee looked up and Ma'Ma' stared off into her soul. "Teach them your heart . . . teach them how to love, how you love them, and I'm sure they will grow to understand . . . then when I pick them up I'll teach them how to do chores and how I whoop me some ass, que no."

Renee' chuckled as Ma'Ma' stood up and headed out the door to her car. She watched as Ma'Ma' pulled away. When she went back inside, Little Romero was sitting quietly on the couch doing nothing. Renee' looked at him for a brief second then went into the bedroom to check on her little one. He was sitting on the edge of his bed doing the same as Little Romero . . . nothing.

Ma'Ma must've really tore into them on the way home, Renee' thought. She went back into the kitchen and started cooking, not saying a word to the boy's. When lunch was finished she called the both of them in to eat.

"Romeo . . . Romero . . . come eat," was all she said.

A few seconds had passed before they both appeared in the doorway. They stood there looking like little soldiers awaiting their next command from their commanding officer. Renee' still said nothing, she just took her seat and began saying grace. The boy's looked at one another confused. This attitude from Renee' was brand new to them. They stood there for another few seconds before taking their seats opposite one another, where Renee' had their plates already placed. When she finished saying grace, they all dug in.

"After you two finish eating we all need to talk," she said breaking the silence.

The boy's remained quiet. They both knew that they were in a world of trouble, due to how they behaved at school.

"Mommy are we in trouble," Little Romeo asked, checking his level of safety.

Renee' said nothing. She just glanced up from her plate at the both of them, then continued to eat.

She finished eating first, and she had dish water already prepared. She got up from the table and washed what the dishes she had used then went into the living-room to watch T.V.

When the boy's were done they followed Renee's lead and washed their dishes. Little Romeo then went into the living-room and sat on the floor in front of the television and Little Romero did the same. Renee' quickly hit the remote turning the T.V. off as she cleared her throat.

"Are you two mad at each other," she asked.

Neither one answered.

"I'll take that as a no," she said. "Well let me ask this . . . do you two love one another . . . because you always say you do."

Little Romeo looked over at Little Romero before answering his mom as if he were waiting for him to answer first.

"He like my brother mama, and that's how much I love'em."

Little Romero was looking at Little Romeo now as if he didn't understand what he was saying. He had never really felt those words he was now hearing from anyone but Ma'Ma'. Renee' studied the looks on their faces and realized Ma'Ma' was right, these are two little confused boy's

"Look you two," she began. "I'm not upset with you because you were fighting . . . I'm angry because you let someone else come between your love for each other. You guys been like brothers every since you were tiny little babies and nobody should've been able to get in between that . . . your not just like brothers, you are brothers . . . just like your dad's . . . they would never let anyone mess up their relationship between them now would they."

"My friend told me that we supposed to hate Black people auntie Ree Ree." Lil Romero said.

"But God said don't hate at all . . . and how can you hate somebody you love?"

"I don't think you supposed to," Little Romeo said.

"That's because you don't . . . do you think me or Ma'Ma' would ever hate one of you?" she asked.

"No."

"Alright then . . . now I'm not trippin' but Ma'Ma' is furious at you two . . . so I think you two might wanna start thinking about your going to smooth this over with her."

"Is she real mad mommy?" Little Romeo asked.

"Yep."

"Awe man Romeo . . . we really messed up . . . what we gon' do?"

"First we say I'm sorry and then we tell her we love her, and then we pray a lot," replied Lil Romeo.

"Sounds like a plan to me," Renee' said. "Now you guys can go and play in the room."

They both jumped up from the floor and shot off to Little Romeo's room. Renee' smiled and picked up the telephone and dialed Ma'Ma' and filled her in on their little discussion.

"How'd it go," she asked.

"Well one thing was for sure . . . it was brief because I almost cried."

They shared a laugh to that reply from Renee'.

"But other than that Ma'Ma', it was just as you had," Renee' went on to say. "Their just confused, because to me it seemed that their feelings for one another is truly genuine."

"Yeah I know sweetie . . . their fathers is the ones that they need to really teach them how to respect and be loyal to their own feelings and beliefs . . . let's just hope and pray they both get home real soon."

"Yeah . . . let's hope and pray," Renee' replied.

CHAPTER TWENTY FOUR

When Romero entered into the chapel he was alone. Romeo greeted him from the shadows of the far corner.

"What up loco . . . what it do boy."

"Man holmes . . . this shit don' got way outta hand and crazy ay," stated Romero.

Romeo was unfazed by Romero's statement as well as his sound of urgency and seriousness. He just laughed it off.

"Outta hand . . . crazy . . . homey this shit been crazy cuz . . . I thought'chu knew."

Quickly changing the subject, Romeo exposed the big manila envelope he possessed.

"Ay . . . I got something' I want you to check out . . . it might help take the edge off yo' ass."

"What?" replied Romero.

"It's some pictures and shit from the little ones homey . . . Renee' took'em and snapped some shots of they lil asses cuz."

Romeo continued his attempt to show Romero the pictures of their little ones, ignoring the issues that Romero was trying to present to him.

"Ay my knott," he said. "You gotta' peep this poem out too, that my little one sent cuz . . . it's deep as a muthafucka' loco."

Romero handed the poem in Romero's direction. He snatched it out of Romeo's hand in frustration.

"Ay holmes this ain't the time for this shit esse' . . . this bullshitin don' got serious fool . . . the homey's son is dead and one of your people sold him bunk shit ay!"

Romeo had hopes of staying out the bullshit, but Romero's tone quickly changed that. "Ay loc," Romeo said through his tightened jaw and gritting teeth. "What the hell you trippin' fo fool!"

"You ay . . . what you think this shit is a joke or something homeboy!"

At that comment, Romeo's whole attitude changed.

"Look muthafucka' . . . first of all don't eva' get at me like you runnin' somp'n in my life like yo' punk ass homeboys nigga' and I aint one of yo' boys, boy and all of a sudden you all high and mighty!"

"Ay homey you the one comin' in here all socially balanced ay . . . I'm trying to get this bullshit resolved ay . . . you bring me this shit like it's gon' be the answer to my fuckin' prayers ay . . . what the fuck is this supposed to do ay!"

Romero was in a fiery rage as was Romeo. The both of them were adamantly stuck on their individual beliefs, in a world where neither mattered to the other.

"Read it asshole!" stated Romeo.

Romero took a breath and decided to quickly give the piece of paper he was holding the benefit of a doubt and buried his eyes into it's words.

As he barely finished reading the first passage he raised his head and looked at Romeo.

"Yeah . . . touching ain't it," Romeo said.

"He continued to read as Romeo paced the floor in front of him. Once again the subject was changed.

"FOOTSTEPS!" Romeo said as he pounded his fist into his palm. "Who's footsteps you think our little ones is following muthafucka'! You prepared to do some time with yo son like these other dumb-ass wannabe gee-ass muthafucka's round here nigga!"

"My son ain't coming to no jail esse'."

"Who said? . . . you! . . . you sho . . . I bet yo' father said the same thing bout yo' ass too."

Romero turned red like a white boy when he got angry. He was pissed now.

"Ay holmes I didn't come here to discuss my son ay . . . this shit is bout respect ay . . . your homeboy crossed the line ay when he sold the lil homey that bullshit ay . . . and now the shits bout to blow up ay!"

Romeo too, was furious, although he didn't show it through turning red. His eyes projected evilness straight ahead and the tone in his voice was humbled but scary.

"Blow up," he laughed. "Fool I don't give a fuck bout no blowin' up . . . them punk ass politics you trying to push is fo' ya'll not us homeyboy!"

"Oh . . . thass' how we getting' down now esse'."

"Hey . . . I'm just keepin' it real my nig . . . ya'll ain't posed to deal with us but muthafucka we can deal or do what the fuck we wanna do . . . that means yo' boy's son should've knew or been taught the rules a little betta' . . . feel me . . . ya'll rules!"

"I thought you had more respect than that carnal," stated Romero.

Romeo sarcastically laughed at what Romero was saying. The blood filled in Romero's head again as his anger rose, yet again.

"Respect," Romeo said nodding his head. "As a thug, yeah . . . but as a man . . . keepin' it real c-a-r-n-a-l," he said sarcastically. "HELL NAW! Mothafuck respect . . . . how the fuck you expect me to respect this bullshit cuz and you muthafucka's following rules from a muthafucka ya'll don't even know and probably wont evea' meet . . . now here you is throwin' some bullshit cuz and you muthafucka's following rules from a muthafucka ya'll don't even know and probably wont eva' meet . . . now here you is throwin' some bullshit at me like I'm some kind'a trick or somp'n."

Romeo smiled and took a breath, then continued.

"Tell me somp'n shot-calla' . . . what's more important to you, yo' son's likfe or the so-called respect of yo' so-called homeboy's!"

Romero was knocked off-guard by Romeo's question. He was standing about ten feet away from the door and just stared at it. In his mind he wanted to leave and just let whatever happen, happen, but his feet wouldn't move. That question hit him like a tazer and literally froze him where he stood.

"Yeah . . . thass' what I thought," Romeo said.

He pointed to the paper Romero had clinched between his fingers.

"You can keep that my nig . . . and keep readin' it so you can figure out whass' mo important . . . me . . . I'm not gon' allow my son to fall fo' my mistakes homey . . . nor am I gon allow him to make the same mistakes I did . . . feel me."

Romero was fixing his mouth to respond when the security alarm sounded. The both of them fell silent and stared at one another. Then they heard the tower guar yell, "GET DOWN ON THE YARD!"

"Shit!" Romeo shouted as he ran for the door.

Romeo shot through the doors of the chapel and headed for the front door leading to the yard. Right before he got there he heard two shots rang out, then another loud, "GET DOWN," from one of the tower guards. Finally he reached the door and peeked out, not realizing that Romero was right besides him. When the peeked out, the yard was in turmoil. It was a full-fledge melee.

With all the running around the guards and inmates were doing, it was hard to tell who was actually involved. There was also a lot of smoke from the tear-gas bombs the guards was tossing. Romeo noticed three Black inmates running and ducking through the smoke. He recognizes one of as being C.J.

Quickly, he and Romero turned and went back into the chapel ara. They got inside and just stared at one another for a brief moment. Romeo noticed a sort of guilty look on Romero's face.

"You knew about this shit huh?" he asked.

Romero remained silent and continued to stare into Romeo's eyes.

"Ay you son-of-a-bitch . . . you . . ."

Romero pointed his finger at Romeo aggressively.

"NO! YOU!," he yelled. "I told you this shit gon' blow up holmes!"

Romero was animated as fuck when he talked now. It was obvious that he really didn't want it to come to this. Just as had finished his statement and holstered his finger, C.J. and two other Blacks burst through the doors of the chapel.

"Get his ass cuz!" C.J. yelled.

Romero's eyes bucked wide open like a deer caught in somebody's headlights. He threw his fist up in his defense, although heknew he had no win.

"Naw . . . Naw cuz," yelled Romeo.

C.J. and the others just looked at him. C.J. attempted to move on Romero again, aggressively.

"I said naw loc!" Romeo shouted. "Go handle yours cuz . . . I got this one!"

C.J. gave Romeo was look of disbelief. He didn't understand why Romeo was calling them off of this Mexican.

"Ay homey . . . I said I got this one," he said again, but more sternly.

C.J. and other two henchmen finally left. Romeo stood now staring off into Romero's eyes. He noticed the fear. Silence was once again the loudest sound in the room. Romeo then made his way to the doors to make sure they was closed.

"Hey what the fuck you doin' ay!" shouted Romero.

"I ain't fuckin' wit' this shit cuz!" Romeo said with his back to Romero.

"What the fuck you mean, you got his one ay?"

"Just what fuck I said . . . ay!" Romeo replied.

"Oh so you just gon' hold me hostage or what ay . . . cause I ain't goin' for that one either fool!"

Romeo turned back around to Romero. His back was now facing the door.

"What!" Romeo snapped back. "Muthafucka I ain't holdin' you shit . . . but I'm goin home when it's my time . . . feel me . . . no later . . . you wanna leave, then get'cho' dumb-ass outta here."

Just as Romeo finished speaking, the doors behind him burst open. He noticed Romero's eyes buck open again. But before he could turn and see who it was, his entire body went limp. He fell to the floor hard.

When he looked up he saw who had some through the doors.

Four Hispanics began punching on Romeo viciously, poking a hole in his body with almost every damaging blow. Romeo felt his own fluid run from his body and soak his shirt with red. A stunned Romero stood back and watched, not doing or saying anything. Romeo looked over at Romero through the pain, while he himself was being brutalized. Their eyes locked on one another's.

Romeo was barely able to blink, but he did. When he reopened his eyes, he saw what looked to him was giant human pickles, which were the same C/O's he despised, were now there to save his life. Officers had burst through the doors of the chapel and subdued Romeo's attackers. Within minutes, Romeo felt himself being lifted, and was hearing an abundance of medical terms being shouted through his ears. The medical staff, assisted by officers, quickly rolled him out on a gurney to an awaiting ambulance. When he reached the outside, the change of light made him gasp for air. He thought life was over as he was choking on his own blood.

Before putting him in the ambulance, medical staff strapped a respirator to Romeo and cleared his breathing passage. Once he was calmed and able to breathe, he was the able to focus his eyes and notice that it was the sun light that spooked him and not he light at the end of life.

The sun was more than bright and the yard was full of smoke and there were bodies everywhere. Some were dead, but most were alive, just injured. Romeo took a brief look around. While the medical personnel was loading him in the ambulance, like he was a piece of furniture. He now regretted the life that he had chosen for himself, and he vowed right then that he would do would do whatever it took to create a better path for his junior.

When the ambulance finally pulled off in hopes to save Romeo's life, Romero and his four accomplices were being escorted out of the chapel in plastic restraints, by nine C.D.C. officers, known as I.S.Us, Institutional Security Unit, aka, The Goon Squad.

A transportation bus was pulled onto the yard and most of the un-injured inmates who were immediately involved in the rioting were loaded onto it. The Goon Squad's lieutenant intercepted the escort, escorting Romero. Right then and there he knew that it was all bad. Especially when the Squad's Sergeant began reading him his rights. Romero was semi resisting as they detoured him into a transportation van alone, to be transported to Ad-Seg, (THE HOLE), to await a D.A. referral.

"Ay holmes . . . I didn't do shit ay . . . he was like a brother to me ay! . . . I didn't do it ay . . . listen to me!" he yelled hysterically.

The officers wanted no part of what he was babbling on about. It was like Lieutenant Booker said," there would be hell to pay". Romero was being charged with the attempted murder of Romeo, and gang affiliation, which will no doubt result in a life sentence. When the officers finally had Romero locked and secured in the van, he laid his head back on the seat and stared straight into the air. He had no questions or no more words to say, all that was left in him was to think of the words Romeo drilled in him, what's more important. At that he closed his eyes, and patiently awaited his fate.

CHAPTER TWENTY FIVE

Renee' was home enjoying some quiet time, relaxing. She only wished her Big Romeo was there to wrap her in his big secure arms. While laying across her bed and imagining him being there, her telephone rang. She started not to answer it, not wanting to interrupt her rest and relaxation. It could be Ma'Ma' or little Romeo, she thought, in which she decided to answer it. She finally grabbed the phone out of it's harness on the fourth ring.

"Hello," she said softly.

A strong and deep voice was on the other end of the call. It was Lieutenant Booker.

"Yes . . . May I please speak to a Mrs. Renee' Jackson please?" he asked politely.

"This is she," Renee' replied.

"Yes, this is Lieutenant Booker at Salinas Valley Maximum Security Prison. Mrs. Jackson I'm calling in regards of your husband."

Renee' went into a state of nervousness quickly. There was an eerie sound a fear in her tone when she said. "Okay . . . . what's happened." Tears had already started to form in her eyes. Somehow, Renee' thought, her Romeo was in trouble and she had to be strong.

"Ma'am," said Lt. Booker. He's been involved in an incident with other inmates. I'm very sorry to have to inform you of this, but he was stabbed and is now being transported to Salina's Emergency Trauma Center . . . Ma'am . . . Ma'am."

Renee' dropped the phone and began to bawl. The thought of losing her Romeo was overwhelmingly painful. Her body went limp and she just laid there on the couch crying and gasping for air.

After a while Renee' ended up crying herself to sleep on the floor in front of her couch. She had managed to come back to life an hour and twenty minutes later. The phone was still on the floor, off the hook. When she looked at it, she realized that what she was hoping was a dream, was in-fact a vicious reality. This realization almost sent Renee' back into a tearful disaster. She pulled herself to her feet and somehow conjured up the strength to walk to the kitchen and get herself something to drink. She felt relieved and rejuvenated from the cold water she drank, although, she knew in her heart, that it would take more than cold water to bring her out of this painful rut. She then made her way into her bedroom, with her eyes full of tears and blurry vision. Still she managed to get to her Bible, on the dresser. When she felt it's coolness in the palms of her hands, she believed that everything was going to be alright. She then dropped to her knees and began to call on God for help.

—◁◦▷—

Two years had passed before Romeo fully recovered from the stabbing. Renee' stood by his side the entire time he was bed-ridden in the hospital. She hated it in the beginning of this journey. She had to be strong as she had ever been, being that Romeo was on life-support. She got sick every time she visited him. Seeing him laid up with breathing and feeding tubes running in and out of his body almost always sent her into a tearful frenzy, however, she hung in there. The beeps from his life support machine gave her hope. Renee' believed that the longer that it continued to beep, the longer her Romeo would still be with her.

When he was taken off the life support, he was released from prison and transferred to a rehab facility. Renee still wouldn't allow little Romeo to visit. She didn't want the little one to see his dad that way. She told Romeo that in order for him to see his son, he had to strengthen himself and get better. Romeo saw it in her eyes that she meant every word of what she said, and he understood it. With Renee' strange ways of encouragement, Romeo recovered fast in rehab. Before the eighteen months the doctor's predicted, Romeo was better and walking on a cane in six.

The day Renee' came to pick him up from the rehab she brought Romeo Jr. and Romero Jr. along with her, at Romeo's request. They had grown into some healthy teens with the assistance of Ma'Ma' and Renee' combined. When Romeo saw his boy's he immediately began crying. He dropped his cane, reached out, and grabbed both of them right at the hospital's front doors. When he finally released his embrace on the boy's, it was Renee's turn. She made her way through the two towering young men and wrapped her softness around her Romeo.

"Oh damn baby girl . . . take it easy now . . . daddy still a little fragile girl." He said.

"I'm sorry babe," she replied.

"She sniffled a little and pulled back, looking Romeo straight in the eyes.

"I love you baby," she said.

"I know," he responded. "And can I ask you somethin' babe?"

"What," she asked.

"Can a man have two best men at his wedding?"

"Ahh . . . I'm sure we can work something out," she said as she smiled at the boys.

They saw the happiness that Romeo Sr. had given Renee' in that moment, and they were all for that.

Romeo grabbed his cane, but before he got in the car he closed his eyes, took a deep breath of fresh air, then began his new life with the ones who truly love him.

CHAPTER TWENTY SIX

Romero was sentenced to twenty-five-to-life for attempted murder, conspiracy to commit murder, gang enhancements, and racial hate crime. Seems his fellow comrades turned the tables on him by throwing him to the wolves. Romero had nineteen witnesses against him and none were Black. All four of the inmates that stabbed Romeo testified that Romero was in-fact their shot-caller and he was in-fact the one that called in the hit on Romeo. They were all then transferred to protective custody with only three years a piece added to their sentence. Romero on the other hand was sent up the river with no get back.

Today he was being transferred from the SHU-program to main population over at Pelican Bay Max. On the bus ride he just laid his head back and rested because he knew it was about time for that meeting with fate.

The van that was transporting Romero and a couple of more hardened criminals finally pulled into the sally port of it's destination. Once the van passed through the security inspection it then proceeded through to R&R,(receiving and release), where Romero and the other inmates were processed in.

"Single file line against the wall," an officer screamed.

When Romero looked up to see who was yelling, he saw an evil-looking, mean-mugging, big black cop, with an intimidating voice looking him straight in the mouth. Shit I hope this mother fucker don't fuck with me today, he thought to himself. He dropped his head to avoid making eye contact. He miraculously made it through processing without being fucked with, but he did feel kind of violated by several of the officers looking up his ass for drugs or weapons.

Romero was given his I.D. and assigned a cell on C-Yard. When he got there he was CTQ'ed, (confirmed to quarters), for seventy-two hours for enemy check. Once the seventy-two hours were up and he was classified, he hit the yard. The first thing that he went looking for was something to get his head right, which didn't take long at all. He ran into one of his young homey's who he had sent on a mission before, and now sending him on another kind of mission to find him some get-high. Cartoon was back in a flash with some high-grade meth. Romero snorted a line and took a deep breath. As he floated above life from the drug, the stench of the air welcomed him to his new home. He tried to enjoy his high and get the day out of the way, even though it really didn't matter rather his day went by fast or not, he wasn't going anywhere no time soon. He and Cartoon did a few more lines together and hug out until yard-recall. At that time Romero headed back into his building. As he was walking to his cell, he noticed a few familiar faces. One in particular, but he couldn't remember where it was that he knew this particular face from. The building's tower guard announced mail-call, and everybody began to gather around the officer's podium. C/O Hampshire started calling the names of those inmates that had mail. Romero stood at the back of the crowd. He didn't believe that he would receive any, only being here but a few days, but what he got to lose, he thought.

"Inmate Phillips," shouted Hampshire.

Phillips was anxious and lit up when he heard his name, as was all the others whose names were called.

"Inmate Riley,"

"Whoop . . . that be me," Riley said.

"Inmate Ramirez."

Two inmates answered, "Yeah," at the same time. It was Romero and that familiar face that he couldn't peg. They both looked at each other as if they had recognized the similarties at the brief moment. Then they both shouted out together, "Which one".

"Hectore Ramirez," Hampshire replied.

Romero grabbed hold of the nearest wall and leaned against it to catch himself from falling. Hector reached in and grabbed a hold of his letter. When he looked at the envelope he saw that it was from Rosa Ramirez, Ma'Ma'. Quickly he tore through the envelope to get it open, pulled the letter out and began reading the few words from his estranged wife, which read;

"Have you met your son?"

Hector turned around quickly. He and Romero's eyes met once again.

That's when fate said, "HELLO," to the both of them.

CHAPTER TWENTY SEVEN

It was sunny day. Romeo Jr. and Romero Jr. woke up bright and early today. It was like the sun was shining just for them, thought Little Romero. Today was their day. It was actually to be a new beginning for the entire urban ghetto, all because of dad, Little Romeo thought to himself.

He and Romeo Jr. was dressed and ready for the day. Renee' had made breakfast and gotten dressed herself. Even she was moving kind of fast this morning, due to her anxiousness of what the day may bring.

The two Juniors' was in the kitchen finishing up their breakfast. They were downing their food like two hungry Lion cubs. Not just because they were extremely hungry, but mainly because they were extremely anxious, as Renee' was.

When the phone rang, Renee' was in her bedroom praying. As it rang a few more times, Little Romero answered it.

"Hello," he said.

"Hey . . . what up . . . ya'll ready fo' the day?" "All the time unc," he replied.

"Ay . . . is that pop's," yelled Little Romeo.

He was at the kitchen sink washing out the dishes that he and Romero used.

"Ay ask pop's, are they ready."

Romero repeated Little Romeo's question to his uncle as Little Romeo requested.

"Tell'em did he have any doubt . . . I'm already here . . . ay tell Renee' I'll be sittin' in the C-section . . . and ya'll need to get here so you can get set . . . put lil Romeo on the horn."

Romero Jr. handed the phone to Little Romeo.

"Here . . . yo' pop wanna holla'."

"Hey pops whass up," he said.

"Heyyy baby boy, you ready?" asked Romeo

"We stay ready . . . it's on pops." He replied.

"Yaee yaee . . . now where my sexy wifey at?"

"She probably in her room praying . . . you want me to take her the horn?"

"Naw naw . . . we don't eva interrupt her praying . . . thass' what keep us above water, feel me . . . look I'll just see you guy's when ya'll get here . . . I'm posted."

"Alright, I love you," stated lil Romeo.

Romero Jr. shouted, I love you, from the background before Lil Romeo hung up the phone.

"I love ya'll too," Romeo replied.

"He said he love us too," stated lil Romeo to Romero Jr.

They turned and jumped in the air slapping each other with hi-five.

"Mamahh," Romeo yelled. "My dad says he's waiting on us."

Renee emerged from her bedroom in what her Romeo would say was the flyest summer fit ever made. When the boy's saw her, they both were wowed.

"Damn mama, you gon' shut down the whole show."

"Uhh . . . boy you betta' watch your mouth."

"Whoa! . . . I'm saying tho' auntie . . . you on fire . . . unc gon' love that."

Renee', being modest, smacked her lips at the boy's comments.

Both of ya'll hush and lets go," she said.

◄○►

Romeo was in Irvine Meadows in the grass, enjoying the sun. He looked over and saw Renee' and the boy's pulling into the parking lot. As they were all getting out of the car, and heading this way, he saw in the distance that Renee' had on something extra sexy. He grabbed his cane and stood to his feet. When he and she finally made physical contact, he laid a nice-gentle wet kiss on her lips.

"Mmmm," she said, "that was nice."

"Naw . . . thass' nice," he replied, looking her up and down. "I got the sexiest piece of chocolate in the box and she wearin' the flyest fit eva' made." he continued.

She was stuntin' some white short-shorts with hot-pink roses bordering them. They wrapped around her thoughs and ass like Christmas ribbons on a million dollar present. The shorts were accented with a hot-pink sheer shawl tied at her waist-line. Her top matched the shorts, but only came halfway down her torso, showing off the pink heart-shaped, four-carat diamond that her Romeo blessed her with. Her hair was in a thick silky-black ponytail, that set her complexion in lights.

"Hm . . . mm . . . mmm," Romeo said. "This gots to be heaven."

"Oh stop it . . . you sound like the boy's."

"I told you auntie."

Loud music was playing, and the meadows was filling up by the second. Romeo turned to the boy's wearing some jeans, heavy boots by Jordan, a fresh T, and baseball cap with a college-like logo that read L.A.U. The T-shirt was all white with dark blue lettering that said, "LOS ANGELES UNITED" across the top.

"This is what ya'll been waiting fo' huh . . . well yo' time has arrived . . . go win this one fo' me."

Romeo kissed both of the boy's on the forehead. They boy's returned the love with a team hug, then turned and headed away. Then went over to the flatbed truck where lil Romeo's rag sixty-four Chevy Impala, and Lil Romero's rag seventy-two Cadillac was sittin with covers over them. As they walked away from where Renee' and Romeo was lounging, they hugged one another as they strolled, highlighting the big bold blue lettering shining across the backs of their shirts that read, Presidents across the top and L.A. UNITED across the bottom. They were the two youngest Presidents of any car-club in America. Their motto was, "Out with the old and in with the new . . . Let's get L.A. UNITED".

Today was their day.

CHAPTER TWENTY EIGHT

It was yard-recall. Romero and his dad, Hector, was shaking their homies and saying their farewells for the day. Today was Romero's birthday and his dad had put together a spread for him, with some of their elite homies.

When the two of them got inside their building the officer was already calling names at the podium for mail. Hector and Romero both were headed to their cell when the officer yelled, "Ramirez".

They both turned and said, "Which one"

This time the officer said, "Romero Ramirez". The envelope was addressed from Romero Jr. and Romeo Jr. Romero smiled as he opened the letter. He pulled the pictures out and was surprised and shocked at the same time. He then read the note.

"Let's get L.A. UNITED . . . . We Love You!!!"

Romero moved quickly to his cell, and Hector followed. They were cellies now. Romeo sat on the edge of his dad's bunk and began flipping through the pictures again as his dad stood over him. They saw the boy's hugged up together holding the first prize trophy and a giant check for fifty-thousand dollars. As Romero analyzed each photo he was handing them to Hector. They were both now sitting on the bottom bunk as Romero was whizzing through the past, whishing he could change it and be part of the future he was gazing at in front of him. Hector saw his son fading into the past, and got up from the bunk.

"Ay . . . you know if you dwell on that shit too hard ay . . . this time gonna seem way harder and longer ay," stated Hector.

Romero just remained silent and continued to stare at the photo of his son and Romeo Jr . . . he silently said, "Thank you Romeo", in his heart and hoped that he heard him, or at least felt his appreciation.

THE END